Thank You, Jeeves

P. G. Wodehouse

CORONET BOOKS
Hodder and Stoughton

First published in Great Britain 1934 by
Herbert Jenkins Limited

This edition © 1975 by P. G. Wodehouse

Coronet Edition 1977

Printed in Great Britain for
Hodder and Stoughton Paperbacks,
a division of Hodder and Stoughton Ltd.,
Mill Road, Dunton Green, Sevenoaks, Kent
(Editorial Office: 47 Bedford Square,
London, WC1 3DP) by
Hazell Watson & Viney Ltd.,
Aylesbury, Bucks

ISBN 0 340 21790 1

PREFACE

This is the first of the full-length novels about Jeeves and Bertie Wooster, and it is the only book of mine which I tried to produce without sitting down at the typewriter and getting a crick in the back.

Not that I ever thought of dictating it to a stenographer. How anybody can compose a story by word of mouth, face to face with a bored looking secretary with a notebook is more than I can imagine. Yet many authors think nothing of saying "Ready, Miss Spelvin? Take dictation. Quote No comma Lord Jasper Murgatroyd comma close quote said no better make it hissed Evangeline comma quote I would not marry you if you were the last man on earth close quote period Quote Well comma, I'm not the last man on earth comma so the point does not arise comma close quote replied Lord Jasper comma twirling his moustache cynically period And so the long day wore on."

If I started to do that sort of thing I should be feeling all the time that the girl was saying to herself as she took it down, "Well comma this beats me period How comma with homes for the feeble-minded touting for customers on every side comma has a fathead like this Wodehouse succeeded in remaining at large all these years mark of interrogation."

But I did get one of those machines where you talk into a mouthpiece and have your observations recorded on wax, and I started *Thank You, Jeeves*, on it. And after the first few paragraphs I thought I would turn back and play the stuff over to hear how it sounded.

It sounded too awful for human consumption. Until that moment I had never realized that I had a voice like that of a very pompous school-master addressing the young scholars in his charge from the pulpit in the school chapel. There was a kind of foggy dreariness about it that chilled the spirits. It stunned me, I had been hoping, if all went well, to make *Thank You, Jeeves*.

an amusing book—gay, if you see what I mean, rollicking if you still follow me and debonair, and it was plain to me that a man with a voice like that could never come within several miles of being debonair. With him at the controls the thing would develop into one of those dim tragedies of peasant life which we return to the library after a quick glance at Page One. I sold the machine next day and felt like the Ancient Mariner when he got rid of the albatross. So now I confine myself to the good old typewriter.

Writing my stories I enjoy. It is the thinking them out that is apt to blot the sunshine from my life. You can't think out plots like mine without getting a suspicion from time to time that something has gone seriously wrong with the brain's two hemispheres and the broad band of transversely running fibres known as the corpus collosum. It is my practice to make about 400 pages of notes before starting a novel, and during this process there always comes a moment when I say to myself "Oh, what a noble mind is here o'erthrown." The odd thing is that just as I am feeling that I must get a proposer and seconder and have myself put up for the loony bin, something always clicks and after that all is joy and jollity.

P. G. Wodehouse

CONTENTS

★ 1 ★

Jeeves Gives Notice

I WAS a shade perturbed. Nothing to signify, really, but still just a spot concerned. As I sat in the old flat, idly touching the strings of my banjolele, an instrument to which I had become greatly addicted of late, you couldn't have said that the brow was actually furrowed, and yet, on the other hand, you couldn't have stated absolutely that it wasn't. Perhaps the word "pensive" about covers it. It seemed to me that a situation fraught with embarrassing potentialities had arisen.

"Jeeves," I said, "do you know what?"

"No, sir."

"Do you know whom I saw last night?"

"No, sir."

"J. Washburn Stoker and his daughter, Pauline."

"Indeed, sir?"

"They must be over here."

"It would seem so, sir."

"Awkward, what?"

"I can conceive that after what occurred in New York it might be distressing for you to encounter Miss Stoker, sir. But I fancy the contingency need scarcely arise."

I weighed this.

"When you start talking about contingencies arising, Jeeves, the brain seems to flicker and I rather miss the gist. Do you mean that I ought to be able to keep out of her way?"

"Yes, sir."

"Avoid her?"

"Yes, sir."

I played five bars of "Old Man River" with something of abandon. His pronouncement had eased my mind. I followed his reasoning. After all, London's a large place. Quite simple not to run into people, if you don't want to.

"It gave me rather a shock, though."

"I can readily imagine so, sir."

"Accentuated by the fact that they were accompanied by Sir Roderick Glossop."

"Indeed, sir?"

"Yes. It was at the Savoy Grill. They were putting on the nosebag together at a table by the window. And here's rather a rummy thing, Jeeves. The fourth member of the party was Lord Chuffnell's aunt, Myrtle. What would she be doing in that gang?"

"Possibly her ladyship is an acquaintance either of Mr. Stoker, Miss Stoker, or Sir Roderick, sir."

"Yes, that may be so. Yes, that might account for it. But it surprised me, I confess."

"Did you enter into conversation with them, sir?"

"Who, me? No, Jeeves. I was out of the room like a streak. Apart from wishing to dodge the Stokers, can you see me wantonly and deliberately going and chatting with old Glossop?"

"Certainly he has never proved a very congenial companion in the past, sir."

"If there is one man in the world I hope never to exchange speech with again, it is that old crumb."

"I forgot to mention, sir, that Sir Roderick called to see you this morning."

"What!"

"Yes, sir."

"He called to see me?"

"Yes, sir."

"After what has passed between us?"

"Yes, sir."

"Well, I'm dashed!"

"Yes, sir. I informed him that you had not yet risen, and he said that he would return later."

"He did, did he?" I laughed. One of those sardonic ones. "Well, when he does, set the dog on him."

"We have no dog, sir."

"Then step down to the flat below and borrow Mrs. Tinkler-Moulke's Pomeranian. Paying social calls after the way he behaved in New York! I never heard of such a thing. Did you ever hear of such a thing, Jeeves?"

"I confess that in the circumstances his advent occasioned me surprise, sir."

"I should think it did. Good Lord! Good heavens! Good gosh! The man must have the crust of a rhinoceros."

And when I have given you the inside story, I think you will agree with me that my heat was justified. Let me marshal my facts and go to it.

About three months before, noting a certain liveliness in my Aunt Agatha, I had deemed it prudent to pop across to New York for a space to give her time to blow over. And about half-way through my first week there, in the course of a beano of some description at the Sherry-Netherland, I made the acquaintance of Pauline Stoker.

She got right in amongst me. Her beauty maddened me like wine.

"Jeeves," I recollect saying, on returning to the apartment, "who was the fellow who on looking at something felt like somebody looking at something? I learned the passage at school, but it has escaped me."

"I fancy the individual you have in mind, sir, is the poet Keats, who compared his emotions on first reading Chapman's Homer to those of stout Cortez when with eagle eyes he stared at the Pacific."

"The Pacific, eh?"

"Yes, sir. And all his men looked at each other with a wild surmise, silent upon a peak in Darien."

"Of course. It all comes back to me. Well, that's how I felt this afternoon on being introduced to Miss Pauline Stoker. Press the trousers with special care tonight, Jeeves. I am dining with her."

In New York, I have always found, one gets off the mark quickly in matters of the heart. This, I believe, is due to something in the air. Two weeks later I proposed to Pauline. She accepted me. So far, so good. But mark the sequel. Scarcely forty-eight hours after that a monkey wrench was bunged into the machinery and the whole thing was off.

The hand that flung that monkey wrench was the hand of Sir Roderick Glossop.

In these memoirs of mine, as you may recall, I have had occasion to make somewhat frequent mention of this old pot of poison. A bald-domed, bushy-browed blighter, ostensibly a nerve specialist, but in reality, as everybody knows, nothing more nor less than a high-priced loony-doctor, he has been cropping up in my path for years, always with the most momentous results. And it so happened that he was in New York when the announcement of my engagement appeared in the papers.

What brought him there was one of his periodical visits to J. Washburn Stoker's second cousin, George. This George was a man who, after a lifetime of doing down the widow and orphan, had begun to feel the strain a bit. His conversation was odd, and he had a tendency to walk on his hands. He had been a patient of Sir Roderick's for some years, and it was the latter's practice to dash over to New York every once in a while to take a look at him. He arrived on the present occasion just in time to read over the morning coffee and egg the news that Bertram Wooster and Pauline Stoker were planning to do the Wedding Glide. And, as far as I can ascertain, he was at the telephone, ringing up the father of the bride-to-be, without so much as stopping to wipe his mouth.

Well, what he told J. Washburn about me I cannot, of course, say: but, as a venture, I imagine he informed him that I had once been engaged to his daughter, Honoria, and that he had broken off the match because he had decided that I was barmy to the core. He would have touched, no doubt, on the incident of the cats and the fish in my bedroom: possibly, also, on the episode of the stolen hat and my habit of climbing down waterspouts: winding up, it may be, with a description of the unfortunate affair of the punctured hot-water bottle at Lady Wickham's.

A close friend of J. Washburn's and a man on whose judgment J. W. relied, I take it that he had little difficulty in persuading the latter that I was not the ideal son-in-law. At any rate, as I say, within a mere forty-eight hours of the holy moment I was notified that it would be unnecessary for me to order the new sponge-bag trousers and gardenia, because my nomination had been cancelled.

And it was this man who was having the cool what's-the-word to come calling at the Wooster home. I mean, I ask you!

I resolved to be pretty terse with him.

I was still playing the banjolele when he arrived. Those who know Bertram Wooster best are aware that he is a man of sudden, strong enthusiasms and that, when in the grip of one of these, he becomes a remorseless machine—tense, absorbed, single-minded.

It was so in the matter of this banjolele-playing of mine. Since the night at the Alhambra when the supreme virtuosity of Ben Bloom and his Sixteen Baltimore Buddies had fired me to take up the study of the instrument, not a day had passed without its couple of hours' assiduous practice. And I was twanging the strings like one inspired when the door opened and Jeeves shovelled in the foul strait-waistcoat specialist to whom I have just been alluding.

In the interval which had elapsed since I had first been apprised of the man's desire to have speech with me, I had been thinking things over: and the only conclusion to which I could come was that he must have had a change of heart of some nature and decided that an apology was due me for the way he had behaved. It was, therefore, a somewhat softened Bertram Wooster who now rose to do the honours.

"Ah, Sir Roderick," I said. "Good morning."

Nothing could have exceeded the courtesy with which I had spoken. Conceive of my astonishment, therefore, when his only reply was a grunt, and an indubitably unpleasant grunt, at that. I felt that my diagnosis of the situation had been wrong. Right off the bull's-eye I had been. Here was no square-shooting apologizer. He couldn't have been glaring at me with more obvious distaste if I had been the germ of *dementia praecox*.

Well, if that was the attitude he was proposing to adopt, well, I mean to say. My geniality waned. I drew myself up coldly, at the same time raising a stiff eyebrow. And I was just about to work off the old To-what-am-I-indebted-for-this-visit gag, when he chipped in ahead of me,

"You ought to be certified!"

"I beg your pardon?"

"You're a public menace. For weeks, it appears, you have been making life a hell for all your neighbours with some hideous musical instrument. I see you have it with you now. How dare you play that thing in a respectable block of flats? Infernal din!"

I remained cool and dignified.

"Did you say 'infernal din'?"

"I did."

"Oh? Well, let me tell you that the man that hath no music in himself . . ." I stepped to the door. "Jeeves," I called down the passage, "what was it Shakespeare said the man who hadn't music in himself was fit for?"

"Treasons, stratagems, and spoils, sir."

"Thank you, Jeeves. Is fit for treasons, stratagems, and spoils," I said, returning.

He danced a step or two.

"Are you aware that the occupant of the flat below, Mrs. Tinkler-Moulke, is one of my patients, a woman in a highly nervous condition. I have had to give her a sedative."

I raised a hand.

"Spare me the gossip from the loony-bin," I said distantly. "Might I inquire, on my side, if you are aware that Mrs. Tinkler-Moulke owns a Pomeranian?"

"Don't drivel."

"I am not drivelling. This animal yaps all day and not infrequently far into the night. So Mrs. Tinkler-Moulke has had the nerve to complain of my banjolele, has she? Ha! Let her first pluck out the Pom which is in her own eye," I said, becoming a bit scriptural.

He chafed visibly.

"I am not here to talk about dogs. I wish for your assurance that you will immediately cease annoying this unfortunate woman."

I shook the head.

"I am sorry she is a cold audience, but my art must come first."

"That is your final word, is it?"

"It is."

"Very good. You will hear more of this."

"And Mrs. Tinkler-Moulke will hear more of this," I replied, brandishing the banjolele.

I touched the buzzer.

"Jeeves," I said, "show Sir R. Glossop out!"

I confess that I was well pleased with the manner in which I had comported myself during this clash of wills. There was a time, you must remember, when the sudden appearance of old Glossop in my sitting-room would have been enough to send me bolting for cover like a rabbit. But since then I had passed through the furnace, and the sight of him no longer filled me with a nameless dread. With a good deal of quiet self-satisfaction I proceeded to play "The Wedding of the Painted Doll", "Singin' In the Rain", "Three Little Words", "Goodnight, Sweetheart",

"My Love Parade", "Spring Is Here", "Whose Baby Are You?" and part of "I Want an Automobile With a Horn That Goes Toot-Toot", in the order named: and it was as I was approaching the end of this last number that the telephone rang.

I went to the instrument and stood listening. And, as I listened, my face grew hard and set.

"Very good, Mr. Manglehoffer," I said coldly. "You may inform Mrs. Tinkler-Moulke and her associates that I choose the latter alternative."

I touched the bell.

"Jeeves," I said, "there has been a spot of trouble."

"Indeed, sir?"

"Unpleasantness is rearing its ugly head in Berkeley Mansions, W.1. I note also a lack of give-and-take and an absence of the neighbourly spirit. I have just been talking to the manager of this building on the telephone, and he has delivered an ultimatum. He says I must either chuck playing the banjolele or clear out."

"Indeed, sir?"

"Complaints, it would seem, have been lodged by the Honourable Mrs. Tinkler-Moulke, of C.6; by Lieutenant-Colonel J. J. Bustard, D.S.O., of B.5; and Sir Everard and Lady Blennerhassett, of B.7. All right. So be it. I don't care. We shall be well rid of these Tinkler-Moulkes, these Bustards, and these Blennerhassetts. I leave them without a pang."

"You are proposing to move, sir?"

I raised the eyebrows.

"Surely, Jeeves, you cannot imagine that I ever considered any other course?"

"But I fear you will encounter a similar hostility elsewhere, sir."

"Not where I am going. It is my intention to retire to the depths of the country. In some old world, sequestered nook I shall find a cottage, and there resume my studies."

"A cottage, sir?"

"A cottage, Jeeves. If possible, honeysuckle-covered."

The next moment, you could have knocked me down with a toothpick. There was a brief pause, and then Jeeves, whom I have nurtured in my bosom, so to speak, for years and years and years, gave a sort of cough and there proceeded from his lips these incredible words:

"In that case, I fear I must give my notice."

There was a tense silence. I stared at the man.

"Jeeves," I said, and you wouldn't be far out in describing me as stunned, "did I hear you correctly?"

"Yes, sir."

"You actually contemplate leaving my entourage?"

"Only with the greatest reluctance, sir. But if it is your intention to play that instrument within the narrow confines of a country cottage . . ."

I drew myself up.

"You say 'that instrument', Jeeves. And you say it in an unpleasant, soupy voice. Am I to understand that you dislike this banjolele?"

"Yes, sir."

"You've stood it all right up to now."

"With grave difficulty, sir."

"And let me tell you that better men than you have stood worse than banjoleles. Are you aware that a certain Bulgarian, Elia Gospodinoff, once played the bagpipes for twenty-four hours without a stop? Ripley vouches for this in his 'Believe It Or Not'."

"Indeed, sir?"

"Well, do you suppose Gospodinoff's personal attendant kicked? A laughable idea. They are made of better stuff than that in Bulgaria. I am convinced that he was behind the young master from start to finish of his attempt on the Central European record, and I have no doubt frequently rallied round with ice packs and other restoratives. Be Bulgarian, Jeeves."

"No, sir. I fear I cannot recede from my position."

"But, dash it, you say you *are* receding from your position."

"I should have said, I cannot abandon the stand which I have taken."

"Oh."

I mused awhile.

"You mean this, Jeeves?"

"Yes, sir."

"You have thought it all out carefully, weighing the pros and cons, balancing this against that?"

"Yes, sir."

"And you are resolved?"

"Yes, sir. If it is really your intention to continue playing that instrument, I have no option but to leave."

The Wooster blood boiled over. Circumstances of recent

years have so shaped themselves as to place this blighter in a position which you might describe as that of a domestic Musso-lini: but, forgetting this and sticking simply to cold fact, what *is* Jeeves, after all? A valet. A salaried attendant. And a fellow simply can't go on truckling—do I mean truckling? I know it begins with a "t"—to his valet for ever. There comes a moment when he must remember that his ancestors did dashed well at the Battle of Crecy and put the old foot down. This moment had now arrived.

"Then, leave, dash it!"

"Very good, sir."

* 2 *

Chuffy

I CONFESS that it was in sombre mood that I assembled the stick, the hat, and the lemon-coloured gloves some half-hour later and strode out into the streets of London. But though I did not care to think what existence would be like without Jeeves, I had no thought of weakening. As I turned the corner into Piccadilly, I was a thing of fire and chilled steel; and I think in about another half-jiffy I should have been snorting, if not actually shouting the ancient battle cry of the Woosters, had I not observed on the skyline a familiar form.

This familiar form was none other than that of my boyhood friend, the fifth Baron Chuffnell—the chap, if you remember, whose Aunt Myrtle I had seen the previous night hobnobbing with the hellhound, Glossop.

The sight of him reminded me that I was in the market for a country cottage and that here was the very chap to supply same.

I wonder if I have ever told you about Chuffy? Stop me if I have. He's a fellow I've known more or less all my life, he and self having been at private school, Eton and Oxford together. We don't see a frightful lot of one another nowadays, however, as he spends most of his time down at Chuffnell Regis on the coast of Somersetshire, where he owns an enormous great place with about a hundred and fifty rooms and miles of rolling parkland.

Don't run away, however, on the strength of this, with the impression that Chuffy is one of my wealthier cronies. He's dashed hard up, poor bloke, like most fellows who own land, and only lives at Chuffnell Hall because he's stuck with it and can't afford to live anywhere else. If somebody came to him and offered to buy the place, he would kiss him on both cheeks. But who wants to buy a house that size in these times? He can't even let it. So he sticks on there most of the year, with nobody to talk to except the local doctor and parson and his Aunt Myrtle and her twelve-year-old son, Seabury, who live at the Dower House in the park. A pretty mouldy existence for one who at the University gave bright promise of becoming one of the lads.

Chuffy also owns the village of Chuffnell Regis—not that that does him much good, either. I mean to say, the taxes on the estate and all the expenses of repairs and what not come to pretty nearly as much as he gets out of the rents, making the thing more or less of a washout. Still, he is the landlord, and, as such, would doubtless have dozens of cottages at his disposal and probably be only too glad of the chance of easing one of them off on to a reputable tenant like myself.

"You're the very chap I wanted to see, Chuffy," I said accordingly, after our initial what-ho-ing. "Come right along with me to the Drones for a bite of lunch. I can put a bit of business in your way."

He shook his head, wistfully, I thought.

"I'd like it, Bertie, but I'm due at the Carlton in five minutes. I'm lunching with a man."

"Give him a miss."

"I couldn't."

"Well, bring him along, then, and we'll make it a threesome."

Chuffy smiled rather wanly.

"I don't think you'd enjoy it, Bertie. He's Sir Roderick Glossop."

I goggled. It's always a bit of a shock, when you've just parted from Bloke A., to meet Bloke B. and have Bloke B. suddenly bring Bloke A. into the conversation.

"Sir Roderick Glossop?"

"Yes."

"But I didn't know you knew him."

"I don't, very well. Just met him a couple of times. He's a great friend of my Aunt Myrtle."

"Ah! That explains it. I saw her dining with him last night."

"Well, if you come to the Carlton, you'll see me lunching with him today."

"But, Chuffy, old man, is this wise? Is this prudent? It's an awful ordeal breaking bread with this man. I know. I've done it."

"I dare say, but I've got to go through with it. I had an urgent wire from him yesterday, telling me to come up and see him without fail, and what I'm hoping is that he wants to take the Hall for the summer or knows somebody who does. He would hardly wire like that unless there was something up. No, I shall have to stick it, Bertie. But I'll tell you what I will do. I'll dine with you tomorrow night."

I would have been all for it, of course, had the circs been different, but I had to refuse. I had formed my plans and made my arrangements and they could not be altered.

"I'm sorry, Chuffy. I'm leaving London tomorrow."

"You are?"

"Yes. The management of the building where I reside has offered me the choice between clearing out immediately or ceasing to play the banjolele. I elected to do the former. I am going to take a cottage in the country somewhere, and that's what I meant when I said I could put business in your way. Can you let me have a cottage?"

"I can give you your choice of half a dozen."

"It must be quiet and secluded. I shall be playing the banjolele a good deal."

"I've got the very shack for you. On the edge of the harbour and not a neighbour within a mile except Police-Sergeant Voules. And he plays the harmonium. You could do duets."

"Fine!"

"And there's a troupe of nigger minstrels down there this year. You could study their technique."

"Chuffy, it sounds like heaven. And we shall be able to see something of each other for a change."

"You don't come playing your damned banjolele at the Hall."

"No, old man. But I'll drop over to lunch with you most days."

"Thanks."

"Don't mention it."

"By the way, what has Jeeves got to say about all this? I

shouldn't have thought he would have cared about leaving London."

I stiffened a little.

"Jeeves has nothing to say on that or any other subject. We have parted brass-rags."

"What!"

I had anticipated that the news would stagger him.

"Yes," I said, "from now on, Jeeves will take the high road and I'll take the low road. He had the immortal rind to tell me that if I didn't give up my banjolele he would resign. I accepted his portfolio."

"You've really let him go?"

"I have."

"Well, well, well!"

I waved a hand nonchalantly.

"These things happen," I said. "I'm not pretending I'm pleased, of course, but I can bite the bullet. My self-respect would not permit me to accept the man's terms. You can push a Wooster just so far. 'Very good, Jeeves,' I said to him. 'So be it. I shall watch your future career with considerable interest.' And that was that."

We walked on for a bit in silence.

"So you've parted with Jeeves, have you?" said Chuffy, in a thoughtful sort of voice. "Well, well, well! Any objection to my looking in and saying good-bye to him?"

"None whatever."

"It would be a graceful act."

"Quite."

"I've always admired his intellect."

"Me too. No one more."

"I'll go round to the flat after lunch."

"Follow the green line," I said, and my manner was airy and even careless. This parting of the ways with Jeeves had made me feel a bit as if I had just stepped on a bomb and was trying to piece myself together again in a bleak world, but we Woosters can keep the stiff upper lip.

I lunched at the Drones and spent the afternoon there. I had much to think of. Chuffy's news that there was a troupe of nigger minstrels performing on the Chuffnell Regis sands had definitely weighed the scale down on the side of the advantages of the place. The fact that I would be in a position to forgather with these experts and possibly pick up a hint or two from their banjoist on fingering and execution enabled me to bear with fortitude the prospect of being in a spot where I would probably have to meet the Dowager Lady Chuffnell and her son Seabury pretty frequently. I had often felt how tough it must be for poor old Chuffy having this pair of pustules popping in and out all the time. And in saying this I am looking straight at little Seabury, a child who should have been strangled at birth. I have no positive proof, but I have always been convinced that it was he who put the lizard in my bed the last time I stayed at the Hall.

But, as I say, I was prepared to put up with this couple in return for the privilege of being in close communication with a really hot banjoist, and most of these nigger minstrel chaps can pick the strings like nobody's business. It was not, therefore, the thought of them which, as I returned to the flat to dress for dinner, was filling me with a strange moodiness.

No. We Woosters can be honest with ourselves. What was giving me the pip was the reflection that Jeeves was about to go out of my life. There never had been anyone like Jeeves, I felt, as I climbed sombrely into the soup and fish, and there never would be. A wave of not unmanly sentiment poured over me. I was conscious of a pang. And when my toilet was completed and I stood before the mirror, surveying that perfectly pressed coat, those superbly creased trousers, I came to a swift decision.

Abruptly, I went into the sitting-room and leaned on the bell.

"Jeeves," I said. "A word."

"Yes, sir?"

"Jeeves," I said, "touching on our conversation this morning."

"Yes, sir?"

"Jeeves," I said, "I have been thinking things over. I have come to the conclusion that we have both been hasty. Let us forget the past. You may stay on."

"It is very kind of you, sir, but . . . are you still proposing to continue the study of that instrument?"

I froze.

"Yes, Jeeves, I am."

"Then I fear, sir . . ."

It was enough. I nodded haughtily.

"Very good, Jeeves. That is all. I will of course, give you an excellent recommendation."

"Thank you, sir. It will not be necessary. This afternoon I entered the employment of Lord Chuffnell."

I started.

"Did Chuffy sneak round here this afternoon and scoop you in?"

"Yes, sir. I go with him to Chuffnell Regis in about a week's time."

"You do, do you? Well, it may interest you to know that I repair to Chuffnell Regis tomorrow."

"Indeed, sir?"

"Yes. I have taken a cottage there. We shall meet at Philippi, Jeeves."

"Yes, sir."

"Or am I thinking of some other spot?"

"No, sir, Philippi is correct."

"Very good, Jeeves."

"Very good, sir."

Such, then, is the sequence of events which led up to Bertram Wooster, on the morning of July the fifteenth, standing at the door of Seaview Cottage, Chuffnell Regis, surveying the scene before him through the aromatic smoke of a meditative cigarette.

⋆ 3 ⋆

Re-enter The Dead Past

YOU know, the longer I live, the more I feel that the great wheeze in life is to be jolly well sure what you want and not let yourself be put off by pals who think they know better than you do. When I had announced at the Drones, on my last day in the metropolis, that I was retiring to this secluded spot for an indeterminate period, practically everybody had begged me, you might say with tears in their eyes, not to dream of doing such a cloth-headed thing. They said I should be bored stiff.

But I had carried on according to plan, and here I was, on the fifth morning of my visit, absolutely in the pink and with no regrets whatsoever. The sun was shining. The sky was blue. And London seemed miles away—which it was, of course. I wouldn't be exaggerating if I said that a great peace enveloped the soul.

A thing I never know when I'm telling a story is how much scenery to bung in. I've asked one or two scriveners of my acquaintance, and their views differ. A fellow I met at a cocktail party in Bloomsbury said that he was all for describing kitchen sinks and frowsty bedrooms and squalor generally, but the beauties of Nature no. Whereas, Freddie Oaker, of the Drones, who does tales of pure love for the weeklies under the pen-name of Alicia Seymour, once told me that he reckoned that flowery meadows in springtime alone were worth at least a hundred quid a year to him.

Personally, I've always rather barred long descriptions of the terrain, so I will be on the brief side. As I stood there that morning, what the eye rested on was the following. There was a nice little splash of garden, containing a bush, a tree, a couple of flower beds, a lily pond with a statue of a nude child with a bit of a tummy on him, and to the right a hedge. Across this hedge, Brinkley, my new man, was chatting with our neighbour, Police Sergeant Voules, who seemed to have looked in with a view to selling eggs.

There was another hedge straight ahead, with the garden gate in it, and over this one espied the placid waters of the harbour, which was much about the same as any other harbour, except that some time during the night a whacking great yacht had rolled up and cast anchor in it. And of all the objects under my immediate advisement I noted this yacht with the most pleasure and approval. White in colour, in size resembling a young liner, it lent a decided tone to the Chuffnell Regis foreshore.

Well, such was the spreading prospect. Add a cat sniffing at a snail on the path and me at the door smoking a gasper, and you have the complete picture.

No, I'm wrong. Not quite the complete picture, because I had left the old two-seater in the road, and I could just see the top part of it. And at this moment the summer stillness was broken by the tooting of its horn, and I buzzed to the gate with all possible speed for fear some fiend in human shape was scratching my paint. Arriving at destination, I found a small boy in the front seat, pensively squeezing the bulb, and was about to administer one on the side of the head when I recognized Chuffy's cousin, Seabury, and stayed the hand.

"Hallo," he said.

"What ho," I replied.

My manner was reserved. The memory of that lizard in my bed still lingered. I don't know if you have ever leaped between the sheets, all ready for a spot of sleep, and received an unforeseen lizard up the left pyjama leg? It is an experience that puts its stamp on a man. And while, as I say, I had no legal proof that this young blighter had been the author of the outrage, I entertained suspicions that were tantamount to certainty. So now I not only spoke with a marked coldness but also gave him the fairly frosty eye.

It didn't seem to jar him. He continued to regard me with that supercilious gaze which had got him so disliked among the right-minded. He was a smallish, freckled kid with aeroplane ears, and he had a way of looking at you as if you were something he had run into in the course of a slumming trip. In my Rogues' Gallery of repulsive small boys I suppose he would come about third—not quite so bad as my Aunt Agatha's son. Young Thos., or Mr. Blumenfeld's Junior, but well ahead of little Sebastian Moon, my Aunt Dahlia's Bonzo, and the field.

After staring at me for a moment as if he were thinking that I had changed for the worse since he last saw me, he spoke.

"You're to come to lunch."

"Is Chuffy back, then?"

"Yes."

Well, of course, if Chuffy had returned, I was at his disposal. I shouted over the hedge to Brinkley that I would be absent from the midday meal and climbed into the car and we rolled off.

"When did he get back?"

"Last night."

"Shall we be lunching alone?"

"No."

"Who's going to be there?"

"Mother and me and some people."

"A party? I'd better go back and put on another suit."

"No."

"You think this one looks all right?"

"No, I don't. I think it looks rotten. But there isn't time."

This point settled, he passed into the silence for a while. A brooding kid. He came out of it to give me some local gossip.

"Mother and I are living at the Hall again."

"What!"

"Yes. There's a smell at the Dower House."

"Even though you've left it?" I said, in my keen way.

He was not amused.

"You needn't try to be funny. If you really want to know, I expect it's my mice."

"Your what?"

"I've started breeding mice and puppies. And, of course, they nif a bit," he added in a dispassionate sort of way. "But mother thinks it's the drains. Can you give me five shillings?"

I simply couldn't follow his train of thought. The way his conversation flitted about gave me that feeling you get in dreams sometimes.

"Five shillings?"

"Five shillings."

"What do you mean, five shillings?"

"I mean five shillings."

"I dare say. But what I want to know is how have we suddenly got on to the subject? We were discussing mice, and you introduce this five shillings motif."

"I want five shillings."

"Admitting that you may possibly want that sum, why the dickens should I give it to you?"

"For protection."

"What!"

"Protection."

"What from?"

"Just protection."

"You don't get any five shillings out of me."

"Oh, all right."

He sat silent for a space.

"Things happen to guys that don't kick in their protection money," he said dreamily.

And on this note of mystery the conversation concluded, for we were moving up the drive of the Hall and on the steps I perceived Chuffy standing. I stopped the car and got out.

"Hallo, Bertie," said Chuffy.

"Welcome to Chuffnell Hall," I replied. I looked round. The kid had vanished. "I say, Chuffy," I said, "young blighted Seabury. What about him?"

"What about him?"

"Well, if you ask me, I should say he had gone off his rocker. He's just been trying to touch me for five bob and babbling about protection."

Chuffy laughed heartily, looking bronzed and fit.

"Oh, that. That's his latest idea."

"How do you mean?"

"He's been seeing gangster films."

The scales fell from my eyes.

"He's turned racketeer?"

"Yes. Rather amusing. He goes round collecting protection money from everybody according to their means. Makes a good thing out of it, too. Enterprising kid. I'd pay up if I were you. I have."

I was shocked. Not so much at the information that the foul child had given this additional evidence of a diseased mind as that Chuffy should be exhibiting this attitude of amused tolerance. I eyed him keenly. Right from the start this morning I had thought his manner strange. Usually, when you meet him, he is brooding over his financial situation and is rather apt to greet you with the lack-lustre eye and the careworn frown. He had been like that a few days ago in London. What, then, had caused him to beam all over the place like this and even to go as far as to speak of little Seabury with what amounted to something perilously near to indulgent affection? I sensed a mystery and decided to apply the acid test.

"How is your Aunt Myrtle?"

"She's fine."

"Living at the Hall now, I hear."

"Yes."

"Indefinitely?"

"Oh, yes."

It was enough.

One of the things, I must mention, which have always made poor old Chuffy's lot so hard is his aunt's attitude toward him. She has never quite been able to get over that matter of the succession. Seabury, you see, was not the son of Chuffy's late uncle, the fourth Baron: he was simply something Lady Chuffnell had picked up *en route* in the course of a former marriage and, consequently, did not come under the head of what the Peerage calls "issue." And, in matters of succession, if you aren't issue, you haven't a hope. When the fourth Baron pegged out, accordingly, it was Chuffy who copped the title and estates. All perfectly square and aboveboard, of course, but you can't get women to see these things, and the relict's manner, Chuffy has often told me, was consistently unpleasant. She had a way of clasping Seabury in her arms and looking reproachfully at Chuffy as if he had slipped over a fast one on mother and child. Nothing actually said, you understand, but her whole attitude that of a woman who considers she has been the victim of sharp practice.

The result of this had been that the Dowager Lady Chuffnell was not one of Chuffy's best-loved buddies. Their relations had always been definitely strained, and what I'm driving at is that usually, when you mention her name, a look of pain comes into Chuffy's clean-cut face and he winces a little, as if you had probed an old wound.

Now he was actually smiling. Even that remark of mine about her living at the Hall had not jarred him. Obviously, there were mysteries here. Something was being kept from Bertram.

I tackled him squarely.

"Chuffy," I said, "what does this mean?"

"What does what mean?"

"This bally cheeriness. You can't deceive me. Not old Hawk-Eye Wooster. Come clean, my lad, something is up. What is all the ruddy happiness about?"

He hesitated. For a moment he eyed me narrowly.

"Can you keep a secret?"

"No."

"Well, it doesn't much matter, because it'll be in the *Morning Post* in a day or two. Bertie," said Chuffy, in a hushed voice, "do you know what's happened? I'm getting Aunt Myrtle off this season."

"You mean somebody wants to marry her?"

"I do."

"Who is this half-wit?"

"Your old friend, Sir Roderick Glossop."

I was stupefied.

"What!"

"I was surprised, too."

"But old Glossop can't be contemplating matrimony."

"Why not? He's been a widower more than two years."

"Oh, I dare say it's possible to make up some kind of a story for him. But what I mean is, he doesn't seem to go with orange blossoms and wedding cake."

"Well, there it is."

"Well, I'm dashed!"

"Yes."

"Well, there's one thing, Chuffy, old man. This means that little Seabury will be getting a really testing stepfather and old Glossop just the stepson I could have wished him. Both have been asking for something on these lines for years. But fancy any woman being mad enough to link her lot with his. Our Humble Heroines!"

"I wouldn't say the heroism was all on one side. About fifty-fifty, I should call it. There is lots of good in this Glossop, Bertie."

I could not accept this. It seemed to me loose thinking.

"Aren't you going a bit far, old man? Admitted that he is taking your Aunt Myrtle off your hands . . ."

"And Seabury."

"And Seabury, true. But, even so, would you really say there was good in the old pest? Remember all the stories I've told you about him from time to time. They show him in a very dubious light."

"Well, he's doing me a bit of good, anyway. Do you know what it was he wanted to see me about so urgently that day in London?"

"What?"

"He's found an American he thinks he can sell the Hall to."

"Not really?"

"Yes. If all goes well, I shall at last get rid of this blasted barracks and have a bit of money in my pocket. And all the credit will be due to Uncle Roderick, as I like to think of him. So you will kindly refrain, Bertie, from nasty cracks at his expense and, in particular, from mentioning him in the same breath with young Seabury. You must learn to love Uncle Roddie for my sake."

I shook my head.

"No, Chuffy, I fear I cannot recede from my positon."

"Well, go to hell, then," said Chuffy agreeably. "Personally, I regard him as a life-saver."

"But are you sure this thing is going to come off? What would this fellow want with a place the size of the Hall?"

"Oh, that part of it is simple enough. He's a great pal of old Glossop's and the idea is that he shall put up the cash and let Glossop run the house as a sort of country club for his nerve patients."

"Why doesn't old Glossop simply rent it from you?"

"My dear ass, what sort of state do you suppose the place is in these days? You talk as if you could open it and step straight into it. Most of the rooms haven't been used for forty years. It wants at least fifteen thousand quid spent on it, to put it in repair. More. Besides new furniture, fittings and so on. If some millionaire like this chap doesn't take it on, I shall have it on my hands the rest of my life."

"Oh, he's a millionaire, is he?"

"Yes, that part of it is all right. All I'm worrying about is getting his signature on the dotted line. Well, he's coming to lunch today, and it's going to be a good one too. He's apt to soften up a good bit after a fat lunch, isn't he?"

"Unless he's got dyspepsia. Many American millionaires have. This man of yours may be one of those fellows who can't get outside more than a glass of milk and a dog biscuit."

Chuffy laughed jovially.

"Not much. Not old Stoker." He suddenly began to leap about like a lamb in the spring-time. "Hullo-ullo-ullo!"

A car had drawn up at the steps and was discharging passengers. Passenger A. was J. Washburn Stoker. Passenger B. was his daughter, Pauline. Passenger C. was his young son, Dwight. And Passenger D. was Sir Roderick Glossop.

* 4 *

Annoying Predicament Of Pauline Stoker

I MUST say I was pretty well a-twitter. It was about as juicy a biff as I had had for years. To have encountered this segment of the dead past in London would have been bad enough. Running into the gang down here like this, with the prospect of a lengthy luncheon party ahead, was a dashed sight worse. I removed the lid with as much courtly grace as I could muster up, but the face had coloured with embarrassment and I was more or less gasping for air.

Chuffy was being the genial host.

"Hullo-ullo-ullo! Here you all are. How are you, Mr. Stoker? How are you, Sir Roderick? Hullo, Dwight. Er—good morning, Miss Stoker. May I introduce my friend, Bertie Wooster? Mr. Stoker, my friend, Bertie Wooster. Dwight, my friend, Bertie Wooster. Miss Stoker, my friend, Bertie Wooster. Sir Roderick Glossop, my friend, Bertie .. Oh, but you know each other already, don't you?"

I was still under the ether. You will agree that all this was enough to rattle any chap. I surveyed the mob. Old Stoker was glaring at me. Old Glossop was glaring at me. Young Dwight was staring at me. Only Pauline appeared to find no awkwardness in the situation. She was as cool as an oyster on the half-shell and as chirpy as a spring breeze. We might have been meeting by appointment. Where Bertram could find only a tentative "Pip-pip!" she bounded forward, full of speech, and grabbed the old hand warmly.

"Well, well, well! Old Colonel Wooster in person! Fancy finding you here, Bertie! I called you up in London, but they told me you had left."

"Yes. I came down here."

"I see you did, you little blob of sunshine. Well, sir, this has certainly made my day. You're looking fine, Bertie. Don't you think he's looking lovely, father?"

Old Stoker appeared reluctant to set himself up as a judge of male beauty. He made a noise like a pig swallowing half a cabbage, but refused to commit himself further. Dwight, a solemn child, was drinking me in in silence. Sir Roderick, who had turned purple, was now fading away to a lighter shade, but still looked as if his finer feelings had sustained a considerable wallop.

At this moment, however, the Dowager Lady Chuffnell came out. She was one of those powerful women who look like female Masters of Hounds, and she handled the mob scene with quiet efficiency. Before I knew where I was, the whole gang had gone indoors, and I was alone with Chuffy. He was staring at me in an odd manner and doing a bit of lower-lip biting.

"I didn't know you knew these people, Bertie."

"I met them in New York."

"You saw something of Miss Stoker there?"

"A little."

"Only a little?"

"Quite a little."

"I thought her manner seemed rather warm."

"Oh, no.   About normal."

"I should have imagined you were great friends."

"Oh, no.   Just fairly pally.   She goes on like that with everyone."

"She does?"

"Oh, yes.   Big-hearted, you see."

"She has got a delightful, impulsive, generous, spontaneous, genuine nature, hasn't she?"

"Absolutely."

"Beautiful girl, Bertie."

"Oh, very."

"And charming."

"Oh, most."

"In fact, attractive."

"Oh, quite."

"I saw a good deal of her in London."

"Yes?"

"We went to the Zoo and Madame Tussaud's together."

"I see.   And what does she seem to feel about this buying the house binge?"

"She seems all for it."

"Tell me, laddie," I said, anxious to get off the current subj., "how do the prospects look?"

He knitted the Chuffnell brow.

"Sometimes good.   Sometimes not."

"I see."

"Uncertain."

"I understand."

"This Stoker chap makes me nervous.   He's friendly enough as a general rule, but I can't help feeling that at any moment he may fly off the handle and scratch the entire fixture.   You can't tell me if there are any special subjects to avoid when talking to him, can you?"

"Special subjects?"

"Well, you know how it is with a stranger.   You say it's a fine day, and he goes all white and tense, because you've reminded him that it was on a fine day that his wife eloped with the chauffeur."

I considered.

"Well, if I were you," I said, "I wouldn't harp too much on the topic of B. Wooster. I mean, if you were thinking of singing my praises . . ."

"I wasn't."

"Well, don't. He doesn't like me."

"Why not?"

"Just one of these unreasonable antipathies. And I was thinking, old man, if it's all the same to you, it might be better if I didn't join the throng at the luncheon table. You can tell your aunt I've got a headache."

"Well, if the sight of you is going to infuriate him . . . What makes him bar you so much?"

"I don't know."

"Well, I'm glad you told me. You had better sneak off."

"I will."

"And I suppose I ought to be joining the others."

He went indoors, and I started to take a turn or two up and down the gravel. I was glad to be alone. I wished to muse upon this matter of his attitude towards Pauline Stoker.

I wonder if you would mind just going back a bit and running the mental eye over that part of our conversation which had had to do with the girl.

Anything strike you about it?

No?

Oh, well, to get the full significance, of course, you ought to have been there and observed him. I am a man who can read faces, and Chuffy's had seemed to me highly suggestive. Not only had its expression, as he spoke of Pauline, been that of a stuffed frog with a touch of the Soul's Awakening about it, but it had also turned a fairly deepish crimson in colour. The tip of the nose had wiggled, and there had been embarrassment in the manner. The result being that I had become firmly convinced that the old schoolmate had copped it properly. Quick work, of course, seeing that he had only known the adored object a few days, but Chuffy is like that. A man of impulse and hot-blooded impetuosity. You find the girl, and he does the rest.

Well, if it was so, it was all right with me. Nothing of the dog in the manger about Bertram. As far as I was concerned,

Pauline Stoker could hitch up with anyone she liked and she would draw a hearty "Go to it!" from the discarded suitor. You know how it is on quiet reflection in these affairs. For a time the broken heart, and then suddenly the healing conviction that one is jolly well out of it. I could still see that Pauline was one of the most beautiful girls I had ever met, but of the ancient fire which had caused me to bung my heart at her feet that night at the Plaza there remained not a trace.

Analysing this, if analysing is the word I want, I came to the conclusion that this changed outlook was due to the fact that she was so dashed dynamic. Unquestionably an eyeful, Pauline Stoker had the grave defect of being one of those girls who want you to come and swim a mile before breakfast and rout you out when you are trying to snatch a wink of sleep after lunch for a merry five sets of tennis. And now that the scales had fallen from my eyes, I could see that what I required for the rôle of Mrs. Bertram Wooster was something rather more on the lines of Janet Gaynor.

But in Chuffy's case these objections fell to the ground. He, you see, is very much on the dynamic side himself. He rides, swims, shoots, chivvies foxes with loud cries, and generally bustles about. He and this P. Stoker would make the perfect pair, and I felt that if there was anything I could do to push the thing along, it should be done unstintedly.

So when at this point I saw Pauline coming out of the house and bearing down on me, obviously with a view to exchanging notes and picking up the old threads and what not, I did not leg it but greeted her with a bright "What ho!" and allowed her to steer me into the shelter of a path that led through the rhododendron shrubbery.

All of which goes to show to what lengths a Wooster will proceed when it is a question of helping a pal, because the last thing I really wanted was to be closeted with this girl. The first shock of meeting her was over, but I was still feeling far from yeasty at the prospect of a heart-to-heart talk. As our relations had been severed by post and the last time we had forgathered we had been an engaged couple, I wasn't quite sure what was the correct note to strike.

However, the thought that I might be able to put in a word for old Chuffy nerved me to the ordeal, and we parked ourselves on a rustic bench and got down to the agenda.

"How perfectly extraordinary finding you here, Bertie," she began. "What are you doing in these parts?"

"I am temporarily in retirement," I replied, pleased to find the conversational exchanges opening on what I might call an unemotional note. "I needed a place where I could play the banjolele in solitude, and I took this cottage."

"What cottage?"

"I've got a cottage down by the harbour."

"You must have been surprised to see us."

"I was."

"More surprised than pleased, eh?"

"Well, of course, old thing, I'm always delighted to meet you, but when it comes to your father *and* old Glossop . . ."

"He's not one of your greatest admirers, is he? By the way, Bertie, *do* you keep cats in your bedroom?"

I stiffened a little.

"There have been cats in my bedroom, but the incident to which you allude is one that is susceptible of a ready . . ."

"All right. Never mind. Take it as read. But you ought to have seen father's face when he heard about it. Talking of father's face, I should get a big laugh if I saw it now."

I could not follow this. Goodness knows, I'm as fond of a chuckle as the next man, but J. Washburn Stoker's face had never made me so much as smile. He was a cove who always reminded me of a pirate of the Spanish Main—a massive blighter and piercing-eyed, to boot. So far from laughing at the sight of him, I had never yet failed to feel absolutely spineless in his presence.

"If he suddenly came round the corner, I mean, and found us with our heads together like this. He's convinced that I'm still pining for you."

"You don't mean that?"

"I do, honestly."

"But, dash it . . ."

"It's true, I tell you. He looks on himself as the stern Victorian father who has parted the young lovers and has got to exercise ceaseless vigilance to keep them from getting together again. Little knowing that you never had a happier moment in your life than when you got my letter."

"No, I say!"

"Bertie, be honest. You know you were delighted."

"I wouldn't say that."

"You don't have to. Mother knows."

"No, dash it, really! I wish you wouldn't talk like that. I always esteemed you most highly."

"You did what? Where do you pick up these expressions?"

"Well, I suppose from Jeeves, mostly. My late man. He had a fine vocabulary."

"When you say 'late', do you mean he's dead? Or just unpunctual?"

"He's left me. He didn't like me playing the banjolele. Words passed, and he is now with Chuffy."

"Chuffy?"

"Lord Chuffnell."

"Oh?"

There was a pause. She sat listening for a moment to a couple of birds who were having an argument in a near-by tree.

"Have you known Lord Chuffnell long?" she asked.

"Oh, rather."

"You're great friends?"

"Bosom is the *mot juste*."

"Good. I hoped you were. I wanted to talk to you about him. I can confide in you, can't I, Bertie?"

"Of course."

"I knew I could. That's the comfort of having been engaged to a man. When you break it off, you feel such a sister."

"I don't regard you as a blister at all," I said warmly. "You had a perfect right . . ."

"Not blister. Sister!"

"Oh, sister? You mean, you look on me as a brother."

"Yes, as a brother. How quick you are. And I want you to be very brotherly now. Tell me about Marmaduke."

"I don't think I know him."

"Lord Chuffnell, idiot."

"Is his name Marmaduke? Well, well! How true it is that one doesn't know how the other half of the world lives, what? Marmaduke!" I said, laughing heartily. "I remember he was always evasive and secretive about it at school."

She seemed annoyed.

"It's a beautiful name!"

I shot one of my swift, keen glances at her. This, I felt,

must mean something. Nobody would say Marmaduke was a beautiful name wantonly and without good reason. And, sure enough, the eyes were gleaming and the epidermis a pretty pink.

"Hullo!" I said. "Hullo, hullo, hullo! Hullo!"

Her demeanour was defiant.

"All right, all right!" she said. "Less of the Sherlock stuff. I'm not trying to hide anything. I was just going to tell you."

"You love this . . . ha, ha! Excuse me . . . this Marmaduke?"

"I'm crazy about him."

"Good! Well, if what you say . . ."

"Don't you worship the way his hair fluffs up behind?"

"I have better things to do than go about staring at the back of Chuffy's head. But, as I was about to remark, if what you say is really so, be prepared for tidings of great joy. I'm a pretty close observer, and a certain bulbous look in the old boy's eyes when a recent conversation happened to turn in your direction has convinced me that he is deeply enamoured of you."

She wiggled her shoulder impatiently, and in a rather peevish manner hoofed a passing earwig with a shapely foot.

"I know that, you chump. Do you think a girl can't tell?"

I was frankly nonplussed.

"Well, if he loves you and you love him, I fail to comprehend what you are beefing about."

"Why, can't you understand? He's obviously dippy about me, but not a yip from him."

"He will not speak?"

"Not a syllable."

"Well, why would he? Surely you realize that there is a certain decency in these matters, a certain decorum? Naturally he wouldn't say anything yet. Dash it, give the man a chance. He's only known you five days."

"I sometimes feel that he was a king in Babylon when I was a Christian slave."

"What makes you think that?"

"I just do."

"Well, you know best, of course. Very doubtful, I should have said myself. And, anyway, what do you want me to do about it?"

"Well, you're a friend of his. You could give him a hint. You could tell him there's no need for cold feet. . . ."

"It is not cold feet. It is delicacy. As I just explained, we men have our code in these matters. We may fall in love pretty nippily, but after that we consider it decorous to back-pedal a while. We are the parfait gentle knights, and we feel that it ill beseems us to make a beeline for a girl like a man charging into a railway restaurant for a bowl of soup. We . . ."

"What utter nonsense! You asked me to marry you after you had known me two weeks."

"Ah, but there you were dealing with one of the Wild Woosters."

"Well, I can't see . . ."

"Yes?" I said "Proceed. You have our ear."

But she was looking past me at something to the south-east; and, turning, I perceived that we were no longer alone.

There, standing in an attitude of respectful courtliness, with the sunshine playing upon his finely-chiselled features, was Jeeves.

✳ 5 ✳

Bertie Takes Things In Hand

I NODDED affably. This man and I might have severed our professional relations, but a Wooster is always debonair.

"Ah, Jeeves."

"Good afternoon, sir."

Pauline appeared interested.

"Is this Jeeves?"

"This is Jeeves."

"So you don't like Mr. Wooster's banjolele?"

"No, miss."

I preferred that this delicate matter be not discussed, and it may be, in consequence, that I spoke a little curtly.

"Well, Jeeves? What is it?"

"Mr. Stoker, sir. He is inquiring after Miss Stoker's whereabouts."

Well, of course, there's always that old one about them being at the wash, but this seemed to me neither the time nor the place. I turned to the girl with an air of courteous dismissal.

"You'd better push along."

"I suppose so.   You won't forget what I said?"

"The matter," I assured her, "shall have my prompt attention."

She legged it, and Jeeves and I were alone together in the great solitude.   I lit a cigarette nonchalantly.

"Well, Jeeves."

"Sir?"

"I mean to say, we meet again."

"Yes, sir."

"Philippi, what?"

"Yes, sir."

"I hope you're getting on all right with Chuffy?"

"Everything is most pleasant, sir.   I trust your new personal attendant is giving satisfaction?"

"Oh, quite.   A sterling fellow."

"I am extremely gratified to hear it, sir."

There was a pause.

"Er, Jeeves," I said.

A rummy thing.   It had been my intention, after exchanging these few civilities, to nod carelessly and leave the fellow.   But it's so dashed difficult to break the habit of years.   I mean to say, here was I and here was Jeeves, and a problem had been put up to me of just the type concerning which I had always been wont to seek his advice and counsel, and now something seemed to keep me rooted to the spot.   And instead of being aloof and distant and passing on with the slight inclination of the head which, as I say, I had been planning, I found myself irresistibly impelled to consult him just as if there had been no rift at all.

"Er—Jeeves," I said.

"Sir?"

"I should rather like, if you have a moment to spare, to split a word with you."

"Certainly, sir."

"I wish to canvass your views regarding old Chuffy."

"Very good, sir."

His face was wearing that expression of quiet intelligence combined with a feudal desire to oblige which I had so often seen upon it, and I hesitated no longer.

"You will agree with me that something's got to be done about the fifth Baron, I take it?"

"I beg your pardon, sir?"

I was impatient with this—what the dickens is the word I want?

"Come, come, Jeeves. You know what I mean as well as I do. A little less coyness and a bit more of the old rallying round spirit. You can't tell me you've been in his employment for nearly a week without observing and deducing and forming your conclusions."

"Am I correct in supposing, sir, that you are alluding to his lordship's feelings towards Miss Stoker?"

"Exactly."

"I am, of course, aware that his lordship is experiencing for the young lady a sentiment deeper and warmer than that of ordinary friendship, sir."

"Would I be going too far if I said that he was potty about her?"

"No, sir. The expression would meet the facts of the case quite adequately."

"Very well, then. Now, mark this. She, too, loves, Jeeves."

"Indeed, sir?"

"She was telling me so specifically when you came along. She confessed herself dippy about the man. And she's very upset, poor fish. Extremely upset. Her feminine intuition has enabled her to read his secret. She detects the lovelight in his eyes. And she is all for it. And what is worrying her is that he does not tell his love, but lets concealment like . . . like what, Jeeves?"

"A worm i' the bud, sir."

"Feed on his something . . ."

"Damask cheek, sir."

"Damask? You're sure?"

"Quite sure, sir."

"Well, then, what on earth is it all about? He loves her. She loves him. So what's the snag? In conversing with her just now, I advanced the theory that what was holding him back was delicacy, but I didn't really believe it. I know Chuffy. A swift performer, if ever there was one. If he didn't propose to a girl by the end of the first week, he would think he was losing his grip. Yet now look at him. Missing on every cylinder. Why?"

"His lordship is a gentleman of scruples, sir."

"How do you mean?"

"He feels that, being of straitened means himself, he has not the right to propose marriage to a young lady as wealthy as Miss Stoker."

"But, dash it, Love laughs at . . . no, it doesn't . . . it's at locksmiths, isn't it?"

"At locksmiths, yes, sir."

"Besides, she isn't as rich as all that. Just comfortably off, I should have said."

"No, sir. Mr. Stoker's fortune amounts to as much as fifty million dollars."

"What! You're talking through your hat, Jeeves."

"No, sir. I understand that that was the sum which he inherited recently under the will of the late Mr. George Stoker."

I was stunned.

"Good Lord, Jeeves! Has Second Cousin George kicked the bucket?"

"Yes, sir."

"And left all his money to old Stoker?"

"Yes, sir."

"Now I see. Now I understand—— This explains everything. I was wondering how he managed to be going about buying vast estates. The yacht in the harbour is his, of course?"

"Yes, sir."

"Well, well, well! But, dash it, George must have had nearer relations."

"Yes, sir. I understand that he disliked them all."

"You know about him, then?"

"Yes, sir. I saw a good deal of his personal attendant when we were in New York. A man named Benstead."

"He was potty, wasn't he?"

"Certainly extremely eccentric, sir."

"Any chance of one of those other relations contesting the will?"

"I do not imagine so, sir. But in such a case Mr. Stoker would rely on Sir Roderick Glossop, of course, to testify that the late Mr. Stoker, while possibly somewhat individual in his habits, was nevertheless perfectly sane. The testimony of so eminent a mental specialist as Sir Roderick would be unassailable."

"You mean he'd say why shouldn't a fellow walk about on his hands, if he wants to? Saves shoe leather, and so forth?"

"Exactly, sir."

"Then there's no chance of Miss Stoker ever being anything except the heiress of a bird with fifty million dollars shoved away behind the brick in the fire-place?"

"Virtually none, sir."

I brooded on this.

"H'm. And unless old Stoker buys the Hall, Chuffy will continue to be Kid Lazarus, the man without a bean. One spots the drama of the situation. And yet, why, Jeeves? Why all this fuss about money? After all, plenty of bust blokes have married oofy girls before now."

"Yes, sir. But his lordship is a gentleman of peculiar views on this particular matter."

I mused. Yes, I reflected, it was quite true. Chuffy is a fellow who has always been odd on the subject of money. It's something to do with the Pride of the Chuffnells, I suppose. I know that for years and years I have been trying to lend him of my plenty, but he has always steadfastly refused to put the bite on me.

"It's difficult," I said. "One fails for the moment to see the way out. And yet you may be wrong, Jeeves. After all, you're only guessing."

"No, sir. His lordship did me the honour to confide in me."

"Really? How did the subject come up?"

"Mr. Stoker had expressed a wish that I should enter his employment. He approached me in the matter. I informed his lordship. His lordship instructed me to hold out hopes."

"You can't mean that he wants you to leave him and go to old Stoker?"

"No, sir. He specifically stated the reverse, with a good deal of vehemence. But he was anxious that I should not break off the negotiations with a definite refusal until the sale of Chuffnell Hall had gone through."

"I see. I follow his strategy. He wanted you to jolly old Stoker along and keep him sweetened till he had signed the fatal papers?"

"Precisely, sir. It was this conversation that led up to his lordship revealing his personal position as concerns Miss Stoker. Until his financial status is sufficiently sound to justify him in doing so, his self-respect will not permit him to propose marriage to the young lady."

"Silly ass!"

"I would not have ventured to employ precisely that term myself, sir, but I confess that I regard his lordship's attitude as somewhat hyper-quixotic."

"We must talk him out of it."

"Impossible, sir, I fear. I endeavoured to do so myself, but my arguments were of no avail. His lordship has a complex."

"A what?"

"A complex, sir. It seems that he once witnessed a musical comedy, in which one of the dramatis personæ was a certain impecunious peer, Lord Wotwotleigh, who was endeavouring to marry an American heiress, and this individual appears to have made a lasting impression on his mind. He stated to me in the most unequivocal terms that he refused to place himself in a position where comparisons might be instituted."

"But suppose the sale of the house does not go through?"

"In that case, I fear, sir . . ."

"The damask cheek will continue to do business at the old stand indefinitely?"

"Exactly, sir."

"You really are sure it is 'damask'?"

"Yes, sir."

"But it doesn't seem to mean anything."

"An archaic adjective, sir. I fancy it is intended to signify a healthy complexion."

"Well, Chuffy's got that."

"Yes, sir."

"But what good's a healthy complexion if you don't get the girl?"

"Very true, sir."

"What would you advise, Jeeves?"

"I fear I have nothing to suggest at the moment, sir."

"Come, come, Jeeves."

"No, sir. The difficulty being essentially a psychological one, I find myself somewhat baffled. As long as the image of Lord Wotwotleigh persists in his lordship's consciousness, I fear that there is nothing to be done."

"Of course there is. Why this strange weakness, Jeeves? It is not like you. Obviously, the fellow must be shoved over the brink."

"I do not quite follow you, sir."

"Of course you do. The thing's perfectly clear. Here's old Chuffy, for the nonce just hanging dumbly round the girl. What he needs is a jolt. If he thought there was grave danger of some other bloke scooping her up, wouldn't that make him forget these dashed silly ideas of his and charge in, breathing fire through the nostrils?"

"Jealously is undoubtedly an extremely powerful motivating force, sir."

"Do you know what I am going to do, Jeeves?"

"No, sir."

"I am going to kiss Miss Stoker and take care that Chuffy sees me do it."

"Really, sir, I should not advocate . . ."

"Peace, Jeeves. I have got the whole thing taped out. It came to me in a flash, as we were talking. After lunch, I shall draw Miss Stoker aside to this seat. You will arrange that Chuffy follows her. Waiting till I see the whites of his eyes, I shall fold her in a close embrace. If that doesn't work, nothing will."

"I consider that you would be taking a decided risk, sir. His lordship is in a highly emotional condition."

"Well, a Wooster can put up with a punch in the eye for the sake of a pal. No, Jeeves, I desire no further discussion. The thing is settled. All that remains is to fix the times. I suppose lunch would be over by about two-thirty. . . . Incidentally, I'm not going in to lunch myself."

"No, sir?"

"No. I cannot face that gang. I shall remain out here. Bring me some sandwiches and a half-bot of the best."

"Very good, sir."

"And, by the way, the french windows of the dining-room will be open in weather like this. Sneak near them from time to time during lunch and bend an ear. Something of importance might be said."

"Very good, sir."

"Put plenty of mustard on the sandwiches."

"Very good, sir."

"And at two-thirty inform Miss Stoker that I would like a word with her. And at two-thirty-one inform Lord Chuffnell that she would like a word with him. The rest you can leave to me."

"Very good, sir."

6

Complications Set In

THERE was a fairly longish interval before Jeeves returned with the food-stuffs. I threw myself on them with some abandon.

"You've been the dickens of a time."

"I followed your instructions, sir, and listened at the dining-room window."

"Oh? With what result?"

"I was not able to hear anything that gave an indication of Mr. Stoker's views regarding the purchase of the house, but he appeared in affable mood."

"That's promising. Full of sparkle, eh?"

"Yes, sir. He was inviting all those present to a party on his yacht."

"He's staying on here, then?"

"For some little time, I gathered, sir. Apparently something has gone wrong with the propeller of the vessel."

"He probably gave it one of his looks. And this party?"

"It appears that it is Master Dwight Stoker's birthday to-morrow, sir. The party, I gathered, was to be in celebration of the event."

"And was the suggestion well received?"

"Extremely, sir. Though Master Seabury appeared to experience a certain chagrin at Master Dwight's somewhat arrogant assertion that he betted this was the first time that Master Seabury had ever so much as smelled a yacht."

"What did he say?"

"He retorted that he had been on millions of yachts. Indeed, if I am not mistaken, trillions was the word he employed."

"And then?"

"From a peculiar noise which he made with his mouth, I received the impression that Master Dwight was sceptical con-cerning this claim. But at this moment Mr. Stoker threw oil upon the troubled waters by announcing his intention of hiring the troupe of negro minstrels to perform at the party. It appears that his lordship had mentioned their presence in Chuffnell Regis."

"And that went well?"

"Very well, indeed, sir. Except that Master Seabury said that he betted Master Dwight had never heard negro minstrels before. From a remark passed shortly afterwards by her ladyship, I gathered that Master Dwight had then thrown a potato at Master Seabury; and for a while a certain unpleasantness seemed to threaten."

I clicked my tongue.

"I wish somebody would muzzle those kids and chain them up. They'll queer the whole thing."

"The imbroglio was fortunately short-lived, sir. I left the whole company on what appeared to be the most amicable terms. Master Dwight protested that his hand had slipped, and the apology was gracefully received."

"Well, bustle back and see if you can hear some more."

"Very good, sir."

I finished my sandwiches and half-bot, and lit a cigarette, wishing that I had told Jeeves to bring me some coffee. But you don't have to tell Jeeves things like that. In due course, up he rolled with the steaming cupful.

"Luncheon has just concluded, sir."

"Ah! Did you see Miss Stoker?"

"Yes, sir. I informed her that you desired a word with her, and she will be here shortly."

"Why not now?"

"His lordship engaged her in conversation immediately after I had given her your message."

"Had you told him to come here, too?"

"Yes, sir."

"No good, Jeeves. I see a flaw. They will arrive together."

"No, sir. On observing his lordship making in this direction, I can easily detain him for a moment on some matter."

"Such as——?"

"I have long been desirous of canvassing his lordship's views as to the desirability of purchasing some new socks."

"H'm! You know what you are when you get on to the subject of socks, Jeeves. Don't get carried away and keep him talking for an hour. I want to get this thing over."

"I quite understand, sir."

"When did you see Miss Stoker?"

"About a quarter of an hour ago, sir."

"Funny, she doesn't turn up. I wonder what they're talking about?"

"I could not say, sir."

"Ah!"

I had observed a gleam of white among the bushes. The next moment, the girl appeared. She was looking more beautiful than ever, her eyes, in particular, shining like twin stars. Nevertheless, I did not waver in my view that I was jolly glad it was Chuffy who, if all went well, was going to marry her, and not me. Odd, how a girl may be a perfect knock-out, and yet one can still feel that to be married to her would give one the absolute pip. That's Life, I suppose.

"Hallo, Bertie," said Pauline. "What's all this about your having a headache? You seem to have been doing yourself pretty well, in spite of it."

"I found I could peck a bit. You had better take these things back, Jeeves."

"Very good, sir."

"And you won't forget that, if his lordship should want me, I'm here."

"No, sir."

He gathered up the plate, cup and bottle and disappeared. And whether I was sorry to see him go or not, I couldn't have said. I was feeling a good deal worked up. Taut, if you know what I mean. On edge. Tense. The best idea I can give you of my emotions at this juncture is to say that they rather resembled those I had once felt when starting to sing "Sonny Boy" at Beefy Bingham's Church Lads entertainment down in the East End.

Pauline had grabbed my arm, and was beginning to make some species of communication.

"Bertie," she was saying . . .

But at this point I caught sight of Chuffy's head over a shrub, and I felt that the moment had come to act. It was one of those things that want doing quickly or not at all. I waited no longer. Folding the girl in my arms, I got home on her right eyebrow. It wasn't one of my best, I will admit, but it was a kiss within the meaning of the act, and I fancied that it ought to produce results.

And so, no doubt, it would have done, had the fellow who

entered left at this critical point been Chuffy. But it wasn't. What with only being able to catch a fleeting glimpse of a Homburg hat through the foliage, I appeared to have made an unfortunate floater. The bloke who now stood before us was old Pop Stoker, and I confess I found myself a prey to a certain embarrassment.

It was, you must admit, not a little awkward. Here was an anxious father who combined with a strong distaste for Bertram Wooster the notion that his daughter was madly in love with him: and the first thing he saw when he took an after-lunch saunter was the two of us locked in a close embrace. It was enough to give any parent the jitters, and I was not surprised that his demeanour was that of stout Cortez staring at the Pacific. A fellow with fifty millions in his kick doesn't have to wear the mask. If he wants to give any selected bloke a nasty look, he gives him a nasty look. He was giving me one now. It was a look that had both alarm and anguish in it, and I realized that Pauline's statement regarding his views had been accurate.

Fortunately, the thing did not go beyond looks. Say what you like against civilization, it comes in dashed handy in a crisis like this. It may be a purely artificial code that keeps a father from hoofing his daughter's kisser when they are fellow guests at a house, but at this moment I felt that I could do with all the purely artificial codes that were going.

There was just one instant when his foot twitched and it seemed as if what you might call the primitive J. Washburn Stoker was about to find self-expression. Then civilization prevailed. With one more of those looks he collected Pauline, and the next moment I was alone and at liberty to think the thing over.

And it was as I was doing so with the help of a soothing cigarette that Chuffy bounded into my little sylvan glade. He too appeared to have something on his mind, for he was noticeably pop-eyed.

"Look here, Bertie," he began without preamble, "what's all this I hear?"

"What's all what you hear, old man?"

"Why didn't you tell me you had been engaged to Pauline Stoker?"

I raised an eyebrow. It seemed to me that a touch of the iron hand would not be out of place. If you see a fellow's going to be austere with you, there's nothing like jumping in and being austere with him first.

"I fail to understand you, Chuffnell," I said stiffly. "Did you expect me to send you a post card?"

"You could have told me this morning."

"I saw no reason to do so. How did you hear about it, anyhow?"

"Sir Roderick Glossop happened to mention it."

"Oh, he did, did he? Well, he's an authority on the subject. He was the bird who broke it off."

"What do you mean?"

"He happened to be in New York at the time, and it was the work of a moment with him to tap old Stoker on the chest and urge him to give me the push. The whole thing didn't last more than forty-eight hours from kick-off to finish."

Chuffy eyed me narrowly.

"You swear that?"

"Certainly."

"Only forty-eight hours?"

"Less."

"And there's nothing between you now?"

His demeanour was not matey, and I began to perceive that in arranging that Stoker and not he should be the witness of the recent embrace the guardian angel of the Woosters had acted dashed shrewdly.

"Nothing."

"You're sure?"

"Nothing whatever. So charge in, Chuffy, old man," I said, patting his shoulder in an elder-brotherly manner. "Follow the dictates of the old heart and fear nothing. The girl is potty about you."

"Who told you that?"

"She did."

"Herself?"

"In person."

"She does really love me?"

"Passionately, I gathered."

A look of relief came into the old egg's care-worn face. He passed a hand over the forehead and general relaxed.

"Well, that's all right, then. Sorry, if I appeared a bit rattled for a moment. When a fellow's just got engaged to a girl, it's rather a jar to find that she was engaged to somebody else about two months before."

I was astounded.

"Are you engaged?   Since when?

"Since shortly after lunch."

"But how about Wotwotleigh?"

"Who told you about Wotwotleigh?"

"Jeeves.   He said the shadow of Wotwotleigh brooded over you like a cloud."

"Jeeves talks too much.   As a matter of fact, Wotwotleigh didn't enter into the matter at all.   Immediately before I fixed things up with Pauline, old Stoker told me he had decided to buy the house."

"Really!"

"Absolutely.   I think it was the port that did it.   I lushed him up on the last of the '85."

"You couldn't have done a wiser thing.   Your own idea?"

"No.   Jeeves's."

I could not restrain a wistful sigh.

"Jeeves is a wonder."

"A marvel."

"What a brain!"

"Size nine-and-a.quarter, I should say."

"He eats a lot of fish.   What a pity he has no ear for music," I said moodily.   Then I stifled regret and tried to think not of my bereavement but of Chuffy's bit of luck.   "Well, this is fine," I said heartily.   "I hope you will be very, very happy.   I can honestly say that I always look on Pauline as one of the nicest girls I was ever engaged to."

"I wish you would stop harping on that engagement."

"Quite."

"I'm trying to forget that you ever were engaged to her."

"Quite, quite."

"When I think that you were once in a position to . . ."

"But I wasn't.   Never lose sight of the fact that the betrothal only lasted two days, during both of which I was in bed with a nasty cold."

"But when she accepted you, you must have . . ."

"No, I didn't.   A waiter came into the room with a tray of beef sandwiches and the moment passed."

"Then you never . . .?"

"Absolutely never."

"She must have had a great time, being engaged to you. One round of excitement. I wonder what on earth made her accept you?"

This had puzzled me too, more than a little. I can only suppose that there is something in me that strikes a chord in the bosoms of these forceful females. I've known it happen before, on the occasion when I got engaged to Honoria Glossop.

"I once consulted a knowledgeable pal," I said, "and his theory was that the sight of me hanging about like a loony sheep awoke the maternal instinct in Woman. There may be something in this."

"Possibly," agreed Chuffy. "Well, I'll be getting along. I suppose Stoker will want to talk to me about the house. You coming?"

"No, thanks. The fact of the matter is, old man, I'm not so dashed keen on mingling with your little troupe. I could stand your Aunt Myrtle. I could even stand little Seabury. But add Stoker and Glossop, and the going becomes too sticky for Bertram. I shall take a stroll about the estate."

This demesne or seat of Chuffy's was a topping place for a stroll, and I should have thought he would have had a certain regret at the thought that it was passing out of his hands, to become a private loony-bin. But I suppose when you've been cooped up in a house for years with an Aunt Myrtle and a cousin Seabury for next-door neighbours, you lose your taste for it. I spent an agreeable two hours messing about, and it was well along into the late afternoon when the imperative need for a cup of tea sent me sauntering round to the back premises, where I anticipated finding Jeeves.

A scullery-maid of sorts directed me to his quarters, and I sat down in the comfortable certainty that ere long the steaming pot and buttered toast would be to the fore. The happy ending of which Chuffy had recently apprised me had induced contentment, and a nice hot cup and slab of toast would, I felt, just top the thing off.

"In fact, Jeeves," I said, "even muffins would scarcely be out of place on an occasion like this. I find it very gratifying to reflect that Chuffy's storm-tossed soul has at last come safely into harbour. You heard about Stoker promising to buy the house?"

"Yes, sir."

"And the engagement?"

"Yes, sir."

"I suppose old Chuffy is feeling great."

"Not altogether, sir."

"Eh?"

"No, sir. I regret to say that there has been something in the nature of a hitch."

"What! They can't have quarrelled already?"

"No, sir. His lordship's relations with Miss Stoker continue uniformly cordial. It is with Mr. Stoker that he is on distant terms."

"Oh, my God!"

"Yes, sir."

"What happened?"

"The origin of the trouble was a physical contest between Master Dwight Stoker and Master Seabury, sir. You may recollect my mentioning that during luncheon there appeared to be a lack of perfect sympathy between the young gentlemen."

"But you said——"

"Yes, sir. Matters were smoothed over at the time, but they came to a head again some forty minutes after the conclusion of the meal. The young gentlemen had gone off together to the small morning-room, and there, it appears, Master Seabury endeavoured to exact from Master Dwight the sum of one shilling and sixpence for what he termed protection."

"Oh, golly!"

"Yes, sir. Master Dwight, I gathered, declined in a somewhat high-spirited manner to kick in, as I believe the expression is, and one word led to another, with the result that at about three-thirty sounds indicative of a brawl were heard proceeding from the morning-room, and the senior members of the party, repairing thither, discovered the young gentlemen on the floor surrounded by the debris of a china cabinet which they had overturned in their struggle. At the moment of their arrival, Master Dwight appeared to be having somewhat the better of the exchanges, for he was seated on Master Seabury's chest, bumping his head on the carpet."

It will give you some idea of the grave concern which this narrative was occasioning me, when I say that my emotion on hearing this was not a sober ecstasy at the thought that after all

these long years somebody had at last been treating little Seabury's head as it ought to be treated, but a sickening dismay.
I could see whither all this was tending.

"Gosh, Jeeves!"

"Yes, sir."

"And then?"

"The action then became, as it were, general, sir."

"The old brigade lent a hand?"

"Yes, sir, the initiative being taken by Lady Chuffnell."

I moaned.

"It would be, Jeeves. Chuffy has often told me that her
attitude towards Seabury resembles that of a tigress towards its
cub. In Seabury's interests she has always been inclined to
stamp on the world's toes and give it the elbow. I have heard
Chuffy's voice absolutely quiver when describing the way in
which, in the days before he contrived to shoot them off to the
Dower House and they were still living at the Hall, she always
collared the best egg at breakfast and slipped it to the little one.
But go on."

"On witnessing the position of affairs, her ladyship uttered a
sharp cry and struck Master Dwight with considerable force on
the right ear."

"Upon which, of course . . .?"

"Precisely, sir. Mr. Stoker, espousing the cause of his son,
aimed a powerful kick at Master Seabury."

"And got him, Jeeves? Tell me he got him."

"Yes, sir. Master Seabury was rising at the moment, and his
attitude was exceptionally well adapted for the receipt of such an
attack. The next moment, a heated altercation had broken out
between her ladyship and Mr. Stoker. Her ladyship called to
Sir Roderick for support, and he—somewhat reluctantly, it
appeared to me—proceeded to take Mr. Stoker to task for the
assault. High words ensued, and the upshot of it was that Mr.
Stoker with a good deal of warmth informed Sir Roderick that if
he supposed that he, Mr. Stoker, intended to purchase Chuffnell
Hall after what had occurred, he, Sir Roderick, was in grave
error."

I buried the head in the hands.

"Upon this . . ."

"Yes, get it over, Jeeves. I can see what's coming."

"Yes, sir. I agree with you that the whole affair has some-

thing of the dark inevitability of Greek tragedy. Upon this,
his lordship, who had been an agitated auditor, gave vent to a
startled exclamation and urged Mr. Stoker to disclaim these
words. It was his lordship's view that Mr. Stoker, having given
his promise to purchase Chuffnell Hall, could not, as an honourable man, recede from his obligation. Upon Mr. Stoker replying that he did not care what he had promised or what he had not
promised and continuing to asseverate that not a penny of his
money should be expended in the direction indicated, his lordship, I regret to say, became somewhat unguarded in his speech."

I moaned another bar or two. I knew what old Chuffy was
capable of when his generous nature was stirred. I had heard
him coaching his college boat at Oxford.

"He ticked Stoker off?"

"With considerable vigour, sir. Stating in an extremely
candid manner his opinion of the latter's character, commercial
probity, and even appearance."

"That must have put the lid on it." ..

"It did appear to create a certain coldness, sir."

"And then?"

"That terminated the distressing scene, sir. Mr. Stoker
returned to the yacht with Miss Stoker and Master Dwight.
Sir Roderick has gone to secure accommodation for himself at
the local inn. Lady Chuffnell is applying arnica to Master
Seabury in his bedroom. His lordship, I believe, is taking the
dog for a run in the west park."

I mused.

"When all this happened, had Chuffy told Stoker he wanted
to marry Miss Stoker?"

"No, sir."

"Well, I don't see how he can very well do it now."

"I fancy the announcement would not be cordially received,
sir."

"They will have to meet by stealth."

"Even that will be a little difficult, sir. I should have mentioned that I chanced to be an auditor of a conversation between
Mr. and Miss Stoker, from the substance of which I gathered
that it was the genetleman's intention to keep Miss Stoker
virtually in durance vile on board the yacht, not permitting her
to go ashore during the remainder of their enforced stay in the
harbour."

"But you said he didn't know anything about the engagement."

"Mr. Stoker's motive in immuring Miss Stoker on the vessel is not to prevent her encountering his lordship, but to obviate any chance of her meeting you, sir. The fact that you embraced the young lady has convinced him that her affection for you has persisted since your parting in New York."

"You're sure you really heard all this?"

"Yes, sir."

"How did you come to do that?"

"I was conversing with his lordship at the moment on one side of a screen of bushes, when the conversation which I have described broke out on the other side. There was no alternative but to overhear Mr. Stoker's remarks."

I started visibly.

"You were talking with Chuffy, did you say?"

"Yes, sir."

"And he heard all that, too?"

"Yes, sir."

"About me kissing Miss Stoker?"

"Yes, sir."

"Did it seem to stir him up?"

"Yes, sir."

"What did he say?"

"He mentioned something about scooping out your inside, sir."

I wiped the brow.

"Jeeves," I said, "this calls for careful thought."

"Yes, sir."

"Advise me, Jeeves."

"Well, sir, I think it might be judicious if you were to attempt to persuade his lordship that the spirit in which you embraced Miss Stoker was a purely brotherly one."

"Brotherly? You think I could get away with that?"

"I fancy so, sir. After all, you are an old friend of the young lady. It would be quite understandable that you should bestow a kindly and dispassionate kiss upon her on learning of her betrothal to so close an intimate as his lordship."

I rose.

"It may work, Jeeves. It is, at least, worth trying. I shall now leave you, to prepare myself for the ordeal before me with silent meditation."

"Your tea will be here in a moment, sir."

"No, Jeeves. This is no time for tea. I must concentrate. I must have that story right before he arrives. I dare say I shall be getting a call from him shortly."

"It would not surprise me if you were to find his lordship awaiting you at your cottage now, sir."

He was absolutely correct. No sooner had I crossed the threshold than something exploded out of the arm-chair and there was Chuffy, gazing bleakly upon me.

"Ah!" he said, speaking the word between clenched teeth and generally comporting himself in an unpleasant and disturbing manner. "Here you are at last!"

I slipped him a sympathetic smile.

"Here I am, yes. And I have heard all. Jeeves told me. Too bad, too bad. I little thought, old man, when I bestowed a brotherly kiss on Pauline Stoker by way of congratulating her on your engagement, that all this trouble would be bobbing up so soon afterwards."

He continued to give me the eye.

"Brotherly?"

"Essentially brotherly."

"Old Stoker didn't seem to think so."

"Well, we know what sort of a mind old Stoker has got, don't we?"

"Brotherly? H'm!"

I registered manly regret.

"I suppose I shouldn't have done it . . ."

"It was lucky for you I wasn't there when you did."

". . . But you know how it is when a fellow you've been at private school, Eton and Oxford with gets engaged to a girl on whom you look as a sister. One is carried away."

It was plain that a struggle was going on in the old boy's bosom. He glowered a bit and paced the room a bit and, happening to trip over a footstool, he kicked it a bit. Then he became calmer. You could see Reason returning to her throne.

"Well, all right," he said. "But in future a little less of this fraternal stuff."

"Quite."

"Switch it off. Resist the impulse."

"Certainly."

"If you want sisters, seek them elsewhere."

"Just so."

"I don't want to feel, when I'm married, that at any moment I may come into the room and find a brother-and-sister act in progress."

"I quite understand, old man. Then you still intend to marry this Pauline?"

"Intend to marry her? Of course I intend to marry her. I'd look a silly ass not marrying a girl like that, wouldn't I?"

"But how about the old Chuffnell scruples?"

"What are you talking about?"

"Well, if Stoker is not going to buy the Hall, aren't you rather by way of being back in the position you were in before, when you would not tell your love, but let the thought of Wotwotleigh like a worm i' the bud feed on your damask cheek?"

He gave a slight shudder.

"Bertie," he said, "don't remind me of a time when I must have been absolutely potty. I can't imagine how I ever felt like that. You can take it as official that my views have changed. I don't care now if I haven't a bean and she's got a packet. If I can dig up seven-and-six for the licence and the couple of quid or whatever it is for the man behind the Prayer Book, this wedding is going through."

"Fine."

"What does money matter?"

"Quite."

"I mean, love's love."

"You never spoke a truer word, laddie. If I were you, I'd write her a letter embodying those views. You see, she may think that, now your finances are rocky once more, you will want to edge out."

"I will. And, by Jove!"

"What?"

"Jeeves shall take it to her. Thus removing any chance of old Stoker intercepting it."

"Could he, do you think?"

"My dear chap! A born letter-intercepter. You can see it in his eye."

"I mean, could Jeeves take it? I don't see how."

"I should have told you that Stoker wanted Jeeves to leave me and enter his service. At the time I thought I had never heard such crust in my life, but now I am all for it. Jeeves shall go to him."

I got on to the ruse or scheme.

"I see what you mean.   Operating under the Stoker banner, he will be free to come and go."

"Exactly."

"He can take a letter from you to her and then one from her to you and then one from you to her and then one from her to you and then one from you to her and then one . . ."

"Yes, yes.   You've got the idea.   And in the course of this correspondence we can fix up some scheme for meeting.   Have you any idea how long it takes to clear the decks for a wedding?"

"I'm not sure.   I believe, if you get a special licence, you can do it like a flash."

"I'll get a special licence.   Two.   Three.   Well, this has certainly put the butter on the spinach.   I feel a new man.   I'll go and tell Jeeves at once.   He can be on that yacht this evening."

At this point he suddenly stopped.   The brow darkened once more and he shot another of those searching looks at me.

"I suppose she really does love me?"

"Dash it, old man, didn't she say so?"

"She said so, yes.   Yes, she said so.   But can you believe what a girl says?"

"My dear chap!"

"Well, they're great kidders.   She may have been fooling me."

"Morbid, laddie."

He brooded a bit.

"It seemed so dashed odd that she should have let you kiss her."

"I took her by surprise."

"She could have sloshed you on the ear."

"Why?   She naturally divined that the embrace was purely brotherly."

"Brotherly, eh?"

"Wholly brotherly."

"Well, it may be so," said Chuffy doubtfully.   "Have you any sisters, Bertie?"

"No."

"But, if you had, you would kiss them?"

"Repeatedly."

"Well . . .   Oh, well . . .   Well, perhaps it's all right."

"You can believe a Wooster's word, can't you?"

"I don't know so much. I remember you once, the morning after the Boat Race our second year at Oxford, telling the magistrates your name was Eustace H. Plimsoll and that you lived at The Laburnams, Alleyn Road, West Dulwich."

"That was a special case, calling for special measures."

"Yes, of course. . . . Yes. . . . Well. . . . Well, I suppose it's all right. You really do swear there's absolutely nothing between you and Pauline now?"

"Nothing. We have often laughed heartily at the thought of that moment's madness in New York."

"I never heard you."

"Well, we have done—frequently."

"Oh? . . . In that case . . . Well, yes, I suppose . . . Well, anyway, I'll go off and write that letter."

For some time after he had left me, I remained with the feet up on the mantelpiece, relaxing. Take it for all in all, it had been a pretty strenuous day, and I was feeling the strain a bit. The recent exchange of thoughts with Chuffy alone had taken it out of the nervous system considerably. And when Brinkley came in and wanted to know when I would have dinner, the thought of sitting down to a solitary steak and fried in the cottage didn't appeal. I felt restless, on edge.

"I shall dine out, Brinkley," I said.

This successor to Jeeves had been sent down by the agency in London, and I'm bound to say he wasn't the fellow I'd have selected if I had had time to go round to the place and make a choice in person. Not at all the man of my dreams. A melancholy blighter, with a long, thin, pimple-studded face and deep, brooding eyes, he had shown himself averse from the start to that agreeable chit-chat between employer and employed to which the society of Jeeves had accustomed me. I had been trying to establish cordial relations ever since he had arrived, but with no success. Outwardly he was all respectfulness, but inwardly you could see that he was a man who was musing on the coming Social Revolution and looked on Bertram as a tyrant and an oppressor.

"Yes, Brinkley, I shall dine out."

He said nothing, merely looking at me as if he were measuring me for my lamp-post.

"I have had a fatiguing day, and I feel a need for the lights and the wine. Both of these, I should imagine, may be had in Bristol. And there ought to be a show of some kind playing there, don't you think? It's one of the Number One touring towns."

He sighed slightly. All this talk of my going to shows was distressing him. What he really wanted was to see me sprinting down Park Lane with the mob after me with dripping knives.

"I shall take the car and drive over there. You can have the evening off."

"Very good, sir," he moaned.

I gave it up. The man annoyed me. I hadn't the slightest objection to his spending his time planning massacres for the bourgeoisie, but I was dashed if I could see why he couldn't do it with a bright and cheerful smile. Dismissing him with a gesture, I went round to the garage and got the car out.

It was only a matter of thirty miles or so to Bristol, and I got there in nice time for a comfortable bite before the theatre. The show was a musical comedy which I had seen on several occasions during its London run, but it stood up quite well on a further visit, and altogether I was feeling rested and refreshed when I started back home.

I suppose it would have been getting on for midnight when I fetched up at the rural retreat: and, being about ready for sleep by now, I lost no time in lighting a candle and toddling upstairs. As I opened the door of my room, I recollect I was thinking how particularly well a dollop of slumber would go: and I was just making for the bed with a song on my lips, so to speak, when something suddenly sat up in it.

The next moment I had dropped the candle and the room was plunged in darkness. But not before I had seen quite enough to be getting along with.

Reading from left to right, the contents of the bed consisted of Pauline Stoker in my heliotrope pyjamas with the old gold stripe.

7

A Visitor For Bertie

THE attitude of fellows towards finding girls in their bedroom shortly after midnight varies. Some like it. Some don't. I didn't. I suppose it's some old Puritan strain in the Wooster blood. I drew myself up censoriously and shot a sternish glance in her direction. Absolutely wasted, of course, because it was pitch dark.

"What . . . What . . . What . . .?"

"It's all right."

"All right?"

"Quite all right."

"Oh?" I said, and I don't pretend to disguise the fact that I spoke bitterly. I definitely meant it to sting.

I stooped to pick up the candle, and the next moment I had uttered a startled cry.

"Don't make such a noise!"

"But there's a corpse on the floor."

"There isn't. I should have noticed it."

"There is, I tell you. I was groping about for the candle, and my fingers touched something cold and still and clammy."

"Oh, that's my swimming suit."

"Your swimming suit?'.

"Well, do you think I came ashore by aeroplane?"

"You swam here from the yacht?"

"Yes."

"When?"

"About half an hour ago."

In that level-headed, practical way of mine, I went straight to the root of the matter.

"Why?" I asked.

A match scratched and a candle by the bed flamed up and lent a bit of light to the scene. Once more I was able to observe those pyjamas, and I'm bound to admit they looked extraordinarily dressy. Pauline was darkish in her general colour scheme, and heliotrope suited her. I said as much, always being ready to give credit where credit is due.

"You look fine in that slumber-wear."

"Thanks."

She blew out the match, and gazed at me in a sort of wondering way.

"You know, Bertie, steps should be taken about you."

"Eh?"

"You ought to be in some sort of a home."

"I am," I replied coldly and rather cleverly. "My own. The point I wish to thresh out is, what are you doing in it?"

Womanlike, she evaded the issue.

"What on earth did you want to kiss me like that for in front of father? You needn't tell me you were carried away by my radiant beauty. No, it was just plain, straight goofiness, and I can quite understand now why Sir Roderick told father that you ought to be under restraint. Why are you still at large? You must have a pull of some kind."

We Woosters are pretty sharp on this sort of thing. I spoke with a good deal of asperity.

"The incident to which you allude is readily explained. I thought he was Chuffy."

"Thought who was Chuffy?"

"Your father."

"If you're trying to make out that Marmaduke looks the least bit like father you must be cuckoo," she replied with a warmth equal to my own. I gathered that she was not a great admirer of the parent's appearance, and I'm not saying she wasn't right. "Besides, I don't see what you mean."

I explained.

"The idea was to let Chuffy observe you in my embrace, so that the generous fire would be stirred within him and he would get keyed up to proposing to you, feeling that if he didn't get action right speedily he might lose you."

Her manner softened.

"You didn't think that out by yourself?"

"I did." I was somewhat nettled. "Why everybody should imagine that I can't get ideas without the assistance of Jeeves . . ."

"But that was very sweet of you."

"We Woosters *are* sweet, exceedingly sweet, when a pal's happiness is in the balance."

"I can see now why I accepted you that night in New York," she said meditatively. "There's a sort of woolly-headed duckiness about you. If I wasn't so crazy about Marmaduke, I could easily marry you, Bertie."

"No, no," I said, with some alarm. "Don't dream of it. I mean to say . . ."

"Oh, it's all right. I'm not going to. I'm going to marry Marmaduke; that's why I'm here."

"And now," I said, "we've come right back to it. Once more we have worked round to the very point concerning which I most desire enlightenment. What on earth is the idea behind all this? You say you swam ashore from the yacht? Why? You came and dumped yourself in my little home. Why?"

"Because I wanted somewhere to lie low till I could get clothes, of course. I can't go to the Hall in a swimming suit."

I began to follow the train of thought.

"Oh, you swam ashore to get to Chuffy?"

"Of course. Father was keeping me a prisoner on board the yacht, and this evening your man Jeeves . . ."

I winced.

"My late man."

"All right. Your late man. Your late man Jeeves arrived with an early letter from Marmaduke. Oh, boy!"

"How do you mean, oh, boy?"

"Was that a letter? I cried six pints when I read it."

"Hot stuff?"

"It was beautiful. It throbbed with poetry."

"It did?"

"Yes."

"This letter?"

"Yes."

"Chuffy's letter?"

"Yes. You seem surprised."

I was a bit. One of the very best, old Chuffy, of course, but I wouldn't have said he could write letters like that. But then one has got to take into consideration the fact that when I've been with him he has generally been eating steak-and-kidney pudding or cursing horses for not running fast enough. On such occasions, the poetic side of a man is not uppermost.

"So this letter stirred you up, did it?"

"You bet it stirred me up. I felt I couldn't wait another day without seeing him. What was that poem about a woman wailing for her demon lover?"

"Ah, there you have me. Jeeves would know."

"Well, that's what I felt like. And, talking of Jeeves, what a man! Sympathy? He drips with it."

"Oh, you confided in Jeeves?"

"Yes. And told him what I was going to do."

"And he didn't try to stop you?"

"Stop me? He was all for it."

"He was, was he?"

"You should have seen him. Such a kind smile. He said you would be delighted to help me."

"He did, eh?"

"He spoke most highly of you."

"Really?"

"Oh, yes, he thinks a lot of you. I remember his very words. 'Mr. Wooster, miss,' he said, 'is, perhaps, mentally somewhat negligible, but he has a heart of gold.' He said that as he was lowering me from the side of the boat by a rope, having first made sure that the coast was clear. I couldn't dive, you see, because of the splash."

I was chewing the lip in some chagrin.

"What the devil did he mean, 'mentally negligible'?"

"Oh, you know. Loopy."

"Tchah!"

"Eh?"

"I said 'Tchah!'"

"Why?"

"Why?" I was a good deal moved. "Well, wouldn't you say 'Tchah!' if your late man was going about the place telling people you were mentally negligible. . . ."

"But with a heart of gold."

"Never mind the heart of gold. The point is that my man, my late man, a fellow I have always looked on more as some sort of an uncle than a personal attendant, is shooting to and fro bellowing out at the top of his voice that I am mentally negligible and filling my bedroom with girls. . . ."

"Bertie! Are you annoyed?"

"Annoyed!"

"You sound annoyed. And I can't see why. I should have thought you would have been only too glad of the chance of helping me get to the man I love. Having this heart of gold I hear so much about."

"The point is not whether I have a heart of gold. Heaps of people have hearts of gold and yet would be upset at finding girls in their bedrooms in the small hours. What you don't seem to realize, what you and this Jeeves of yours have omitted to take into your calculations, is that I have a reputation to keep up, an unspotted name to maintain in its pristine purity. This cannot be done by entertaining girls who come in, in the middle of the night, without so much as a by-your-leave and coolly pinch your heliotrope pyjamas . . ." . .

"You didn't expect me to sleep in a wet swimming suit?"

". . . and leap into your bed . . ."

She uttered an exclamation.

"I know what this reminds me of. I've been trying to think ever since you came in. The story of the Three Bears. You must have been told it as a kid. 'There's somebody in my bed. . . .' Wasn't that what the Big Bear said?"

I frowned doubtfully.

"As I recollect it, it was something about porridge. 'Who's been eating my porridge?'"

"I'm sure there was a bed in it."

"Bed? Bed? I can't remember any bed. On the subject of the porridge, however, I am absolutely. . . . But we are wandering from the point once more. What I was saying was that a reputable bachelor like myself, who has never had his licence so much as endorsed, can scarcely be blamed for looking askance at girls in heliotrope pyjamas in his bed. . . ."

"You said they suited me."

"They do suit you."

"You said I looked fine in them."

"You do look fine in them, but once more you are refusing to meet the issue squarely. The point is . . ."

"How many points is that? I seem to have counted about a dozen."

"There is only one point, and I am endeavouring to make it clear. In a nutshell, what will people say when they find you here?"

"But they won't find me here."

"You think so? Ha! What about Brinkley?"

"Who's he?"

"My man."

"Your late man?"

I clicked the tongue.

"My new man. At nine tomorrow morning he will bring me tea."

"Well, you'll like that."

"He will bring it to this room. He will approach the bed. He will place it on the table."

"What on earth for?"

"To facilitate my getting at the cup and sipping."

"Oh, you mean he will put the tea on the table. You said he would put the bed on the table."

"I never said anything of the sort."

"You did. Distinctly."

I tried to reason with the girl.

"My dear child," I said, "I must really ask you to use your intelligence. Brinkley is not a juggler. He is a well-trained gentleman's gentleman, and would consider it a liberty to put beds on tables. And why should he put beds on tables? The idea would never occur to him. He . . ."

She interrupted my reasoning.

"But wait a minute. You keep babbling about Brinkley, but there isn't a Brinkley."

"There is a Brinkley. One Brinkley. And one Brinkley coming into this room at nine o'clock tomorrow morning and finding you in that bed will be enough to start a scandal which will stagger humanity."

"I mean, he can't be in the house."

"Of course he's in the house."

"Well, he must be deaf, then. I made enough noise getting in to wake six gentlemen's gentlemen. Apart from smashing a window at the back . . ."

"Did you smash a window at the back?"

"I had to, or I couldn't have got in. It was the window of some sort of bedroom on the ground floor."

"Why, dash it, that's Brinkley's bedroom."

"Well, he wasn't in it."

"Why on earth not? I gave him the evening off, not the night."

"I can see what has happened. He's away on a toot some-where, and won't be back for days. Father had a man who did that once. He went out for his evening from our house on East Sixty-Seventh Street, New York, on April the fourth in a

bowler hat, grey gloves and a check suit, and the next we heard
of him was a telegram from Portland, Oregon, on April the
tenth, saying he had overslept himself and would be back
shortly. That's what your Brinkley must have done."

I must say I drew a good deal of comfort from the idea.

"Let us hope so," I said. "If he is really trying to drown his
sorrows, it ought to take him weeks."

"So, you see, you've been making a fuss about nothing. I
always say . . ."

But what it was she always said, I was not privileged to learn.
For at that moment she broke off with a sharp squeak.

Somebody was knocking on the front door.

* 8 *

Police Persecution

WE looked at each other with a wild surmise, silent upon a
first-floor back in Chuffnell Regis. That frightful sound,
coming unexpectedly like that in the middle of the peaceful
summer night, had been enough to strike the chit-chat from anybody's lips. And what rendered it so particularly unpleasant
to us, personally, was the fact that we had both jumped simul-
taneously to the same ghastly conclusion.

"It's father!" Pauline gargled, and with a swift flip of her
finger she doused the candle.

"What did you do that for?" I said, a good deal pipped.
The sudden darkness seemed to make things worse.

"So that he shouldn't see a light in the window, of course.
If he thinks you're asleep he may go away."

"What a hope!" I retorted, as the knocking, which had eased
off for a moment, started again with more follow-through than
ever.

"Well, I suppose you had better go down," said the girl in a
subdued sort of voice. "Or" —she seemed to brighten—"shall
we pour water on him from the staircase window?"

I started violently. She had made the suggestion as if she
considered it one of her best and brightest, and I suddenly

realized what it meant to play the host to a girl of her temperament and personality. All that I had ever heard or read about the reckless younger generation seemed to come back to me.

"Don't dream of it!" I whispered urgently. "Dismiss the project utterly and absolutely from your mind."

I mean to say, a dry J. Washburn Stoker seeking an errant daughter was bad enough. A J. Washburn Stoker stimulated to additional acerbity by a jugful of H_2O on his head, I declined to contemplate. Goodness knows, I wasn't keen on going down and passing the time of night with the man, but if the alternative was to allow his loved one to drench him to the skin and then wait while he tore the walls down with his bare hands I proposed to do so immediately.

"I'll have to see him," I said.

"Well, be careful."

"How do you mean, careful?"

"Oh, just careful. Still, of course, he may not have a gun."

I swallowed a trifle.

"What exactly would you say the odds were, for and against?"

She mused awhile.

"I'm trying to remember if father is a Southerner or not."

"A what?"

"I know he was born at a place called Carterville, but I can't recollect if it was Carterville, Kentucky, or Carterville, Massachusetts."

"What the dickens difference does it make?"

"Well, if you smirch the honour of a Southerner's family, he's apt to shoot."

"Would your father consider it smirched the family honour, your being here?"

"Bound to, I should think."

I couldn't help agreeing with her. It did seem to me offhand that a purist might consider the smirching pretty good, but I hadn't time to weigh the point, because the knocker got going again with renewed vim.

"Well, dash it," I said, "wherever this ghastly parent of yours was born, I shall have to go down and talk to him. That door will be splitting asunder soon."

"Don't get closer to him than you can help."

"I won't."

"He was a great wrestler when he was a young man."

"You needn't tell me any more about your father."

"I only meant, I wouldn't let him get hold of you, if you can help.   Is there anywhere I can hide?"

"No."

"Why not?"

"I don't know why not," I replied, a little curtly.   "They don't build these country cottages with secret rooms and underground passages.   When you hear me open the front door, stop breathing."

"Do you want me to suffocate?"

Well, of course, a Wooster does not put such thoughts into words, but I'm bound to say this struck me as a jolly good idea. Forbearing the reply, I hurried down the stairs and flung open the front door.   Well, when I say flung, I opened it a matter of six inches, not omitting to keep it on the chain.

"Hallo?" I said.   "Yes?"

I don't know when I've felt such a chunk of relief as surged over me the next moment.

"Oy!" said a voice.   "Taken your time, haven't you?   What's the matter with you, young man?   Deaf or something?"

It wasn't in its essentials a musical voice, being on the thick side and a shade roopy.   If I'd been its owner, I'd have given more than a little thought to the subject of tonsils.   But it had one supreme merit which out-weighed all its defects.   It wasn't the voice of J. Washburn Stoker.

"Frightfully sorry," I said.   "I was thinking of this and that. Sort of reverie, if you know what I mean."

The voice spoke again, not without a pretty goodish modicum of suavity this time.

"Oh, I beg your pardon, sir.   I thought you was the young man Brinkley."

"Brinkley's out," I said, feeling that if he ever returned I would have a word to say to him about the hours at which his pals paid social calls.   "Who are you?"

"Sergeant Voules, sir."

I opened the door.   It was pretty dark outside, but I could recognize the arm of the Law all right.   This Voules was a bird built rather on the lines of the Albert Hall, round in the middle and not much above.   He always looked to me as if Nature had really intended to make two police sergeants and had forgotten to split them up.

"Ah, Sergeant!" I said.

Careless, debonair. Not a thing on Bertram's mind, you would have supposed, but his hair.

"Anything I can do for you, Sergeant?"

My eyes were getting accustomed to the darkness by this time, and I was enabled to spot certain objects of interest by the wayside. The principal one was another policeman. Tall and lean and stringy, this one.

"This is my young nephew, sir. Constable Dobson."

Well, I wasn't exactly in the mood for a social reunion, and I could have wished that the sergeant, if he wanted to make me one of the family and all pals together, so to speak, had selected some other time, but I inclined the bean gracefully in the constable's direction and uttered a kindly "Ah, Dobson!" I rather think, if I remember, that I also said something about its being a fine night.

But apparently this wasn't just one of those chummy gatherings which recall the old-time *salon*.

"Are you aware, sir, that there's a window broke at the back of your residence? My young nephew here spotted it and thought best to wake me up and have me investigate. A ground-floor window, sir, with a whole pane of glass gone from it."

I simpered slightly.

"Oh, that? Yes, Brinkley did that yesterday. Silly ass!"

"You knew about it, then, sir?"

"Oh, yes. Oh, yes. Quite all right, Sergeant."

"Well, you know best if it's quite all right, sir, but I should say there was a danger of marauders getting through."

And at this juncture the chump of a constable, who had hitherto not spoken, shoved his oar in.

"I thought I did see a marauder getting through, Uncle Ted."

"What! Then why didn't you tell me before, you young muttonhead? And don't call me Uncle Ted when we're on duty."

"No, Uncle Ted."

"You'd best let us make a search of the 'ouse, sir," said Sergeant Voules.

Well, I put the presidential veto on this pretty quick.

"Certainly not, Sergeant," I said. "Quite out of the q."

"It would be wiser, sir."

"I'm sorry," I said, "but it can't be done."

He seemed piqued and discontented.

"Well, please yourself, sir, but you're shackling the police, that's what you're doing. There's too much shackling of the police these days. There was a piece in the *Mail* about it yesterday. Perhaps you read it?"

"No."

"On the middle page. Unshackle the police, it said because public alarm is growing in Great Britain owing to the continuous increase of crime in the lonely rural districts. I clipped it out to paste in my album. The number of indictable offences, it said, has rose from one three four five eight one in 1929 to one four seven nought three one in 1930, with a marked increase of seven per cent in crimes of violence, and is this disturbing state of things due to slackness on the part of the police, it said? No, it said, it's not. It's because the police are shackled."

The man was obviously cut to the quick. Dashed awkward.

"Well, I'm sorry," I said.

"Yes, sir, and you're going to be sorrier when you go upstairs to your bedroom and a marauder cuts your throat from ear to ear."

"Fight against these gloomy views, my dear old police sergeant," I said. "I anticipate no such contingency. I've just come from upstairs, and I give you my word there were no marauders."

"Probably lurking, sir."

"Biding their time," suggested Constable Dobson.

Sergeant Voules sighed heavily.

"I wouldn't like nothing to happen to you, sir, seein' you're a close friend of his lordship's. But as you prove obdurate . . ."

"Oh, nothing could happen to anyone in a place like Chuffnell Regis."

"Don't you believe it, sir. Chuffnell Regis is going down. I would never have thought to have seen a troupe of nigger minstrels singing comic songs within a stone's-throw of my police station."

"You view them with concern?"

"There's been fowls missing," said Sergeant Voules darkly. "Several fowls. And I have my suspicions. Well, come along, Constable. If we're to be shackled, there's nothing to keep us here. Good night, sir."

"Good night."

I shut the door and buzzed back to the bedroom. Pauline was sitting up in bed, more or less agog.

"Who was it?"

"The constabulary."

"What did they want?"

"Apparently they saw you getting in."

"What a lot of trouble I'm giving you, Bertie."

"Oh, no. Only too pleased. Well, I suppose I might as well be pushing along."

"Are you going?"

"In the circumstances," I replied a little frigidly. "I can hardly doss on the premises. I shall withdraw to the garage."

"Isn't there a sofa downstairs?"

"There is. Noah's. He brought it ashore on Mount Ararat. I shall be better off in the car."

"Oh, Bertie, I *am* giving you a lot of trouble."

I softened slightly. After all, the poor girl was scarcely to be blamed for what had occurred. As Chuffy had remarked earlier in the evening, love's love.

"Don't you worry, old thing. We Woosters can rough it when it is a matter of giving two fond hearts a leg-up. You put your little head on the pillow and curl your little pink toes up and doze off. I shall be all right."

And, so saying, I uncorked a kindly smile, popped off, trickled down the stairs, opened the front door, and out into the scented night; and I don't suppose I was a dozen yards from the house when a heavy hand fell on my shoulder, occasioning me both mental and physical distress, and a shadowy form said: "Gotcher!"

"Ouch!" I replied.

The shadowy form now revealed itself as that of Constable Dobson of the Chuffnell Regis police force. He was in apologetic vein.

"I'm sure I beg your pardon, sir. I thought you was the marauder."

I forced myself to be airy and affable. The young squire setting the lower orders at their ease.

"Quite all right, Constable. Quite all right. Just going for a stroll."

"I understand, sir. Breath of air."

"You have put it in a nutshell. A breath, as you astutely observe, of air. The house is quite close."

"Yes, sir. Just over there."

"I mean stuffy."

"Oh, yes, sir. Well, good night, sir."

"Tra-la, Constable."

I proceeded on my way, a little shaken. I had left the garage door open, and I felt my way to the old two-seater, glad to be alone once more. In certain moods, no doubt, one would have found Constable Dobson a delightful and stimulating companion, but tonight I preferred his absence. I climbed into the car and, leaning back, endeavoured to compose myself for sleep.

Now, whether I should have been able to achieve the dreamless had the conditions remained right, I cannot say. The point is pretty moot. As two-seaters go, I had always found mine fairly comfortable, but then I had never before tried to get the eight hours in it, and you would be surprised at the number of knobs and protuberances which seem suddenly to sprout out of a car's upholstery when you seek to convert it into a bed.

But, as it happened, I was not given a square chance of making the test. I don't suppose I could have counted more than about a platoon and a half of sheep when a light suddenly flashed on the features and a voice instructed me to come on out of it.

I sat up.

"Ah, Sergeant!" I said.

Another awkward meeting. Embarrassment on both sides.

"Is that you, sir?"

"Yes."

"Sorry to have disturbed you, sir."

"Not at all."

"Can't say it occurred to me that it might be you in here, sir."

"I thought I'd try to get a bit of sleep in the old car, Sergeant."

"Yes, sir."

"Such a warm night."

"Just so, sir."

His voice was respectful, but I could not conquer a suspicion that he was beginning to look a bit askance. There was something in his manner that gave me the idea that he considered Bertram eccentric.

"Stuffy indoors."

"Yes, sir?"

"I often park myself in the car in the summertime."

"Yes, sir?"

"Good night, Sergeant."

"Good night, sir."

Well, you know how it is when someone butts in on you just as you are shaping for the beauty sleep. It breaks the spell, if you know what I mean. I curled up again, but I soon saw that all efforts in the direction of the restful night in my present environment would be fruitless. I counted about five more medium-sized flocks, but it was no good. Steps, I realized, would have to be taken through other channels.

I hadn't done a great deal of exploring in these grounds of mine, but it so happened that one morning a sharp shower had driven me to the shelter of a species of shed or outhouse down in the south-west corner of the estate where the gardener-by-the-day stacked his tools and flower-pots and what not. And, unless memory deceived me, there had been in that outhouse or shed a pile of sacking on the floor.

Well, you may say that sacking, considered in the light of a bed, isn't everybody's money, and in saying so you would be perfectly correct. But after half an hour in the seat of a Widgeon Seven, even sacking begins to look pretty good to you. It may be a little hardish on the frame, and it may smell a good deal of mice and the deep-delved earth, but there remains just one point to be put forward in its favour—viz. that it enables one to stretch the limbs. And stretching the limbs was the thing I felt now that I wanted to do most.

In addition to smelling of mice and mould, the particular segment of sacking on which some two minutes later I was reclining had a marked aroma of by-the-day gardener; and there was a moment when I had to ask myself if the mixture wasn't a shade too rich. But these things grow on one in time, and at the end of about a quarter of an hour I was rather enjoying the blend of scents than otherwise. I can recall inflating the lungs and more or less drinking it in. At the end of about half an hour a soothing drowsiness had begun to steal over me.

And at the end of about thirty-five minutes the door flew open and there was the old, familiar lantern shining in again.

"Ah!" said Sergeant Voules.

And Constable Dobson said the same.

I realized that the time had come to strike a forceful note with these two pests. I am all for not shackling the police, but what I maintain is that if the police come dodging about a householder's garden all night, routing him out every time he is on the point of snatching a little repose, they have jolly well got to be shackled.

"Yes?" I said, and there was a touch of the imperious old aristocrat in my manner. "What is it now?"

Constable Dobson had been saying something in a pretty self-satisfied sort of way about having seen me creeping through the darkness and tracking me like a leopard, and Sergeant Voules, who was a man who believed in keeping nephews in their place, was remarking that he had seen me first and had tracked me just as much like a leopard as Constable Dobson: but at these crisp words a sudden silence fell upon them.

"Is that you *again*, sir?" inquired the sergeant in rather an awed voice.

"Yes, it is, dash it! What, may I ask, is the meaning of this incessant chivying? Sleep under these conditions becomes impossible."

"Very sorry, sir. It never occurred to me that it could be you."

"And why not?"

"Well, sleeping in a shed, sir . . ."

"You do not dispute the fact that it is my shed?"

"No, sir. But it sort of seems funny."

"I see nothing funny in it whatsoever."

"Uncle Ted means 'odd', sir."

"Not so much of what Uncle Ted means. And don't call me Uncle Ted. What it sort of seemed to us, sir, was peculiar."

"I cannot subscribe to your opinion, Sergeant," I said stiffly. "I have a perfect right, have I not, to sleep where I please?"

"Yes, sir."

"Exactly. It might be the coal cellar. It might be the front-door steps. It happens to be this shed. I will now thank you, Sergeant, to withdraw. At this rate, I shan't drop off till daybreak."

"Are you intending to remain here the rest of the night, sir?"

"Certainly. Why not?"

I had got him. He was at a loss.

"Well, I suppose there's no reason why you shouldn't, if you want to, sir. But it seems . . ."

"Odd," said Constable Dobson.

"Peculiar," said Sergeant Voules. "It seems peculiar, having a bed of your own, sir, if I might say so . . ."

I had had enough of this.

"I hate beds," I said curtly. "Can't stand them. Never could."

"Very good, sir." He paused a moment. "Quite a warm day today, sir."

"Quite."

"My young nephew here pretty near got a touch of the sun. Didn't you, Constable?"

"Ah!" said Constable Dobson.

"Made him come over all funny."

"Indeed?"

"Yes, sir. Sort of seemed to addle the brain."

I endeavoured without undue brusqueness to convey to this man the idea that I did not consider one in the morning a suitable time for discussing his nephew's addled brain.

"You must give me all the family medical gossip another day," I said. "At the moment, I wish to be alone."

"Yes, sir. Good night, sir."

"Good night, Sergeant."

"If I might ask the question, sir, do you feel a sort of burning feeling about the temples?"

"I beg your pardon?"

"Does your head throb, sir?"

"It's beginning to."

"Ah! Well, good night, sir, again."

"Good night, Sergeant."

"Good night, sir."

"Good night, Constable."

"Good night, sir."

The door closed softly. I could hear them whispering for a moment or two, like a couple of specialists holding a conference outside the sick-room. Then they appeared to ooze off, for all became quiet save for the lapping of the waves on the shore. And, by Jove, so sedulously did these waves lap that gradually a drowsiness crept over me and not ten minutes after I had made up my mind that I should never get to sleep again in this world I was off as comfortably as a babe or suckling.

It couldn't last, of course—not in a place like Chuffnell Regis, a hamlet containing more Nosey Parkers to the square foot than any other spot in England. The next thing I remember is someone joggling my arm.

I sat up. There was the good old lantern once more.

"Now, listen . . ." I was beginning, with a generous strength, when the words froze on my lips.

The fellow who was joggling my arm was Chuffy.

∗ 9 ∗

Lovers' Meetings

IT has been well said of Bertram Wooster that he is a man who is at all times glad to see his friends and can be relied upon to greet them with a cheery smile and a gay quip. But though in the main this is correct, I make one proviso—viz. that the conditions be right. On the present occasion they were not. When an old schoolmate's fiancée is roosting in your bed in a suit of your personal pyjamas, it is hard to frisk round this old schoolmate with any abandon when he suddenly appears in the immediate vicinity.

I uttered, accordingly, no gay quip. I couldn't even manage the cheery smile. I just sat goggling at the man, wondering how he had got there, how long he proposed to remain, and what the chances were of Pauline Stoker suddenly shoving her head out of window and shouting to me to come and grapple with a mouse or something.

Chuffy was bending over me with a sort of bedside manner. In the background I could see Sergeant Voules hovering with something of the air of a trained nurse. What had become of Constable Dobson, I did not know. It seemed too jolly to think that he was dead, so I took it that he had returned to his beat.

"It's all right, Bertie," said Chuffy soothingly. "It's me, old man."

"I found his lordship by the side of the harbour," explained the sergeant.

I must say I chafed a bit. I saw what had happened. When

you tear a lover of Chuffy's calibre from the girl of his heart, he
does not just mix himself a final spot and turn in—he goes and
stands beneath her window.   And if she's on a yacht, anchored
out in the middle of a harbour, this can only be done, of course,
by infesting the water-front.   All quite in order, no doubt, but
in the present circs dashed inconvenient, to use the mildest term.
And what was making me chafe was the thought that if only he
had got to his parking place a bit earlier he would have been in a
position to welcome the girl as she came ashore, thus obviating
all the present awkwardness.

"The sergeant was worried about you, Bertie.   He seemed
to think your manner was strange.   So he brought me along to
have a look at you.   Very sensible of you, Voules."

"Thank you, m'lord."

"A sound move."

"Thank you, m'lord."

"You couldn't have done a wiser thing."

"Thank you, m'lord."

It was sickening to hear them.

"So you've got a touch of the sun, Bertie?"

"I have not got a touch of any bally sun."

"Voules thought so."

"Voules is an ass."

The sergeant bridled somewhat.

"Begging your pardon, sir, you informed me that your head
throbbed, and I assumed that the brain was addled."

"Exactly.   You must have gone slightly off your rocker, old
chap," said Chuffy gently, "mustn't you?   To be sleeping out
here, I mean, what?"

"Why shouldn't I sleep out here?"

I saw Chuffy and the sergeant exchange glances.

"But you've got a bedroom, old fellow.   You've got a nice
bedroom, haven't you?   I should have thought you would have
found it so much snugger and jollier in your cosy little bedroom."

The Woosters have all been pretty quick thinkers.   I saw that
I had got to make this move of mine seem plausible.

"There's a spider in my bedroom."

"A spider, eh?   Pink?"

"Pinkish."

"With long legs?"

"Fairly long legs."

"And hairy, I shouldn't wonder?"

"Very hairy."

The rays of the lantern were falling on Chuffy's face, and at this point I observed a subtle change come into his expression. A moment before, he had been solicitous old Doctor Chuffnell, gravely concerned about the sorely sick patient whom he had been called in to treat. He now grinned in a most unpleasant manner and, rising, drew Sergeant Voules aside and addressed a remark to him which told me that he had placed an entirely wrong construction on the matter.

"It's all right, Sergeant. Nothing to worry about. He's simply as tight as an owl."

I think he imagined he was speaking in a tactful undertone, but his words came clearly to my ears, as did the sergeant's reply.

"Is that so, m'lord?" said Sergeant Voules. And his voice was the voice of a sergeant to whom all things have been made clear.

"That's all that's the trouble. Completely boiled. You notice the glassy look in the eyes?"

"Yes, m'lord."

"I've seen him like this before. Once, after a bump-supper at Oxford, he insisted that he was a mermaid and wanted to dive into the college fountain and play the harp there."

"Young gents will be young gents," said Sergeant Voules in a tolerant and broad-minded manner.

"We must put him to bed."

I jumped up. Horror-stricken. Trembling like a leaf.

"I don't want to go to bed!"

Chuffy stroked my arm soothingly.

"It's all right, Bertie. Quite all right. We understand. No wonder you were frightened. Beastly great spider. Enough to frighten any one. But it's all right now. Voules and I will come up to your room with you and kill it. You aren't scared of spiders, Voules?"

"No, m'lord."

"You hear that, Bertie? Voules will stand by you. Voules can tackle any spider. How many spiders was it you were telling me you took on in India once, Voules?"

"Ninety-six, m'lord."

"Big ones, if I remember rightly?"

"Whackers, m'lord."

"There, Bertie. You see there's nothing to be afraid of. You take this arm, Sergeant. I'll take the other. Just relax, Bertie. We'll hold you up."

Looking back, I am not certain whether I didn't do the wrong thing at this juncture. It may be that a few well-chosen words would have served me better. But you know how it is about well-chosen words. When you need them most, you can't find any. The sergeant had begun to freeze on to my left arm, and I couldn't think of a single remark. So, in lieu of conversation, I punched him in the tummy and made a dash for the open spaces.

Well, you can't go far at a high rate of speed in a dark shed littered with the belongings of a by-the-day gardener. I suppose there were quite half a dozen things I could have come a purler over. The one which actually caused me to take the toss was a watering-can. I fell with a dull, sickening thud, and when reason returned to her throne I found I was being carried through the summer night in the direction of the house. Chuffy had got me under the arms, and Sergeant Voules was attached to my feet. And, thus linked, we passed through the front door and up the stairs. It wasn't, perhaps, actually the frog's march, but it was quite near enough to it to wound my *amour propre*.

Not that I was thinking such a frightful lot about my *amour propre* at the moment. We had reached the bedroom door now, and what I was asking myself was, What would the harvest be when Chuffy opened it and noted contents?

"Chuffy," I said, and I spoke earnestly, "don't go into that room!"

But it's no good speaking earnestly if your head's hanging down and your tongue has got tangled up with your back teeth. All that actually emerged was a sort of gargle, and Chuffy completely misunderstood it.

"I know, I know," he said. "Never mind. Soon be in beddy-bye now."

I considered his manner offensive, and would have said so, but at this moment speech was, so to speak, wiped from my lips, as it were, by amazement. With a quick heave, my bearers had suddenly dumped me on the bed, and all that the frame had encountered was a blanket and pillow. Of anything in the nature of a girl in heliotrope pyjamas there was absolutely no trace.

I lay there, wondering. Chuffy had found the candle and lighted it, and I was now in a position to look about me.

Pauline Stoker had absolutely disappeared. Leaving not a wrack behind, as I remember Jeeves saying once.

Dashed odd.

Chuffy was dismissing his assistant.

"Thanks, Sergeant. I can manage now."

"You're sure, m'lord?"

"Yes, it's quite all right. He always drops off to sleep on these occasions."

"Then I think I'll be going, m'lord. It's a bit late for me."

"Yes, pop off. Good night."

"Good night, m'lord."

The sergeant clumped down the stairs, making enough row for two sergeants, and Chuffy, with something of the air of a mother brooding over a sleeping child, took off my boots.

"That's my little man," he said. "Now you lie quite quiet, Bertie, and take things easy."

It is a thing I have often wondered, whether I would or would not have commented upon what I considered the insufferably patronizing note in his voice as he called me his little man. I wanted to, but I saw that it would be fruitless unless I could think of something more than a little biting: and it was while I was searching in my mind for the telling phrase that the door of the hanging cupboard outside the room opened and Pauline Stoker came strolling in as if she hadn't a care in the world. In fact, she seemed distinctly entertained.

"What a night, what a night!" she said amusedly. "A close call that, Bertie. Who were those men I heard going out?"

And then she suddenly sighted Chuffy, gave a kind of gasping squeak, and the love light came into her eyes as if somebody had pressed a switch.

"Marmaduke!" she cried, and stood there, staring.

But, by Jove, it was the poor old schoolmate who was doing the real staring, in the truest and fullest sense of the word. I've seen starers in my time, many of them, but never one who came within a mile of putting up the performance which Chuffy did then. The eyebrows had shot up, the jaw had fallen, and the eyes were protruding from one to two inches from the parent sockets. He also appeared to be trying to say something, but in this he flopped badly. Nothing came through except a rather unpleasant whistling sound, not quite so loud as the row your radio makes when you twiddle the twiddler a bit too hard but in other respects closely resembling it.

Pauline, meanwhile, had begun to advance with the air of a woman getting together with her demon lover, and a sort of pity for the girl shot through the Wooster bosom. I mean to say, any observant outsider like myself could see so clearly that she had got quite the wrong angle on the situation. I could read Chuffy like a book, and I knew that she was totally mistaken in what she supposed to be his emotions at this juncture. That odd noise he was making I could diagnose, not as the love call which she appeared to think it, but as the stern and censorious gruffle of a man who, finding his loved one on alien premises in heliotrope pyjamas, is stricken to the core, cut to the quick, and as sore as a gumboil.

But she, poor simp, being so dashed glad to behold him, had not so much as begun to suspect that he, the circs being what they were, might possibly not be equally glad to behold her. With the result that when at this juncture he stepped back and folded his arms with a bitter sneer, it was as if he had jabbed her in the eye with a burnt stick. The light faded from her face, and in its stead there appeared the hurt, bewildered look of a bare-foot dancer who, while half-way through The Vision of Salome, steps on a tin tack.

"Marmaduke!"

Chuffy unleashed another bitter sneer.

"So!" he said, finding speech—if you can call that speech.

"What do you mean? Why are you looking like that?"

I thought it about time that I put in a word. I had risen from the bed on Pauline's entry and for some moments had been teetering towards the door with a sort of sketchy idea of making for the great open spaces. But partly because I felt that it ill beseemed a Wooster to leg it at such a time and partly because I had no boots on, I had decided to remain. I now intervened, coming across with the word in season.

"What you want on an occasion like this, Chuffy, old man," I said, "is simple faith. The poet Tennyson tells us . . ."

"Shut up," said Chuffy. "I don't want to hear anything from you."

"Right ho," I said. "But, all the same, simple faith *is* better than Norman blood, and you can't get away from it."

Pauline was looking a bit fogged.

"Simple faith? What . . . Oh!" she said, abruptly signing off. And I noted that the features were suffused with a crimson blush.

"Oh!" she said.

The cheeks continued to glow. But now it was not the blush of modesty that hotted them up. That first "*Oh!*" I take it, had been caused by her catching sight of her pyjamaed limbs and suddenly getting on to the equivocal nature of her position. The second one was different. It was the heart cry of a woman who is madder than a hornet.

I mean, you know how it is. A sensitive and high-spirited girl goes through the deuce of an ordeal to win through to the bloke she loves, jumping off yachts, swimming through dashed cold water, climbing into cottages, and borrowing other people's pyjamas, and then, when she has come to journey's end, so to speak, and is expecting the tender smile and the whispered endearments, gets instead the lowering frown, the curled lip, the suspicious eye, and—in a word—the raspberry. Naturally, she's a bit upset.

"Oh!" she said, for the third time, and her teeth gave a little click, most unpleasant. "So that's what you think?"

Chuffy shook his head in an impatient sort of way.

"Of course I don't."

"You do."

"I don't."

"Yes, you do."

"I don't think anything of the kind," said Chuffy. "I know that Bertie has been . . ."

". . . Scrupulously correct in his behaviour throughout," I suggested.

". . . sleeping in a potting shed," continued Chuffy, and I must say it didn't sound half as good as my version. "That's not the point. The fact remains that in spite of being engaged to me and pretending this afternoon that you were tickled pink to be engaged to me, you are still so much in love with Bertie that you can't keep away from him. You think I don't know all about your being engaged to him in New York, but I do. Oh, I'm not complaining," said Chuffy, looking rather like Saint Sebastian on receipt of about the fifteenth arrow. "You have a perfect right to love who you like . . ."

Whom, old man," I couldn't help saying.   Jeeves has made me rather a purist in these matters.

"Will you keep quiet!"

"Of course, of course."

"You keep shoving your oar in. . . ."

"Sorry, sorry.   Shan't occur again."

Chuffy, who had been gazing at me as if he would have liked to strike me with a blunt instrument, gazed once more at Pauline as if he would have liked to strike her with a blunt instrument. "But . . ."   He paused.   "Now you've made me forget what I was going to say," he said in a rather peevish manner.

Pauline took the floor.   She was still on the pink side, and her eyes were gleaming glitteringly.   I've seen my Aunt Agatha's eyes gleam just like that when she prepared to tick me off for some fancied misdemeanour.   Of the love light no traces remained.

"Well, then, perhaps you'll listen to what *I'm* going to say. I suppose you have no objection to my putting in a word?"

"None," said Chuffy.

"None, none," I said.

Pauline was beyond a question stirred to the core.   I could see her toes wiggling.

"In the first place, you make me sick!"

"Indeed?"

"Yes, indeed.   In the second place, I hope I shall never see you again in this world or the next."

"Really?"

"Yes, really.   I hate you.   I wish I'd never met you.   I think you're a worse pig than any you've got up at that beastly house of yours."

This interested me.

"I didn't know you kept pigs, Chuffy."

"Black Berkshires," he said absently.   "Well, if that's how you . . ."

"There's money in pigs."

"Well, all right," said Chuffy.   "If that's how you feel, well, all right."

"You bet it's all right."

"That's what I said, it's all right."

"My Uncle Henry . . ."

"Bertie," said Chuffy.

"Hallo?"

"I don't want to hear about your Uncle Henry. I am not interested in your Uncle Henry. It will be all right with me if your damned Uncle Henry trips over his feet and breaks his blasted neck."

"Too late, old man. He passed away three years ago. Pneumonia. I was only saying he kept pigs. Made a good thing out of them, too."

"Will you stop . . ."

"Yes, and will you," said Pauline. "Are you going to spend the night here? I wish you would leave off talking and go."

"I will," said Chuffy.

"Do," said Pauline.

"Good night," said Chuffy.

He strode to the head of the stairs.

"But one last word . . ." he said with a wide, passionate gesture.

Well, I could have told the poor old chap that you can't do that sort of thing in these old-world country cottages. His knuckles hit a projecting beam, he danced in agony, over-balanced, and the next moment was on his way to the ground floor like a sack of coals.

Pauline Stoker ran to the banisters and looked over.

"Are you hurt?" she cried.

"Yes," yelled Chuffy.

"Good," cried Pauline.

She came back into the room, and the front door slammed like the bursting of an over-wrought heart.

⋆ 10 ⋆

Another Visitor

I DREW a deepish breath. With the departure of the male half of the sketch a certain strain seemed to have gone out of the atmosphere. Excellent companion though I had always found him in the past, Chuffy had not shown himself at his chummiest during the recent scene, with the result that for some little time I had been feeling rather like Daniel in the lions' den.

Pauline was panting somewhat. Not exactly snorting, but

coming very near to what you might call the borderland of the snort. Her eyes were hard and bright. Deeply moved. She picked up her bathing suit.

"Push off, Bertie," she said.

I had been hoping for a quiet chat, in the course of which we would review the situation, touching on this point and on that, and strive to ascertain what to do for the best.

"But listen. . . ."

"I want to change."

"Change what?"

"Put on my swimming suit."

I could not follow her.

"Why?"

"Because I am going to swim."

"Swim?"

"Swim."

I stared.

"You aren't going back to the yacht?"

"I am going back to the yacht."

"But I wanted to talk about Chuffy."

"I never wish to hear his name mentioned again."

It seemed time to be the wise old mediator.

"Oh, come!"

"Well?"

"When I say 'Oh, come!'" I explained, "I mean surely you don't intend to give the poor blighter the permanent air on account of a trifling lovers' tiff?"

She looked at me in rather a peculiar manner.

"Would you mind repeating that? Just the last three words."

"Trifling lovers' tiff?"

She breathed heavily, and for a moment I experienced a return of that lions' den sensation.

"I wasn't sure I had caught them correctly," she said.

"I mean to say you get (a) a girl and (b) a bloke and stir up their generous natures, and the result is that each says lots of things she or he doesn't mean."

"Oh? Well, let me tell you I meant every word I said. I told him I never wanted to speak to him again. I don't. I told him I hated him. I do. I called him a pig. He is."

"Now, that's rummy about Chuffy's pigs. I had no notion he kept them."

"Why not? Birds of a feather."

There seemed nothing much more to say about pigs.

"Aren't you a bit hard?"

"Am I?"

"And rather rough on Chuffy?"

"Am I?"

"You wouldn't say his attitude was excusable?"

"I would not."

"Must have been a shock for the poor old chap, I mean, barging in and finding you here."

"Bertie."

"Hallo?"

"Ever been hit over the head with a chair?"

"No."

"Well, you soon may be."

I began to see she was in difficult mood.

"Oh, well!"

"Does that mean the same as 'Oh, come!'?"

"No. All I was driving at was that it seems a pity. Two loving hearts sundered for ever—*bingo!*"

"Yes?"

"Still, if that's the way you feel, well, that's the way you feel, what?"

"Yes."

"We now come to this idea of swimming home. Potty, it strikes me as."

"There's nothing to keep me here now, is there?"

"No. But the midnight swim. . . . You're going to find it pretty cold."

"And wet. I don't care."

"And how are you going to get aboard?"

"I'll get aboard. I can climb up by the thing they hang the anchor from. I've done it before. So will you remove yourself and let me change."

I went out on to the landing. And presently she emerged in the bathing suit.

"You needn't see me out."

"Of course I will, if you're really going."

"I'm going, all right."

"Well, if you must."

Outside the front door the air seemed nippier than ever.

The mere thought of plunging into the harbour gave me the shivers. But it had no effect on her. She slipped off into the darkness without a word, and I went upstairs to bed.

You might have thought that after garages and potting sheds the fact that I was in a bed would have resulted in instant slumber. But no. I couldn't get off. The more I tried, the more I found the mind turning to what you might call the tragedy in which I had so recently participated. I don't mind admitting that my heart ached for Chuffy. It also ached for Pauline. It ached for both of them.

I mean to say, consider the facts. Two thoroughly sound eggs, destined for each other, you might almost say, through all eternity, giving each other the bird like this for no reason whatever, really. Pitiful. Rotten. No good to man or beast. The more I thought of it, the sillier it seemed.

And yet there it was. Words had passed. Relations had been severed. The whole binge was irrevocably off.

There is only one thing for the sympathetic bystander to do on these occasions, and I realized now that it was madness not to have done it before going to bed and attempting sleep. I slid out from between the sheets and went downstairs.

The whisky bottle was in the cupboard. So was the siphon. So was the glass. I mixed myself a healing beaker and sat down. And, as I did so, I observed on the table a sheet of paper.

It was a note from Pauline Stoker.

DEAR BERTIE,
  You were right about it being cold. I couldn't face the swim. But there's a boat down by the landing stage. I shall row to the yacht and set it adrift. I've come back to borrow your overcoat. I didn't want to disturb you, so I climbed in through the window. I'm afraid you will have to sacrifice the coat, as of course I shall have to throw it overboard when I get to the yacht. Sorry.

P. S.

You notice the style? Curt. Staccato. Evidence of the wounded heart and the heavy mind. I felt sorrier for her than ever, but glad she probably wasn't going to get a cold in the head. As for the coat, a careless shrug of the shoulders covered that. I did not grudge it her, though new and silk-lined. Only too pleased, about summed up my attitude in the matter.

I tore up the note and returned to my spot.

There is nothing like a strong w-and-s for calming the system. In about another quarter of an hour I was feeling so soothed that I could contemplate bed once more, this time confident that the betting was at least eight to three that a refreshing slumber would be my portion.

I rose accordingly, and was just about to ankle upstairs, when for the second time that night there was the dickens of a knocking on the front door.

I don't know that you would call me an irascible man. I rather think not. Ask them about me at the Drones, and they will probably tell you that Bertram Wooster, wind and weather permitting, is as a general rule suavity itself. But, as I had been compelled to show Jeeves in the matter of the banjolele, I can be pushed too far. It was with drawn brow and cold eye that I now undid the chain. I was just about ready to give Sergeant Voules—for I assumed that it was he—the ticking-off of a lifetime.

"Voules," I was preparing to say, "enough is enough. This police persecution must stop. It is monstrous and uncalled-for. We are not in Russia, Voules. There are such things, I would have you remember, Voules, as strong letters to *The Times*."

That, or something like it, is what I would have said to Sergeant Voules: and what caused me to refrain was not weakness or pity, but the fact that the man attached to the knocker wasn't Voules at all. It was J. Washburn Stoker, and he was regarding me with a sort of hard-boiled fury which, but for the fact that I had just finished a life-giving snort and knew that his daughter Pauline was safely off the premises, would undoubtedly have tickled me up not a little.

As it was, I remained tranquil.

"Yes?" I said.

I had packed so much cold surprise and hauteur into the word that a lesser man might well have keeled over backwards as if hit by a bullet. J. W. Stoker took it without blinking. He pushed past me into the house, then turned and grabbed me by the shoulder.

"Now, then!" he said.

I disengaged myself coldly. I had to wriggle out of my pyjama jacket to do so, but I managed it.

"I beg your pardon?"

"Where's my daughter?"

"Your daughter Pauline?"

"I have only one daughter."

"And you ask me where this one daughter is?"

"I know where she is."

"Then why did you ask?"

"She's here."

"Then give me my pyjama jacket and tell her to come in," I said.

I've never actually seen a man grind his teeth, so I wouldn't care to state definitely that this is what J. Washburn Stoker did at this juncture. He may have done. He may not have done. All I can say authoritatively is that the muscles stood out on his cheeks and his jaws began to work as if he were chewing gum. It was not a pleasant spectacle, but thanks to the fact that I had mixed that whisky and splash particularly strong so as to facilitate sleep I was enabled to endure it with fortitude and phlegm.

"She's in this house!" he said, continuing to grind, if he was grinding.

"What makes you think that?"

"I'll tell you what makes me think that. I went to her state-room half an hour ago, and it was empty."

"But why on earth should you suppose she's come here?"

"Because I know she's infatuated with you."

"Not at all. She regards me as a sister."

"I am going to search this house."

"Charge right ahead."

He dashed upstairs and I returned to my spot. Not the same spot. Another one. I felt that in the circumstances a repeat was justified. And presently my visitor, who had gone up like a lion, came down like a lamb. I suppose a parent who has barged into a comparative stranger's cottage in the small hours in search of a missing daughter, feels more or less of a silly ass. I know I should, and apparently this Stoker did, for he shuffled a bit and I could see that a lot of the steam or motive force had gone out of him.

"I owe you an apology, Mr. Wooster."

"Don't give it a thought."

"I took it for granted whan I found Pauline gone . . ."

"Dismiss the whole thing from your mind. Might have

happened to anybody. Faults on both sides and so forth. You'll have a certain something before you go?"

It seemed to me that it would be a prudent move to detain him on the premises for as long as possible, so as to give Pauline plenty of time to get back to the old boat. But he wouldn't be tempted. His mind was evidently too occupied for spots.

"It beats me where she can have gone," he said, and you would have been astounded at the mildness and even chummy pathos with which he spoke. It was as if Bertram had been some wise old friend to whom he was bringing his little troubles. The man seemed positively punctured. A child could have played with him.

I endeavoured to throw out a word of cheer.

"I expect she's gone for a swim."

"At this time of night?"

"Girls do rummy things."

"And she's a curious girl. This infatuation of hers for you, for instance."

This seemed to me lacking in tact, and I would have frowned slightly, had I not remembered that I wished to disabuse him, if disabuse is what I'm driving at, of the idea that any such infatuation existed.

"Correct this notion that Miss Stoker is under my fatal spell." I urged him. "She laughs herself sick at the sight of me."

"I did not get that impression this afternoon."

"Oh, that? Just brother and sister stuff. It shan't occur again."

"It had better not," he said, returning for a moment to what I might call his earlier manner. "Well, I won't keep you up, Mr. Wooster. I apologize again for making a darned fool of myself."

I did not quite slap him on the back, but I made a sort of back-slapping gesture.

"Not at all," I said. "Not at all. I wish I had a quid for every time I've made a darned fool of *my*self."

And on these cordial terms we parted. He went down the garden path, and I, having waited up about ten minutes on the chance that somebody else might come paying a social call, drained my glass and popped up to bed.

Something attempted, something done, had earned a night's repose, or as near as you can get to a night's repose in a place full of Stokers and Paulines and Vouleses and Chuffys and

Dobsons.   It was not long before the weary eyelids closed and I was off.

It seems almost incredible, considering what the night life of Chuffnell Regis was like, but the next thing that woke me was not a girl leaping out from under the bed, her father bounding in with blood in his eye, or a police sergeant playing ragtime on the knocker, but actually the birds outside my window heralding in a new day.

Well, when I say heralding, it was about ten-thirty of a fine summer morning, and the sunshine streaming in through the window seemed to be calling to me to get up and see what I could do to an egg, a rasher, and the good old pot of coff.

I had a hasty bath and shave and trotted down to the kitchen, full of *joie de vivre*.

∗ 11 ∗

Sinister Behaviour Of A Yacht-Owner

IT was not until I had finished breakfast and was playing the banjolele in the front garden that something seemed to whisper reproachfully in my ear that I had no right to be feeling as perky as this on what was so essentially the morning after. Dirty work had been perpetrated overnight.   Tragedy had stalked through the home.   Scarcely ten hours earlier I had been a witness of a scene which, if I were the man of fine fibre I liked to think myself, should have removed all the sunshine from my life. Two loving hearts, one of which I had been at school and Oxford with, had gone to the mat together in my presence and having chewed holes in one another had parted in anger, never—according to present schedule—to meet again.   And here I was, care-free and callous, playing "I Lift Up My Finger And I Say Tweet-Tweet" on the banjolele.

All wrong.   I switched to "Body and Soul", and a sober sadness came upon me.

Something, I felt, must be done.   Steps must be taken and avenues explored.

But I could not conceal from myself that the situation was

complex. Usually, in my experience, when one of my pals has broken off diplomatic relations with a girl or vice versa they have been staying in a country house together or at least living in London, where it wasn't so dashed difficult to arrange a meeting and join their hands with a benevolent smile. But in this matter of Chuffy and Pauline Stoker, consider the facts. She was on the yacht, virtually in irons. He was at the Hall, three miles inland. And anybody who wanted to do any hand-joining had got to be a much more mobile force than I was. True, my standing with old Stoker had improved a bit overnight, but there had been no hint on his part of any disposition to give me the run of his yacht. I seemed to have about as much chance of getting in touch with Pauline and endeavouring to reason with her as if she had never come over from America at all.

Quite a prob., I mean to say, and I was still brooding on it when the garden gate clicked and I perceived Jeeves walking up the path.

"Ah, Jeeves," I said.

My manner probably seemed to him a little distant, and I jolly well meant it to. What Pauline had told me about his loose and unconsidered remarks with reference to my mentality had piqued me considerably. It was not the first time he had said that sort of thing, and one has one's feelings.

But if he sensed the hauteur, he affected to ignore it. His bearing continued placid and unmoved.

"Good morning, sir."

"Have you come from the yacht?"

"Yes, sir."

"Was Miss Stoker there?"

"Yes, sir. She appeared at the breakfast table. I was somewhat surprised to see her. I had assumed that it was her intention to remain ashore and establish communication with his lordship."

I laughed shortly.

"They established communication, all right?"

"Sir?"

I put down the banjolele and looked at him sternly.

"A nice thing you let all and sundry in for last night!" I said.

"Sir?"

"You can't get out of it by saying 'Sir?'. Why on earth didn't you stop Miss Stoker from swimming ashore yestreen?"

"I could scarcely take the liberty, sir, of thwarting the young lady in an enterprise on which her heart was so plainly set."

"She says you urged her on with word and gesture."

"No, sir. I merely expressed sympathy with her stated aims."

"You said I would be delighted to put her up for the night."

"She had already decided to seek refuge in your house, sir. I did nothing more than hazard the opinion that you would do all that lay in your power to assist her."

"Well, do you know what the outcome was—the upshot, if I may use the term? I was pursued by the police."

"Indeed, sir?"

"Yes. Naturally I couldn't sleep in the house, with every nook and cranny bulging with blighted girls, so I withdrew to the garage. I had hardly been there ten minutes before Sergeant Voules arrived."

"I have not met Sergeant Voules, sir."

"With him Constable Dobson."

"I am acquainted with Constable Dobson. A nice young fellow. He is keeping company with Mary, the parlourmaid at the Hall. A red-haired girl, sir."

"Resist the urge to talk about the colour of parlourmaids' hair, Jeeves," I said coldly. "It is not germane to the issue. Stick to the point. Which is that I spent a sleepless night, chased to and fro by the gendarmerie."

"I am sorry to hear that, sir."

"Eventually Chuffy arrived. Forming a totally erroneous diagnosis of the case, he insisted on helping me to my room, removing my boots, and putting me to bed. He was thus occupied when Miss Stoker strolled in, wearing my heliotrope pyjamas."

"Most disturbing, sir."

"It was. They had the dickens of a row, Jeeves."

"Indeed, sir?"

"Eyes flashed, voices were raised. Eventually Chuffy fell downstairs and went moodily out into the night. And the point is—the nub of the thing is—what is to be done about it?"

"It is a situation that will require careful thought, sir."

"You mean you have not had any ideas yet?"

"I have only this moment heard what transpired, sir."

"True. I was forgetting that. Have you had speech with Miss Stoker this morning?"

"No, sir."

"Well, I can see no point in your going to the Hall and tackling Chuffy. I have given this matter a good deal of thought, Jeeves, and it is plain to me that Miss Stoker is the one who will require the persuasive word, the nicely reasoned argument—in short, the old oil. Last night Chuffy wounded her deepest feelings, and it's going to take a lot of spadework to bring her round. In comparison, the problem of Chuffy is simple. I shouldn't be surprised if even now he was kicking himself soundly for having behaved so like a perfect chump. One day of quiet meditation, at the outside, should be enough to convince him that he wronged the girl. To go and reason with Chuffy is simply a waste of time. Leave him alone, and Nature will effect the cure. You had better go straight back to the yacht and see what you can do at the other end."

"It was not with the intention of interviewing his lordship that I came ashore, sir. Once more I must reiterate that, until you informed me just now, I was not aware that anything in the nature of a rift had occurred. My motive in coming here was to hand you a note from Mr. Stoker."

I was puzzled.

"A note?"

"Here it is, sir."

I opened it, still fogged, and read contents. I can't say I felt much clearer when I had done so.

"Rummy, Jeeves."

"Sir?"

"This is a letter of invitation."

"Indeed, sir?"

"Absolutely. Bidding me to the feast. 'Dear Mr. Wooster,' writes Pop Stoker, 'I shall be frightfully bucked if you will come and mangle a spot of garbage on the boat tonight. Don't dress.' I give you the gist of the thing. Peculiar, Jeeves."

"Certainly unforeseen, sir."

"I forgot to tell you that among my visitors last night was this same Stoker. He bounded in, shouting that his daughter was on the premises, and searched the house."

"Indeed, sir?"

"Well, of course, he didn't find any daughter, because she was already on her way back to the yacht, and he seemed conscious of having made rather an ass of himself. His manner on departing was chastened. He actually spoke to me civilly—a thing I'd have taken eleven to four on that he didn't know how to do. But does that explain this sudden gush of hospitality? I don't think so. Last night he seemed apologetic rather than matey. There was no indication whatever that he wished to start one of those great friendships."

"I think it is possible that a conversation which I had this morning with the gentleman, sir . . ."

"Ah! It was you, was it, who caused this pro-Bertram sentiment?"

"Immediately after breakfast, sir, Mr. Stoker sent for me and inquired if I had once been in your employment. He said that he fancied that he recalled having seen me at your apartment in New York. On my replying in the affirmative, he proceeded to question me with regard to certain incidents in the past."

"The cats in the bedroom?"

"And the hot-water bottle episode."

"The purloined hat?"

"And also the matter of your sliding down pipes, sir."

"And you said——?"

"I explained that Sir Roderick Glossop had taken a biased view of these occurrences, sir and proceeded to relate their inner history."

"And he——?"

"—seemed pleased, sir. He appeared to think that he had mis-judged you. He said that he ought to have known better than to believe information proceeding from Sir Roderick—to whom he alluded as a bald-headed old son of a something which for the moment has escaped my memory. It was, I imagine, shortly after this that he must have written this letter inviting you to dinner, sir."

I was pleased with the man. When Bertram Wooster finds the old feudal spirit flourishing, he views it with approval and puts that approval into words.

"Thank you, Jeeves."

"Not at all, sir."

"You have done well. Regarding the matter from one aspect, of course, it is negligible whether Pop Stoker thinks I'm a loony or not. I mean to say, a fellow closely connected by ties of blood with a man who used to walk about on his hands is scarcely in a position, where the question of sanity is concerned, to put on dog and set himself up as an . . ."

"*Arbiter elegentiarum*, sir?"

"Quite.   It matters little to me, therefore, from one point of view, what old Stoker thinks about my upper storey.   One shrugs the shoulders.   But, setting that aside, I admit that this change of heart is welcome.   It has come at the right time.   I shall accept his invitation.   I regard it as . . ."

"The *amende honorable*, sir?"

"I was going to say olive branch."

"Or olive branch.   The two terms are virtually synonymous. The French phrase I would be inclined to consider perhaps slightly the more exact in the circumstances—carrying with it, as it does, the implication of remorse, of the desire to make restitution.   But if you prefer the expression 'olive branch', by all means employ it, sir."

"Thank you, Jeeves."

"Not at all, sir."

"I suppose you know that you have made me completely forget what I was saying?"

"I beg your pardon, sir.   I should not have interrupted.   If I recollect, you were observing that it was your intention to accept Mr. Stoker's invitation."

"Ah, yes.   Very well, then.   I shall accept his invitation— whether as an olive branch or an *amende honorable* is wholly immaterial and doesn't matter a single, solitary damn, Jeeves. . . ."

"No, sir."

"And shall I tell you why I shall accept his invitation?   Because it will enable me to get together with Miss Stoker and plead Chuffy's cause."

"I understand, sir."

"Not that it's going to be easy.   I hardly know what line to take."

"If I might make the suggestion, sir, I should imagine that the young lady would respond most satisfactorily to the statement that his lordship was in poor health."

"She knows he's as fit as a fiddle."

"Poor health induced since her parting from him by distress of mind."

"Ah!   I get you.   Distraught?"

"Precisely, sir."

"Contemplating self-destruction?"

"Exactly, sir."

"Her gentle heart would be touched by that, you think?"

"Very conceivably, sir."

"Then that is the vein I shall work. I see this invitation says dinner at seven. A bit on the early side, what?"

"I presume that the arrangements have been made with a view to the convenience of Master Dwight, sir. This would be the birthday-party of which I informed you yesterday."

"Of course, yes. With nigger minstrel entertainment to follow. They are coming all right, I take it?"

"Yes, sir. The Negroes will be present."

"I wonder if there would be any chance of a word with the one who plays the banjo. There are certain points in his execution I would like to consult him about."

"No doubt it could be arranged, sir."

He seemed to speak with a certain reserve, and I could see that he felt that the conversation had taken an embarrassing turn. Probing the old sore, I mean.

Well, the best thing to do on these occasions, I've always found, is to be open and direct.

"I'm making great progress with the banjolele, Jeeves."

"Indeed, sir?"

"Would you like me to play you 'What Is This Thing Called Love?'"

"No, sir."

"Your views on the instrument are unchanged?"

"Yes, sir."

"Ah, well! A pity we could not see eye to eye on that matter."

"Yes, sir."

"Still, it can't be helped. No hard feelings."

"No, sir."

"Unfortunate, though."

"Most unfortunate, sir."

"Well, tell old Stoker that I shall be there at seven prompt with my hair in a braid."

"Yes, sir."

"Or should I write a brief, civil note?"

"No, sir. I was instructed to bring back a verbal reply."

"Right ho, then."

"Very good, sir."

At seven on the dot, accordingly, I stepped aboard the yacht and handed the hat and light overcoat to a passing salt. It was with mixed feelings that I did so, for conflicting emotions were warring in the bosom. On the one hand, the keen ozone of Chuffnell Regis had given me a good appetite, and I knew from recollections of his hosp. in New York that J. Washburn Stoker did his guests well. On the other, I had never been what you might call tranquil in his society, and I was not looking forward to it particularly now. You might put it like this if you cared to—The fleshly or corporeal Wooster was anticipating the binge with pleasure, but his spiritual side rather recoiled a bit.

In my experience, there are two kinds of elderly American. One, the stout and horn-rimmed, is matiness itself. He greets you as if you were a favourite son, starts agitating the cocktail shaker before you know where you are, slips a couple into you with a merry laugh, claps you on the back, tells you a dialect story about two Irishmen named Pat and Mike, and, in a word, makes life one grand, sweet song.

The other, which runs a good deal to the cold, grey stare and the square jaw, seems to view the English cousin with concern. It is not Elfin. It broods. It says little. It sucks in its breath in a pained way. And every now and again you catch its eye, and it is like colliding with a raw oyster.

Of this latter class or species J. Washburn Stoker had always been the perpetual vice-president.

It was with considerable relief, therefore, that I found that tonight he had eased off a bit. While not precisely affable, he gave a distinct impression of being as nearly affable as he knew how.

"I hope you have no objection to a quiet family dinner, Mr. Wooster?" he said, having shaken the hand.

"Rather not. Dashed good of you to ask me," I replied, not to be outdone in the courtesies.

"Just you and Dwight and myself. My daughter is lying down. She has a headache."

This was something of a jar. In fact, it seemed to me to take what you might describe as the whole meaning out of this expedition.

"Oh?" I said.

"I am afraid she found her exertions last night a little too much for her," said Pop Stoker, with something of the old fish-like expression in the eye: and, reading between the lines, I rather gathered that Pauline had been sent to bed without her supper, in disgrace. Old Stoker was not one of your broad-minded, modern parents. There was, as I had had occasion to notice before, a distinct touch of the stern and rockbound old Pilgrim Father about him. A man, in short, who, in his dealings with his family, believed in the firm hand.

Observing that eye, I found it a bit difficult to shape the kindly inquiries.

"Then you—er . . . she—er——?"

"Yes. You were quite right, Mr. Wooster. She had gone for a swim."

And once more, as he spoke, I caught a flash of the fishlike. I could see that Pauline's stock was far from high this p.m., and I would have liked to put in a word for the poor young blighter. But beyond an idea of saying that girls would be girls, which I abandoned, I could think of nothing.

At this moment, however, a steward of sorts announced dinner, and we pushed in.

I must say that there were moments during that dinner when I regretted that occurrences which could not be overlooked had resulted in the absence from the board of the Hall party. You will question this statement, no doubt, inclining to the view that all a dinner-party needs to make it a success is for Sir Roderick Glossop, the Dowager Lady Chuffnell, and the latter's son, Seabury, not to be there. Nevertheless, I stick to my opinion. There was a certain uncomfortable something about the atmosphere which more or less turned the food to ashes in my mouth. If it hadn't been that this man, this Stoker, had gone out of his way to invite me, I should have said that I was giving him a pain in the neck. Most of the time he just sat and champed in a sort of dark silence, like a man with something on his mind. And when he did speak it was with a marked what-d'you-call-it. I mean to say, not actually out of the corner of his mouth, but very near it.

I did my best to promote a flow of conversation. But it was not till young Dwight had left the table and we were lighting the cigars that I seemed to hit on a topic that interested, elevated, and amused.

"A fine boat, this, Mr. Stoker," I said.

For the first time, something approaching animation came into the face.

"Not many better."

"I've never done much yachting. And, except at Cowes one year, I've never been on a boat this size."

He puffed at his cigar. An eye came swivelling round in my direction, then pushed off again.

"There are advantages in having a yacht."

"Oh, rather."

"Plenty of room to put your friends up."

"Heaps."

"And, when you've got 'em, they can't get away so easy as they could ashore."

It seemed a rummy way of looking at it, but I supposed a man like Stoker would naturally have a difficulty in keeping guests. I mean, I took it that he had had painful experiences in the past. And nothing, of course, makes a host look sillier to have somebody arrive at his country house for a long visit and then to find, round about lunch-time the second day, that he has made a quiet sneak for the railway station.

"Care to look over the boat?" he asked.

"Fine," I said.

"I'd be glad to show it to you. This is the main saloon we're in."

"Ah," I said.

"I'll show you the state-rooms."

He rose, and we went along passages and things. We came to a door. He opened it and switched on the light.

"This is one of our larger guest-rooms."

"Very nice, too."

"Go in and take a look round."

Well, there wasn't much to see that I couldn't focus from the threshold, but one has to do the civil thing on these occasions. I toddled over and gave the bed a prod.

And, as I did so, the door slammed. And when I nipped round, the old boy had disappeared.

Rather rummy, was my verdict. In fact, distinctly rummy. I went across and gave the handle a twist.

The bally door was locked.

"Hoy!" I called.

No answer.

"Hey!" I said. "Mr. Stoker."

Only silence, and lots of it.

I went and sat down on the bed. This seemed to me to want thinking out.

Start Smearing, Jeeves!

I CAN'T say I liked the look of things. In addition to being at a loss and completely unable to follow the scenario, I was also distinctly on the uneasy side. I don't know if you ever read a book called "The Masked Seven"? It's one of those goose-fleshers and there's a chap in it, Drexdale Yeats, a private investigator, who starts looking for clues in a cellar one night, and he's hardly collected a couple when—*bingo*—there's a metallic clang and there he is with the trapdoor shut and someone sniggering nastily on the other side. For a moment his heart stood still, and so did mine. Excluding the nasty snigger (which Stoker might quite well have uttered without my hearing it), it seemed to me that my case was more or less on all fours with his. Like jolly old Drexdale, I sensed some lurking peril.

Of course, mark you, if something on these lines had occurred at some country house where I was staying, and the hand that had turned the key had been that of a pal of mine, a ready explanation would have presented itself. I should have set it down as a spot of hearty humour. My circle of friends is crammed with fellows who would consider it dashed diverting to bung you into a room and lock the door. But on the present occasion I could not see this being the solution. There was nothing roguish about old Stoker. Whatever view you might take of this fishy-eyed man, you would never call him playful. If Pop Stoker put his guests in cold storage, his motive in so doing was sinister.

Little wonder, then, that as he sat on the edge of the bed pensively sucking at his cigar, Bertram was feeling uneasy. The thought of Stoker's second cousin, George, forced itself upon the mind. Dotty, beyond a question. And who knew but what that dottiness might not run in the family? It didn't seem such a long step, I mean to say, from a Stoker locking people in state-rooms to a Stoker with slavering jaws and wild, animal eyes coming back and doing them a bit of no good with the meat axe.

When, therefore, there was a click and the door opened,

revealing mine host on the threshold, I confess that I rather drew myself together somewhat and pretty well prepared myself for the worst.

His manner, however, was reassuring. Puff-faced, yes, but not fiend-in-human-shape-y. The eyes were steady and the mouth lacked foam. And he was still smoking his cigar, which I felt was promising. I mean, I've never met any homicidal loonies, but I should imagine that the first thing they would do before setting about a fellow would be to throw away their cigars.

"Well, Mr. Wooster?"

I never have known quite what to answer when blokes say "Well?" to me, and I didn't now.

"I must apologize for leaving you so abruptly," proceeded the Stoker, "but I had to get the concert started."

"I'm looking forward to the concert," I said.

"A pity," said Pop Stoker. "Because you're going to miss it."

He eyed me musingly.

"There was a time, when I was younger, when I would have broken your neck," he said.

I didn't like the trend the conversation was taking. After all, a man is as young as he feels, and there was no knowing that he wouldn't suddenly get one of these—what do you call them?—illusions of youth. I had an uncle once, aged seventy-six, who, under the influence of old crusted port, would climb trees.

"Look here," I said civilly but with what you might call a certain urgency, "I know it's trespassing on your time, but could you tell me what all this is about?"

"You don't know?"

"No, I'm hanged if I do."

"And you can't guess?"

"No, I'm dashed if I can."

"Then I had best tell you from the beginning. Perhaps you recall my visiting you last night?"

I said I hadn't forgotten.

"I thought my daughter was in your cottage. I searched it. I did not find her."

I twiddled a hand magnanimously.

"We all make mistakes."

He nodded.

"Yes. So I went away. And do you know what happened after I left you, Mr. Wooster? I was coming out of the garden gate when your local police sergeant stopped me. He seemed suspicious."

I waved my cigar sympathetically.

"Something will have to be done about Voules," I said. "The man is a pest. I hope you were pretty terse with him."

"Not at all. I supposed he was only doing his duty. I told him who I was and where I lived. On learning that I came from this yacht, he asked me to accompany him to the police station."

I was amazed.

"What bally cheek! You mean he pinched you?"

"No, he was not arresting me. He wished me to identify someone who was in custody."

"Bally cheek, all the same. What on earth did he bother you with that sort of job for? Besides, how on earth could you identify anyone? I mean, a stranger in these parts, and all that sort of thing."

"In this instance it was simple. The prisoner happened to be my daughter, Pauline."

"What!"

"Yes, Mr. Wooster. It seems that this man Voules was in his back garden late last night—it adjoins yours, if you recollect—and he saw a figure climbing out of one of the lower windows of your house. He ran down the garden and caught this individual. It was my daughter Pauline. She was wearing a swimming suit and an overcoat belonging to you. So, you see, you were right when you told me she had probably gone for a swim."

He knocked the ash carefully off his cigar. I didn't need to do it to mine.

"She must have been with you a few moments before I arrived. Now, perhaps, Mr. Wooster, you can understand what I meant when I said that, when I was a younger man, I would have broken your neck."

I hadn't anything much to say. One hasn't sometimes.

"Nowadays, I'm more sensible," he proceeded. "I take the easier way. I say to myself that Mr. Wooster is not the son-in-law I would have chosen personally, but if my hand has been forced that is all there is to it. Anyway, you're not the gibbering idiot I thought you at one time, I'm glad to say. I have heard since that those stories which caused me to break off

Pauline's engagement to you in New York were untrue. So we can consider everything just as it was three months ago. We will look upon that letter of Pauline's as unwritten."

You can't reel when you're sitting on a bed. Otherwise, I would have done so, and right heartily. I was feeling as if a hidden hand had socked me in the solar plexus.

"Do you mean——?"

He let me have an eye squarely in the pupil. A beastly sort of eye, cold and yet hot, if you follow me. If this was the Boss's Eye you read so much about in the advertisements in American magazines, I was dashed if I could see why any ambitious young shipping clerk should be so bally anxious to catch it. It went clean through me, and I lost the thread of my remarks.

"I am assuming that you wish to marry my daughter?"

Well, of course . . . I mean, dash it . . . I mean, there isn't much you can say to an observation like that. I just weighed in with a mild "Oh, ah!"

"I am not quite sure if I understand the precise significance of the expression 'Oh, ah!'" he said, and, by Jove, I wonder if you notice a rather rummy thing. I mean to say, this man had had the advantage of Jeeves's society for only about twenty-four hours, and here he was—except that Jeeves would have said "wholly" instead of "quite" and stuck in a "Sir" or two—talking just like him. I mean, it just shows. I remember putting young Catsmeat Potter-Pirbright up at the flat for a week once, and the very second day he said something to me about gauging somebody's latent potentialities. And Catsmeat a fellow who had always thought you were kidding him when you assured him that there were words in the language that had more than one syllable. As I say, it simply goes to show. . . .

However, where was I?

"I am not quite sure if I understand the precise significance of the expression 'Oh, ah!'" said this Stoker, "but I will take it to mean that you do. I won't pretend that I'm delighted, but one can't have everything. What are your views upon engagements, Mr. Wooster?"

"Engagements?"

"Should they be short or long?"

"Well . . ."

"I prefer them short. I feel that we had best put this wedding through as quickly as possible. I shall have to find out how soon that is on this side. I believe you cannot simply go to the nearest minister, as in my country. There are formalities. While these are being attended to, you will, of course, be my guest. I'm afraid I can't offer you the freedom of the boat, because you are a pretty slippery young gentleman and might suddenly remember a date elsewhere—some unfortunate appointment which would necessitate your leaving. But I shall do my best to make you comfortable in this room for the next few days. There are books on that shelf—I assume you can read?—and cigarettes on the table. I will send my man along in a few minutes with some pyjamas and so on. And now I will wish you good night, Mr. Wooster. I must be getting back to the concert. I can't stay away from my son's birthday-party, can I, even for the pleasure of talking to you?"

He slipped through the door and oozed out, and I was alone.

Now, it so happened that twice in my career I had had the experience of sitting in a cell and listening to keys turning in locks. The first time was the one to which Chuffy had alluded, when I had been compelled to assure the magistrate that I was one of the West Dulwich Plimsolls. The other—and both, oddly enough, had occurred on Boat Race night—was when I had gone into partnership with my old friend, Oliver Sipperley, to pick up a policeman's helmet as a souvenir, only to discover that there was a policeman inside it. On both these occasions I had ended up behind the bars, and you might suppose that an old lag like myself would have been getting used to it by now.

But this present binge was something quite different. Before, I had been faced merely with the prospect of a moderate fine. Now, a life sentence stared me in the eyeball.

A casual observer, noting Pauline's pre-eminent pulchritude and bearing in mind the fact that she was heiress to a sum amounting to more than fifty million fish, might have considered that in writhing, as I did, in agony of spirit at the prospect of having to marry her, I was making a lot of fuss about nothing. Such an observer, no doubt, would have wished that he had half my complaint. But the fact remains that I did writhe, and writhe pretty considerably.

Apart from the fact that I didn't want to marry Pauline Stoker, there was the dashed serious snag that I knew jolly well that she didn't want to marry me. She might have ticked him off with great breadth and freedom at their recent parting, but I was certain that deep down in her the old love for Chuffy still persisted and only needed a bit of corkscrew work to get it to the surface again. And Chuffy, for all that he had hurled himself downstairs and stalked out into the night, still loved her. So that what it amounted to, when you came to tot up the pros and cons, was that by marrying this girl I should not only be landing myself in the soup but breaking both her heart and that of the old school friend. And if that doesn't justify a fellow in writhing, I should very much like to know what does.

Only one gleam of light appeared in the darkness—viz. that old Stoker had said that he was sending his man along with the necessaries for the night. It might be that Jeeves would find the way.

Though how even Jeeves could get me out of the current jam was more than I could envisage. It was with the feeling that no bookie would hesitate to lay a hundred to one against that I finished my cigar and threw myself on the bed.

I was still picking at the coverlet when the door opened and a respectful cough informed me that he was in my midst. His arms were full of clothing of various species. He laid these on a chair and regarded me with what I might describe as commiseration.

"Mr. Stoker instructed me to bring your pyjamas, sir."

I emitted a hollow g.

"It is not pyjamas I need, Jeeves, but the wings of a dove. Are you abreast of the latest development?"

"Yes, sir."

"Who told you?"

"My informant was Miss Stoker, sir."

"You've been having a talk with her?"

"Yes, sir. She related to me an outline of the plans which Mr. Stoker had made."

The first spot of hope I had had since the start of this ghastly affair now shot through my bosom.

"By Jove, Jeeves, an idea occurs to me. Things aren't quite as bad as I thought they were."

"No, sir?"

"No. Can't you see? It's all very well for old Stoker to talk—er——"

"Glibly, sir?"

"Airily."

"Airily or glibly, sir, whichever you prefer."

"It's all very well for old Stoker to talk with airy glibness about marrying us off, but he can't do it, Jeeves. Miss Stoker will simply put her ears back and refuse to co-operate. You can lead a horse to the altar, Jeeves, but you can't make it drink."

"In my recent conversation with the young lady, sir, I did not receive the impression that she was antagonistic to the arrangements."

"What!"

"No, sir. She seemed, if I may say so, resigned and defiant."

"She couldn't be both."

"Yes, sir. Miss Stoker's attitude was partly one of listless-ness, as if she felt that nothing mattered now, but I gathered that she was also influenced by the thought that in contracting a matrimonial alliance with you, she would be making—shall I say, a defiant gesture at his lordship."

"A defiant gesture?"

"Yes, sir."

"Scoring off him, you mean?"

"Precisely, sir."

"What a damn silly idea. The girl must be cuckoo."

"Feminine psychology is admittedly odd, sir. The poet Pope . . ."

"Never mind about the poet Pope, Jeeves."

"No, sir."

"There are times when one wants to hear all about the poet Pope and times when one doesn't."

"Very true, sir."

"The point is, I seem to be up against it. If that's the way she feels, nothing can save me. I am a pipped man."

"Yes, sir. Unless——"

"Unless?"

"Well, I was wondering, sir, if on the whole it would not be best if you were to obviate all unpleasantness and embarrassment by removing yourself from the yacht."

"What!"

"Yacht, sir."

"I know you said 'Yacht'. And I said 'What!' Jeeves," I went on, and there was a quiver in the voice, "it is not like you to come in here at a crisis like this with straws in your hair and talk absolute drip. How the devil can I leave the yacht?"

"The matter could be readily arranged, if you are agreeable, sir. It would, of course, involve certain inconveniences . . ."

"Jeeves," I said, "short of squeezing through the port-hole, which can't be done, I am ready to undergo any little passing inconvenience if it will get me off this bally floating dungeon and restore me to terra firma." I paused and regarded him anxiously. "This is not mere gibbering, is it? You really have a scheme?"

"Yes, sir. The reason I hesitated to advance it was that I feared you might not approve of the idea of covering your face with boot polish."

"What!"

"Time being of the essence, sir, I think it would not be advisable to employ burnt cork."

I turned my face to the wall. It was the end.

"Leave me, Jeeves," I said. "You've been having a couple."

And I'm not sure that what cut me like a knife, more even than any agony at my fearful predicament, was not the realization that my original suspicions had been correct and that, after all these years, that superb brain had at last come unstuck. For, though I had tactfully affected to set all this talk of burnt cork and boot polish down to mere squiffiness, in my heart I was convinced that the fellow had gone off his onion.

He coughed.

"If you will permit me to explain, sir. The entertainers are just concluding their performance. In a short time they will be leaving the boat."

I sat up. Hope dawned once more, and remorse gnawed me like a bullpup worrying a rubber bone at the thought that I should have so misjudged this man. I saw what that giant brain was driving at.

"You mean——?"

"I have a small tin of boot polish here, sir. I brought it with me in anticipation of this move. It would be a simple task to apply it to your face and hands in such a manner as to create the illusion, should you encounter Mr. Stoker, that you were a member of this troupe of negroid entertainers."

"Jeeves!"

"The suggestion I would make, sir, is that, if you are amenable to what I propose, we should wait until these black-faced persons have left for the shore. I could then inform the captain that one of them, a personal friend of mine, had lingered behind to talk with me and so had missed the motor launch. I have little doubt that he would accord me permission to row you ashore in one of the smaller boats."

I stared at the man. Years of intimate acquaintance, the memory of swift ones he had pulled in the past, the knowledge that he lived largely on fish, thus causing his brain to be about as full of phosphorus as the human brain can jolly well stick, had not prepared me for this supreme effort.

"Jeeves," I said, "as I have so often had occasion to say before, you stand alone."

"Thank you, sir."

"Others abide our question. Thou art free."

"I endeavour to give satisfaction, sir."

"You think it would work?"

"Yes, sir."

"The scheme carries your personal guarantee?"

"Yes, sir."

"And you say you have the stuff handy?"

"Yes, sir."

I flung myself into a chair and turned the features ceiling-wards.

"Then start smearing, Jeeves," I said, "and continue to smear till your trained senses tell you that you have smeared enough."

★ 13 ★

A Valet Exceeds His Duties

I MUST say, as a general rule, I always bar stories where the chap who's telling them skips lightly from point to point and leaves you to work it out for yourself as best you can just what has happened in the interim. I mean to say, the sort of story where Chapter Ten ends with the hero trapped in the underground den and Chapter Eleven starts with him being the life and soul of a gay party at the Spanish Embassy. And, strictly speaking, I suppose, I ought at this juncture to describe step by step the various moves which led me to safety and freedom, if you see what I mean.

But when a tactician like Jeeves is in charge of the arrangements, it all seems so unnecessary. Simply a waste of time. If Jeeves sets out to shift a fellow from Spot A to Spot B, from a state-room on a yacht, for instance, to the shore in front of his cottage, he just does it. No hitches. No difficulties. No fuss. No excitement. Absolutely nothing to report. I mean, one just reaches for the nearest tin of boot polish, blacks one's face, strolls across the deck, saunters down the gangway, waves a genial farewell to such members of the crew as may be leaning over the side, spitting into the water, steps into a boat, and in about ten minutes there one is, sniffing the cool night air on the mainland. A smooth bit of work.

I mentioned this to Jeeves as we tied up at the landing stage, and he said it was extremely kind of me to say so.

"Not at all, Jeeves," I said. "I repeat. An exceedingly smooth bit of work, and a credit to you."

"Thank you, sir."

"Thank *you*, Jeeves. And now what?"

We had left the landing stage and were standing on the road that ran past my garden gate. All was still. The stars twinkled above. We were alone with Nature. There was not even a sign of Police-Sergeant Voules or Constable Dobson. Chuffnell Regis slept, as you might say. And yet, looking at my watch, I found that the hour was only a few minutes after nine. It gave me quite a start, I recall. What with stress of emotion, so to speak, and the spirit having been on the rack, as it were, I had got the impression that the night was particularly well advanced, and wouldn't have been surprised to find it one in the morning.

"And now what, Jeeves?" I said.

I noted a soft smile playing over the finely-chiselled face and resented same. I was grateful to the man, of course, for having saved me from the fate that is worse than death, but one has to check this sort of thing. I gave him one of my looks.

"Something is tickling you, Jeeves?" I said, coldly.

"I beg your pardon, sir. I had not intended to betray amusement, but I could not help being a little entertained by your appearance. It is somewhat odd, sir."

"Most people would look somewhat odd with boot polish all over them, Jeeves."

"Yes, sir."

"Greta Garbo, to name but one."

"Yes, sir."

"Or Dean Inge."

"Very true, sir."

"Then spare me these personal comments, Jeeves, and reply to my question."

"I fear I have forgotten what it was that you asked me, sir."

"My question was—and is—'Now what?'"

"You desire a suggestion respecting your next move, sir?"

"I do."

"I would advise repairing to your cottage, sir, and cleansing your face and hands."

"So far, sound. It is just what I was thinking of doing."

"After which, if I might hazard the advice, sir, I think it would be well if you were to catch the next train to London."

"Again, sound."

"Once there, sir, I would advocate a visit to some Continental resort, such as Paris or Berlin or even perhaps, as far afield as Italy."

"Or Sunny Spain?"

"Yes, sir. Possibly Spain."

"Or even Egypt?"

"You would find Egypt somewhat warm at this season of the year, sir."

"Not half so warm as England, if Pop Stoker re-establishes connection."

"Very true, sir."

"There's a lad, Jeeves! There's a tough citizen! There's a fellow who chews broken glass and drives nails into the back of his neck instead of using a collar stud!"

"Mr. Stoker's personality is decidedly forceful, sir."

"Bless my soul, Jeeves, I can remember the time when I thought Sir Roderick Glossop a man-eater. And even my Aunt Agatha. They pale in comparison, Jeeves. Positively pale. Which brings us to a consideration of your position. Do you intend to go back to the yacht and continue mingling with that gruesome bird?"

"No, sir. I fancy Mr. Stoker would not receive me cordially. It will be readily apparent to a gentleman of his intelligence, when he discovers your flight, that I must have been instrumental in assisting you to leave the boat. I shall return to his lordship's employment, sir."

"He'll be glad to get you back."

"It is very kind of you to say so, sir."

"Not at all, Jeeves.   Anybody would be."

"Thank you, sir."

"Then you'll push on to the Hall?"

"Yes, sir."

"A very hearty good night, then.   I will drop you a line to let you know where I am and how I have made out."

"Thank you, sir."

"Thank *you*, Jeeves.   There will be a slight testimonial of my appreciation wedged into the envelope."

"Extremely generous of you, sir."

"Generous, Jeeves?   Do you realize that if it hadn't been for you I should now be behind locked doors on that bloodsome yacht?   But you know how I feel."

"Yes, sir."

"By the way, *is* there a train to London tonight?"

"Yes, sir.   The 10.21.   You should be able to catch it comfortably, sir.   I fear it is not an express."

I waved a hand.

"As long as it moves, Jeeves, as long as the wheels revolve and it trickles from point to point, it will do me nicely.   Good night, then."

"Good night, sir."

It was with uplifted heart that I entered the cottage.   Nor was my satisfaction lessened by the discovery that Brinkley had not yet returned.   As an employer, I might look a bit askance at the idea of the blighter being given the evening off and taking a night and a day, but in the capacity of a private citizen with boot polish on his face, I was all for it.   On such occasions, solitude is, as Jeeves would have said, of the essence.

I went up to the bedroom with all possible speed, and poured water from the jug into the basin, bath-rooms not being provided in Chuffy's little homes.   This done, I dipped the face and instituted a hearty soaping.   Then, having rinsed thoroughly, I moved to the mirror, and picture my chagrin and dismay when I discovered that I was still as black as ever.   You might say I had hardly so much as scratched the surface.

These are the moments that make a fellow think a bit, and it wasn't long before I saw where the snag was.   I remembered hearing or reading somewhere that in crises like this you have to have butter. I was just about to go downstairs and get some, when suddenly I heard a noise.

Now, a fellow in my positon—virtually the hunted stag, I mean to say—has got to take considerable thought as to what his next move shall be when he hears a noise on the premises. Quite possibly, I felt, this might be J. Washburn Stoker baying on the trail, for if he had happened to drop into the state-room and observe that it was empty, the first thing he would do would be to come dashing to my cottage. So there was nothing of the lion leaping from its den about the way I now left the bedroom, but rather a bit more than a suggestion of a fairly diffident snail poking its head out of its shell during a thunderstorm. For the nonce, I merely stood in the doorway and listened.

There was plenty to listen to. Whoever was making the row was down in the sitting-room, and he seemed to me to be throwing the furniture about. And I think it was the reflection that a keen, practical man like Pop Stoker, if on my track, would hardly waste time doing this sort of thing that braced me at length to the point of tiptoeing to the banisters and peeping over.

What I describe as the sitting-room, I must tell you, was really more in the nature of a sort of lounge-hall. It was rather liberally furnished for such a smallish place, and contained a table, a grandfather clock, a sofa, two chairs, and from one to three glass cases with stuffed birds in them. From where I stood, looking over the banisters, I had a complete view of the entire lay-out. It was fairly dim down there, but I could see pretty well, because there was an oil lamp burning on the mantelpiece. By its light I was able to observe that the sofa had been upset, the two chairs thrown through the window, and the stuffed-bird cases smashed; and at the moment of going to press, a shadowy form was in the far corner, wrestling with the grandfather clock.

It was difficult to say with any certainty which of the pair was getting the better of it, If in sporting vein, I think I should have been inclined to put my money on the clock. But I was not in sporting vein. A sudden twist of the combatants had revealed to me the face of the shadowy f., and with a considerable rush of emotion I perceived that it was Brinkley. Like a sheep wandering back to the fold, this blighted Bolshevik had rolled home, twenty-four hours late, plainly stewed to the gills.

All the householder awoke in me. I forgot that it was in-judicious of me to allow myself to be seen. All I could think of was that this bally Five-Year-Planner was smashing up the Wooster home.

"Brinkley!" I bellowed.

I imagine he thought at first that it was the voice of the clock, for he flung himself upon it with renewed energy. Then, suddenly, his eye fell on me, and he broke away and stood staring. The clock, after rocking to and fro for a moment, settled into the perpendicular with a jerk and, having struck thirteen, relapsed into silence.

"Brinkley!" I repeated, and was about to add "Dash it!" when a sort of gleam came into his eyes, the gleam of the man who understands all. For an instant he stood there, goggling. Then he uttered a cry.

"Lor lumme! The Devil!"

And, snatching up a carving knife which he appeared to have placed on the mantelpiece with a sort of idea that you never knew when these things may not come in useful, he came bound-ing up the stairs.

Well, it was a close thing. If I ever have grandchildren—which, at the moment, seems a longish shot—and they come clustering round my knee of an evening for a story, the one I shall tell them is about my getting back into the bedroom just one split second ahead of that carving knife. And if as a result they have convulsions during the night and wake up screaming, they will have got some rough idea of their aged relative's emo-tions at this juncture. To say that Bertram, even when he had slammed the door, locked it, shoved a chair against it, and a bed against the chair, felt wholly at his ease would be a wilful overstatement. I cannot put my mental attitude more clearly than by saying that, if J. Washburn Stoker had happened to drop in at that moment, I would have welcomed him like a brother.

Brinkley was at the keyhole, begging me to come out and let him ascertain the colour of my insides; and, by Jove, what seemed to me to add the final touch to the whole unpleasantness was that he spoke in the same respectful voice he always used. Kept calling me "Sir", too, which struck me as dashed silly. I mean, if you're asking a fellow to come out of a room so that you can dismember him with a carving knife, it's absurd to tack a "Sir" on to every sentence. The two things don't go together.

At this point it seemed to me that my first move ought to be to clear up the obvious misunderstanding that existed in his mind.

I put the lips to the woodwork.

"It's all right, Brinkley."

"It will be if you come out, sir," he said civilly.

"I mean, I'm not the Devil."

"Oh, yes, you are, sir."

"I'm not, I tell you."

"Oh, yes, sir."

"I'm Mr. Wooster."

He uttered a piercing cry.

"He's got Mr. Wooster in there!"

You don't get the old-fashioned soliloquy much nowadays, so I took it that he was addressing some third party. And, sure enough, there was a sort of rumbling puffing and a tonsil-ridden voice spoke.

"What's all this?"

It was my sleepless neighbour, Police-Sergeant Voules.

My first emotion on realizing that the Law was in our midst was one of pretty sizeable relief. There were lots of things about this vigilant man I didn't like—his habit of poking his nose into people's garages and potting sheds, for one—but, whatever you might feel about some of his habits, there was no denying that he was a useful chap to have around in a situation like this. Tackling a loony valet is not everyone's job. You need a certain personality and presence. These this outsize guardian of the peace had got in full measure. And I was just about to urge him on with encouraging noises through the door, when something seemed to whisper to me that it would be more prudent to refrain.

You see, the whole thing about these vigilant police-sergeants is that they detain and question. Finding Bertram Wooster in the equivocal position of going about the place with his face blacked up, Sergeant Voules would not just pass the thing off with a shrug of the shoulders and a light good night. He would, as I say, detain and question. Recalling our encounters of the previous night, he would view with concern. He would insist on my accompanying him to the police station while he sent for

Chuffy to come and advise what to do for the best. Doctors would be summoned, ice packs applied. With the result that I would most certainly be confined to the neighbourhood quite long enough for old Stoker to discover that my room was empty and my bed had not been slept in and to come rushing ashore to scoop me up and carry me back to the yacht again.

On second thoughts, therefore, I said nothing. Merely breathed softly through the nose.

Outside the door, snappy dialogue was in progress; and I give you my honest word that, if I hadn't had authoritative information to the contrary, I should have said that this extraordinary bird, Brinkley, was as sober as a teetotal Girl Guide. All that one of the biggest toots in history had done to him was to put a sort of precise edge on his speech and cause him to articulate with a crystal clearness which was more like a silver bell than anything.

"The Devil is in there, murdering Mr. Wooster, sir," he was saying. And, except in radio announcers, I've never heard anything more beautifully modulated.

You would call that a fairly sensational announcement, I suppose; but it didn't seem to register immediately with Sergeant Voules. The sergeant was one of those men who like to take things in their proper order and tidy up as they go along; and for the moment, it seemed, he was interested exclusively in the carving knife.

"What are you doing with that knife?" he inquired.

Nothing could have been more civil and deferential than Brinkley's response.

"I caught it up to attack the Devil, sir."

"What devil?" asked Sergeant Voules, taking the next point in rotation.

"A black devil, sir."

"Black?"

"Yes, sir. He is in this room, murdering Mr. Wooster."

Now that he had at last got round to it, Sergeant Voules seemed interested.

"In this room?"

"Yes, sir."

"Murdering Mr. Wooster?"

"Yes, sir."

"We can't have that sort of thing," said Sergeant Voules, rather austerely. And I heard him click his tongue.

There was an authoritative rap on the door.

"Oy!"

I preserved a prudent silence.

"Excuse me, sir," I heard Brinkley say, and from the sound of feet on the stairs I took it that he was leaving our little symposium. Possibly to have another go at the clock.

Knuckles smote the woodwork again.

"In there. Oy!"

I made no remark.

"Are you in there, Mr. Wooster?"

I was beginning to feel that this conversation was a bit one-sided, but I didn't see what could be done about it. I moved to the window and looked out, more with the idea of just doing something to pass the time than anything else, and it was now—and only now, if you'll believe me—that the idea came to me that it might be possible to edge away from this distasteful scene. It wasn't so much of a drop to the ground, and with a good deal of relief I started to tie knots in a sheet with a view to the get-away.

It was at this moment that I heard Sergeant Voules suddenly give tongue.

"Oy!"

And from down below Brinkley's voice.

"Sir?"

"Look out what you're doing with that lamp."

"Yes, sir."

"You'll upset it."

"Yes, sir."

"Oy!"

"Sir?"

"You'll set the house on fire!"

"Yes, sir."

And then there came a far-off crash of glass, and the Sergeant went bounding down the stairs. This was followed by a sound which gave me the impression that Brinkley, feeling that he had done his bit, had galloped to the front door and slammed it after him. And after that another slam, as if the Sergeant, too, had made a break for the open. And then, filtering through the keyhole, came a little puff of smoke.

I don't suppose there is anything that makes much better burning than one of these old country cottages. You just put a match to them—or upset a lamp in the hall, as the case may be—and up they go.   It couldn't have been more than half a minute before a merry crackling came to my ears and a bit of the floor over in the corner suddenly burst into a cheerful flame.

It was enough for Bertram.   A moment before, I had been messing about with knotted sheets with a view to what you might call the departure *de luxe* and generally loafing about and taking my time over the thing.   I now quickened up quite a good deal. It was borne in upon me that anything in the nature of leisurely comfort was off.   In the next thirty seconds cats on hot bricks could have picked up hints from me.

I remember reading in a paper once one of those Interesting Problem things about Suppose You were in a Burning House, what would you save?   If I recollect rightly, a baby entered into it.   Also a priceless picture and, if I am not mistaken, a bed-ridden aunt.   I know there was a wide choice, and you were supposed to knit the brow and think the thing out from every angle.

On the present occasion I did not hesitate.   I looked round immediately for my banjolele.   Conceive my dismay when I remembered that I had left it in the sitting-room.

Well, I wasn't going down to that sitting-room even for the faithful old musical instrument.   Already it was beginning to be a very moot point whether I wouldn't get cooked to a crisp, because that genial glow over in the corner had now spread not a little.   With a regretful sigh I hopped hurriedly to the window, and the next moment I was dropping like the gentle dew upon the place beneath.

Or is it rain?   I always forget.

Jeeves would know.

I made a smooth landing and shot silently through the hedge at the junction between my back garden and Sergeant Voules's little bit, and continued to leg it till I was in a sort of wood—I suppose about half a mile from the pulsing centre of affairs. The sky was all lit up, and in the distance I could hear the sound of the local fire brigade going about its duties.

I sat down on a stump, and took time off to pass the situation under review.

Wasn't it Robinson Crusoe or someone who, when things were working out a bit messily for him, used to draw up a sort of

Credit and Debit account, in order to see exactly where he stood and ascertain whether he was behind or ahead of the game at that particular moment? I know it was someone, and I had always thought it rather a sound idea.

This was what I did now. In my head, of course, and keeping a wary eye out for possible pursuers.

The thing came out about as follows:

Credit	*Debit*
Well, here I am, what?	Yes, but your bally house has burned down.
Not mine, Chuffy's.	Yes, I know, but all your things are in it.
Nothing of value.	How about the banjolele?
Oh, my gosh! That's true.	I thought that would make you think a bit.
You needn't rub it in.	I'm not rubbing it in. I am merely saying that your banjolele has been reduced to a heap of ashes.
Well, I'd have looked a damn sight sillier if it had been me.	A footling bit of reasoning.
Well, anyway, I've got away from old Stoker.	How do you know you have?
He hasn't caught me yet.	No, but he may.
I've still time to get that 10.21 train.	My poor ass, you can't go getting on trains with your face all black.
Butter will remove the blacking.	Yes, but you have no butter.
I can buy some.	How? Got any money on you?
Well, no.	Ah!
Why shouldn't I get someone to give me butter?	Who?
Why, Jeeves, of course. All I have to do is to go to the Hall and put the whole case before Jeeves and tell him to rally round, and there I'll be, as right as rain, with nothing more to worry about. Jeeves will know where to lay his hand on seas of butter. You see! It's perfectly simple if you think it out and don't lose your head.	

And, by Jove, there didn't seem a single Debit to shove against that. I examined the position thoroughly, trying to find one, but at the end of five minutes I saw that I had got the Debit account stymied. I had baffled it. It hadn't a thing to say.

Of course, I mused, I ought to have thought of this solution right from the start. Dashed obvious, the whole thing, when you came to think of it. I mean, Jeeves would be back at the Hall by now. I had only to go and get in touch with him and he would bring out pounds of butter on a lordly dish. And not only that, but he would lend me enough of the needful to pay my fare to London and possibly even to purchase a packet of milk chocolate from the slot machine at the station. The thing was a walk-over.

I rose from my stump, braced to a degree, and started off. In the race for life, as you might term it, I had lost my bearings a bit, but I pretty soon hit the main road, and I don't suppose it was more than a quarter of an hour later that I was rapping at the back door of the Hall.

It was opened by a small female—a scullerymaid of sorts, I put her down as—who, on observing me, gaped for a moment with a sort of shocked horror, and then with a piercing squeal keeled over and started to roll about and drum her heels on the floor. And I'm not so dashed sure she wasn't frothing at the mouth.

★ 14 ★

The Butter Situation

I MUST admit it was a fairly nasty shock. I had never realized before what an important part one's complexion plays in life. I mean to say, a Bertram Wooster with merely a pretty tan calling at the back door of Chuffnell Hall would have been received with respect and deference. Indeed, I shouldn't wonder if a girl of the social standing of a scullerymaid might not actually have curtsied. And I don't suppose matters would have been so substantially different if I had had an interesting pallor or pimples. But purely and simply because there happened to be a little boot polish on my face, here was this female tying herself in knots on the doormat and throwing fits up and down the passage.

Well, there was only one thing to do, of course. Already voices from along the corridor were making inquiries, and in another half-second I presumed that I might expect a regular susurration of domestics on the scene. I picked up the feet and pushed off. And, taking it that the neighbourhood of the back door was liable to be searched pretty soon, I hared round to the front and came to roost in a patch of bushes not far from the main entrance.

Here I paused. It seemed to me that before going any farther, I had better try to analyse the situation and find out what to do next.

In other circs—if, let us say, I had been reclining in a deck-chair with a cigarette, instead of squatting in a beastly jungle with beetles falling down my neck—I should probably have got a good deal of entertainment and uplift out of the scene and surroundings generally. I've always been rather a lad for the peace of the old-world English garden round about the time between the end of dinner and the mixing of the bedtime spot. From where I sat, I could see the great mass of the Hall standing out against the sky, and very impressive it was, too. Birds were rustling in the trees, and I think there must have been a flower-bed fairly close by with stocks and tobacco plants in it, for the air was full of a pretty goodish sort of smell. Add the perfect stillness of a summer night, and there you are.

At the end of about ten minutes, however, the stillness of the summer night rather sprang a leak. From one of the rooms there proceeded a loud yelling. I recognized the voice of little Seabury, and I remembered feeling thankful that he had his troubles, too. After a bit, he cheesed it—I assumed the friction had arisen from the fact that somebody wanted to put him to bed and he didn't want to go—and all was quiet again.

Directly after that there came a sound of footsteps. Somebody was walking up the drive to the front door.

My first idea was that it was Sergeant Voules. Chuffy, you see, is a local Justice of the Peace, and I imagined that one of the first things Voules would do after the affair at the cottage would be to call on the big chief and report. I wedged myself a bit tighter into the bushes.

No, it wasn't Sergeant Voules. I had just got him against a patch of sky and I could see he was taller and not nearly so round. He went up the steps and started knocking at the door.

And when I say knocking I mean knocking. I had thought Voules's performance at the cottage on the previous night a pretty good exhibition of wrist-work, but this chap put it all over him. In a different class, altogether. He was giving that knocker more exercise than I suppose it had ever had since the first Chuffnell, or whoever it was, had it screwed on.

In the intervals of slamming the knocker, he was also singing a hymn in a meditative sort of voice. It was, if I recollect rightly, "Lead, Kindly Light", and it enabled me to place him. I had heard that reedy tenor before. One of the first things I had had to put my foot down about, on arriving at the cottage, was Brinkley's habit of singing hymns in the kitchen while I was trying to play foxtrots on the banjolele in the sitting-room. There could not be two voices like that in Chuffnell Regis. This nocturnal visitor was none other than my plastered personal attendant, and what he wanted at the Hall was more than I could understand.

Lights flashed up in the house, and the front door was wrenched open. A voice spoke. It was a pretty peevish voice, and it was Chuffy's. As a rule, of course, the Squire of Chuffnell Regis shoves the task of answering the door off on to the domestic staff, but I suppose he felt that a ghastly din like this constituted a special case. Anyway, here he was, and he didn't seem too pleased.

"What on earth are you making that foul noise for?"

"Good evening, sir."

"What do you mean, good evening? What . . ."

I think he would have gone to some length, for he was evidently much stirred, but at this point Brinkley interrupted.

"Is the Devil in?"

It was a simple question, capable of being answered with a Yes or No, but it seemed to take Chuffy aback somewhat.

"Is—who?"

"The Devil, sir."

I must say I had never looked on old Chuffy as a fellow of very swift intelligence, he having always run rather to thews and sinews than the grey cells, but I'm bound to say that at this juncture he exhibited a keen intuition which did him credit.

"You're tight."

"Yes, sir."

Chuffy seemed to explode like a paper bag. I could follow

his mental processes, if you know what I mean, pretty clearly. Ever since that unfortunate episode at the cottage, when the girl he loved had handed him the mitten and gone out of his life, I imagine he had been seething and brooding and sizzling and what not like a soul in torment, yearning for some outlet for his repressed emotions, and here he had found one. Ever since that regrettable scene he had been wishing that he could work off the stored-up venom on somebody, and, by Jove, Heaven had sent this knocker-slamming inebriate.

To run Brinkley down the steps and up the drive, kicking him about every other yard, was with the fifth Baron Chuffnell the work of a moment. They passed my little clump of bushes at about forty m.p.h., and rolled away into the distance. And after a while I heard footsteps and the sound of someone whistling as if a bit of a load had been removed from his soul, and Chuffy came legging it back.

Just about opposite my lair he paused to light a cigarette, and it seemed to me that the moment had come to get in touch.

Mark you, I wasn't any too keen on chatting with old Chuffy, for his manner at our last parting had been far from bonhomous, and had my outlook been a shade rosier I would most certainly have given him a miss. But he was by way of being my last hope. What with platoons of scullerymaids having hysterics every time I went near the back door, it seemed impossible to connect with Jeeves tonight. It was just as impossible to go the round of the neighbourhood, calling on perfect strangers and asking for butter. I mean, you know yourself how you feel when a fellow you've never met drops in at your house with his face all black and tries to touch you for a bit of butter. You just aren't in sympathy.

No, everything pointed to Chuffy as the logical saviour of the situation. He was a man who had butter at his command, and it might be that, now that he had worked off some of the hard feelings on Brinkley, he would be in a frame of mind to oblige an old school friend with a quarter of a pound or so. So I crawled softly out of the undergrowth and came up in his immediate rear.

"Chuffy!" I said.

I can see now it would have been better to have given him a bit more warning of my presence. Nobody likes to have unexpected voices speaking suddenly down the back of their neck, and in calmer mood I should have recognized this. I don't say it was exactly a repetition of the scullerymaid episode, but for a moment it looked like coming very near it. The poor old lad distinctly leaped. The cigarette flew out of his hand, his teeth came together with a snap, and he shook visibly. The whole effect being much as if I had spiked him in the trousering with a gimlet or bodkin. I have seen salmon behave in a rather similar way during the spawning season.

I did my best to lull the storm with soothing words.

"It's only me, Chuffy."

"Who?"

"Bertie."

"Bertie?"

"That's right."

"Oh!"

I didn't much like the sound of that "Oh!" It hadn't a welcoming ring. One learns to sense when one is popular and when one is not. It was pretty plain to me at this point that I was not, and I thought it might be wise if, before proceeding to the main topic, I were to start off with a stately compliment.

"You put it across that fellow properly, Chuffy," I said. "I liked your work. It was particularly agreeable to me to see him so adequately handled, because I had been wishing I had the nerve to kick him myself."

"Who was he?"

"My man, Brinkley."

"What was he doing here?"

"I fancy he was looking for me."

"Why wasn't he at the cottage, then?"

I had been hoping for a good opportunity of breaking the news.

"I'm afraid you're a cottage short, Chuffy," I said. "I regret to report that Brinkley has just burned it down."

"What!"

"Insured, I trust?"

"He burned the cottage? How? Why?"

"Just a whim. I suppose it seemed a good idea to him at the moment."

Chuffy took it rather hard. I could see that he was brooding, and I would have liked to allow him to brood all he wanted. But if I was going to catch that 10.21 it was necessary to push along. Time was of the essence.

"Well," I said, "I hate to bother you, old man . . ."

"Why on earth should he burn a cottage?"

"One cannot attempt to fathom the psychology of blokes like Brinkley. They move in a mysterious way their wonders to perform. Suffice it that he did."

"Are you sure it wasn't you?"

"My dear chap!"

"It sounds the sort of silly, fat-headed thing you would do," said Chuffy, and I was distressed to note in his voice much evidence of the old rancour. "What do you want here, anyway? Who asked you to come? If you think, after what has happened, that you can stroll in and out . . ."

"I know, I know. I understand. Painful misunderstanding. Coolness. A disposition to disapprove of Bertram. But . . ."

"And where did you spring from just now? I never saw you."

"I was sitting in a bush."

"Sitting in a bush?"

The tone in which he said the words told me that, always too prone to misjudge an old friend, he had once more formed a wrong conclusion. I heard a match scratch on its box, and the next moment he was examining me by its light. The light went out, and I heard him breathing deeply in the darkness.

I could follow the workings of his mind. He was evidently struggling with his feelings. The disinclination to have anything more to do with me after last night's painful rift was contending with the reflection that the fact that we had been pals for years carried with it a certain obligation. A chap, he was thinking, may have ceased to be on cordial terms with an old schoolmate, but he can hardly let him go wandering about the country-side in the condition he supposed I was in.

"You'd better come in and sleep it off," he said in a weary sort of way. "Can you walk?"

"It's all right," I hastened to assure him. "It's not what you think. Listen."

And with convincing fluency I rattled off "British Constitution", "She sells sea-shells", and "He stood at the entrance of Burgess's fish-sauce shop, welcoming him in".

The demonstration had its effect.

"Then you're not tight?"

"Not a bit."

"But you sit in bushes."

"Yes. But . . ."

"And your face is black."

"I know. Hold the line, old man, and I will tell you all."

I dare say you have had the experience of telling someone a longish story and getting on to the fact, half-way through, that you haven't got the sympathy of the audience. Most unpleasant sensation. I had it now. It was not that he said anything. But a sort of deleterious animal magnetism seemed to exude from him as I passed from point to point. More and more, as I proceeded, did the conviction steal over me that I was getting the silent raspberry.

However, I carried on stoutly and, having related the salient facts, wound up with a pretty eloquent plea for the stearic matter.

"Butter, Chuffy, old man," I said. "Slabs of butter. If you have butter, prepare to shed it now. I'll just saunter about out here, shall I, while you pop to the kitchen and secure the stuff? And you realize, don't you, that time is of the essence? I shall only just be able to catch that train, as it is."

He did not speak for a moment or two. When he did, there was such a nasty tinkle in his voice that I confess the heart sank.

"Let me get all this straight," he said. "You want me to bring you butter?"

"That's the idea."

"So that you can clean your face and go off on this train to London."

"Yes."

"Thus escaping from Mr. Stoker."

"That's right. Amazing the way you've followed it all," I said in a congratulatory sort of voice, deeming it best to suck up a bit and apply the old salve. "I don't suppose I know six fellows who would have grasped the plot with the same unerring accuracy. I've always thought highly of your intelligence, Chuffy, old man—very highly."

But the heart was still sinking. And when I heard him snort emotionally in the darkness it touched a new low.

"I see," he said. "In other words, you wish me to help you back out of your honourable obligations, what?"

"What?"

"That's what I said—'What?' Good God!" cried Chuffy,

and I dare say he quivered from head to foot, but I couldn't see properly, it being too dark. "I didn't interrupt when you were telling me your degrading story, because I wanted to get it quite clear. Now, perhaps, you will let me say a word."

He snorted a bit more.

"You want to catch trains to London, do you? I see. Well, I don't know what you think of yourself, Wooster, but, if you would care to know how your conduct strikes a perfectly un-prejudiced outsider, I don't mind informing you that in my opinion you are behaving like a hound, a skunk, a worm, a tick, and a wart-hog. Good gosh! This beautiful girl loves you. Her father very decently consents to an early wedding. And instead of being delighted and pleased and tickled as—er—as any-body else would be, you are planning to edge away."

"But, Chuffy . . ."

"I repeat, to edge away. You are brutally and callously scheming to oil out, leaving this lovely girl to break her heart— deserted, abandoned, flung aside like a . . . like a . . . I shall forget my own name next . . . like a soiled glove."

"But, Chuffy . . ."

"Don't try to deny it."

"But, dash it, it isn't as if she were in love with me."

"Ha! Isn't she so infatuated with you that she swims ashore from yachts to get at you?"

"She loves you."

"Ha!"

"She does, I tell you. It was you she swam ashore last night to see. And she only took on this binge of marrying me to score off you because you doubted her."

"Ha!"

"So take the sensible viewpoint, old man, and bring me butter."

"Ha!"

"I wish you wouldn't keep saying 'Ha!' It doesn't advance the issue, and it sounds rotten. I must have butter, Chuffy. It is of the essence. If it be only a small pat, bring it out. Wooster speaking, old man—the chap you were at school with, the fellow you've known since he was so high."

I paused. For a moment I had an idea that this had done the trick. I felt his hand fall on my shoulder with a distinct knead-ing movement. At that instant I would have put my shirt on it that he was softened.

And so he was, but not along the right lines.

"I will tell you exactly how I feel about all this, Bertie," he said, and there was a sort of beastly gentleness in his manner. "I won't pretend that I don't love this girl. Even after what has happened, I still love her. I shall always love her. I loved her from the first moment we met. It was at the Savoy Grill, I remember, and she was sitting on one of those chairs in that lobby place half-way through a medium dry Martini, because Sir Roderick and I were a bit late getting there and her father had thought they might as well be having a cocktail instead of just sitting. Our eyes met, and I knew that I had found the only girl in the world for me, not having the foggiest that she was really crazy about you."

"She isn't!"

"I realize it now, and I know, of course, that I can never win her for myself. But I can do this, Bertie. Having this great love for her, I can see to it that she is not robbed of her happiness. If she is happy, that is all that matters. For some reason her heart is set on being your wife. Why, one cannot say, and we need not go into it. But for some unexplained reason she wants you, and she shall jolly well get you. Funny that you should have come to me, of all people, to help you shatter her girlish dreams and rob her of her sweet, childlike trust in the goodness of human nature! You think I will sit in with you on this foul project? My left foot I will! You get no butter from me, my lad. You will remain exactly as you are, and, after thinking it over, I have no doubt that you will find your better self pointing the way and that you will go back to the yacht, prepared to fulfil your obligations like an English gentleman."

"But, Chuffy . . ."

"And, if you wish, I will be your best man. Agony, of course, but I'll do it if you want me to."

I clutched at his arm.

"Butter, Chuffy!"

He shook his head.

"No butter, Wooster. You are better without it."

And, flinging aside my hand like a soiled glove, he stalked past me into the night.

I don't know how long it was that I stood there, rooted to the s. It may have been a short time. It may have been quite a stretch.

Despair was gripping me, and when that happens you don't keep looking at your watch.

Let us say, then, that at some point—five, ten, fifteen, or it may have been twenty minutes later—I became aware of somebody coughing softly at my side like a respectful sheep trying to attract the attention of its shepherd, and how can I describe with what thankfulness and astonishment I perceived Jeeves.

* 15 *

Development Of The Butter Situation

A BALLY miracle it seemed to me at the moment, but of course there was a simple explanation.

"I was hoping that you would not have left the grounds, sir," he said. "I have been searching for you for some little time. On learning that the scullerymaid had become a victim of hysterics as the result of opening the back door and observing a black man, I sprang to the conclusion that you must have been calling there, no doubt with a view to seeing me. Has something gone wrong, sir?"

I wiped the brow.

"Jeeves," I said, "I feel like a lost child that has found its mother."

"Indeed, sir?"

"If you don't mind me calling you a mother?"

"Not at all, sir."

"Thank you, Jeeves."

"Then there is something wrong, sir?"

"Wrong! You said it. What are those sore things people find themselves in?"

"Straits, sir."

"I am in the sorest straits, Jeeves. To start with, I found that soap and water won't get this stuff off."

"No, sir. I should have informed you that butter is a *sine qua non*."

"Well, I was on the point of getting butter when Brinkley—my man, you know—suddenly blew in and burned the house down."

"Too bad, sir."

"The expression 'Too bad' scarcely overstates it, Jeeves. It landed me in the dickens of a hole. I came here. I tried to get in touch with you. But that scullerymaid gummed up that project."

"A temperamental girl, sir. And by an unfortunate coincidence she and the cook, at the moment of your arrival, had just been occupying themselves with the Ouija board—with, I believe, some interesting results. She appears to have regarded you as a materialized spirit."

I quivered a bit.

"If cooks would stick to their roasts and hashes," I said rather severely, "and not waste their time in psychical research, life would be a very different thing."

"Quite true, sir."

"Well, then I ran into Chuffy. He stoutly declined to lend me butter."

"Indeed, sir?"

"He was in a very unpleasant mood."

"His lordship is undergoing a good deal of mental anguish at the moment, sir."

"I could see that. He left me apparently to go for a country ramble. At this time of night!"

"Physical exercise is a recognized palliative when the heart is aching, sir."

"Well, I mustn't think too harshly of Chuffy. I must always remember that he kicked Brinkley properly. It did me good to watch him. And now you've turned up, all is well. The happy ending, what?"

"Precisely, sir. I shall be delighted to procure you butter."

"But can I still catch that 10.21?"

"I fear not, sir. But I have ascertained that there is another train as late as 11.50."

"Then I'm on velvet."

"Yes, sir."

I breathed deeply. The relief was great.

"I shouldn't wonder if you couldn't even dig me up a packet of sandwiches for the journey, what?"

"Certainly, sir."

"And a drop of something?"

"Undoubtedly, sir."

"Then if you happened to have such a thing as a cigarette on your person at this moment, everything would be more or less perfect."

"Turkish or Virginian, sir?"

"Both."

There is nothing like a quiet cigarette for soothing the system. For some moments I puffed luxuriously, and my nerves, which had been sticking out of my body an inch long and curled at the ends, gradually slipped into place again. I felt restored and invigorated and in a mood for conversation.

"What was all that yelling about, Jeeves?"

"Sir?"

"Just before I met Chuffy, animal cries started to proceed from somewhere in the house. It sounded like Seabury."

"It was Master Seabury, sir. He is a little fractious tonight."

"What's biting him?"

"He is somewhat acutely disappointed, sir, at having missed the negro entertainment on the yacht."

"Absolutely his own fault, the silly little geezer. If he wanted to go to Dwight's birthday-party, he shouldn't have started a scrap with him."

"Just so, sir."

"To attempt to touch your host for one and sixpence protection money on the eve of a birthday-party is the act of a fathead."

"Very true, sir."

"What did they do about it? He seems to have stopped yelling. Did they chloroform him?"

"No, sir. I understand that steps are being taken to provide something in the nature of an alternative entertainment for the little fellow."

"How do you mean, Jeeves? Are they having the niggers up here?"

"No, sir. The expense rules that project out of the sphere of practical politics. But I understand that her ladyship has induced Sir Roderick Glossop to offer his services."

I could not follow this.

"Old Glossop?"

"Yes, sir."

"But what can he do?"

"It appears, sir, that he has a pleasing baritone voice and as a younger man—in the days when he was a medical student—was often accustomed to render songs at smoking concerts and similar entertainments."

"Old Glossop!"

"Yes, sir. I overheard him telling her ladyship so."

"Well, I would never have thought it."

"I agree that one would scarcely suspect such a thing from his bearing nowadays, sir. *Tempora mutantur, nos et mutamur in illis.*"

"Then you mean that he is going to soothe young Seabury with song?"

"Yes, sir. Accompanied by her ladyship on the piano."

I spotted the snag.

"It won't work, Jeeves. Reason it out for yourself."

"Sir!"

"Well, here is a kid who has been looking forward to seeing a troupe of nigger minstrels do their stuff. Is he likely to accept as an adequate substitute a white-faced loony-doctor accompanied by his mother on the piano?"

"Not white-faced, sir."

"What!"

"No, sir. The question was debated, and it was her ladyship's view that something in the nature of a negroid performance was indispensable. The young gentleman, when in his present frame of mind, is always extremely exigent."

I swallowed a puff of smoke the wrong way in my emotion.

"Old Glossop isn't blacking up?"

"Yes, sir."

"Jeeves, pull yourself together. This can't be true. He is blacking his face?"

"Yes, sir."

"It isn't possible."

"Sir Roderick is very amenable at the moment, sir, you must remember, to any suggestion emanating from her ladyship."

"You mean he's in love?"

"Yes, sir."

"And Love conquers all?"

"Yes, sir."

"But even so. . . . If you were in love, Jeeves, would you black up to entertain the son of the adored object?"

"No, sir. But we are not all constituted alike."

"True."

"Sir Roderick did endeavour to protest, but her ladyship overruled his objections. And, as a matter of fact, sir, I think that, on the whole, it is a good thing that she did. Sir Roderick's kindly act will serve to heal the breach between Master Seabury and himself. I happen to know that the young gentleman has been unsuccessful in his endeavour to extract protection money from Sir Roderick, and was resenting the fact keenly."

"He tried to gouge the old boy?"

"Yes, sir. For ten shillings. I have the information from the young gentleman himself."

"They all confide in you, Jeeves."

"Yes, sir."

"And old Glossop wouldn't kick in?"

"No, sir. Instead, he read the young gentleman something of a lecture. What the young gentleman described as 'pi-jaws'. And I happen to know that hard feelings existed as a consequence on the latter's side. So much so, indeed, that I received the impression that he had been planning something in the nature of a reprisal."

"He wouldn't have the nerve to do the dirty on a future stepfather, would he?"

"Young gentlemen are headstrong, sir."

"True. One recalls the case of my Aunt Agatha's son, young Thos., and the Cabinet Minister."

"Yes, sir."

"In a spirit of ill-will he marooned him on an island in the lake with a swan."

"Yes, sir."

"How is the swanning in these parts? I confess that I would like to see old Glossop shinning up something with a bilious bird after him."

"I fancy that Master Seabury's thoughts turned more towards something on the order of a booby trap, sir."

"They would. No imagination, that kid. No vision. I've often noticed it. His fancy is—what's the word?"

"Pedestrian, sir?"

"Exactly. With all the limitless opportunities of a large country house at his disposal, he is content to put soot and water on top of the door, a thing you could do in a suburban villa. I have never thought highly of Seabury, and this confirms my low opinion."

"Not soot and water, sir. I think what the young gentleman had in mind was the old-fashioned butter-slide, sir. He was asking me yesterday where the butter was kept, and referred guardedly to a humorous film he had seen not long ago in Bristol, in which something of that nature occurred."

I was disgusted. Goodness knows that any outrage perpetrated on the person of a bloke like Sir Roderick Glossop touches a ready chord in Bertram Wooster's bosom, but a butter-slide . . . the lowest depths, as you might say. The merest A B C of the booby-trapping art. There isn't a fellow at the Drones who would sink to such a thing.

I started to utter a scornful laugh, then stopped. The word had reminded me that life was stern and earnest and that time was passing.

"Butter, Jeeves! Here we are, standing idly here, talking of butter, and all the time you ought to have been racing to the larder, getting me some."

"I will go immediately, sir."

"You know where to lay your hand on it all right?"

"Yes, sir."

"And you're sure it will do the trick?"

"Quite sure, sir."

"Then shift-ho, Jeeves. And don't loiter."

I sat down on an upturned flower-pot, and resumed my vigil. My feelings were very different now from what they had been when first I had begun to roost on this desirable property. Then, I had been a penniless outcast, so to speak, with nothing much of a future before me. Now, I could see daylight. Presently Jeeves would return with the fixings. Shortly after that, I should be the old pink-cheeked clubman once more. And, in due season, I should be safely inside the 11.50 train, on my way to London and safety.

I was a good deal uplifted. I drank in the night air with a light heart. And it was while I was drinking it in that a sudden uproar proceeded from the house.

Seabury appeared to be contributing most of it. He was yelling his bally head off. From time to time, one caught the fainter, yet penetrating note of the Dowager Lady Chuffnell. She seemed to be reproaching or upbraiding someone. Blending with this, there could be discerned a deeper voice, the unmistakable baritone woofle of Sir Roderick Glossop. The whole appeared to be proceeding from the drawing-room, and, except for one time when I was sauntering in Hyde Park and suddenly found myself mixed up in a Community Singing, I've never heard anything like it.

It couldn't have been very long after this when the front door was suddenly flung open. Somebody emerged. The door slammed. And then the emerger started to stump rapidly down the drive in the direction of the gates.

There had been just a moment when the light from the hall shone upon this bloke. It had been long enough for me to identify him.

This sudden exiter, who was now padding away into the darkness with every outward sign of being fed to the eye-teeth, was none other than Sir Roderick Glossop. And his face, I noted, was as black as the ace of spades.

A few moments later, while I was still wondering what it was all about and generally turning the thing over in my mind, I observed Jeeves looming up on the right flank.

I was glad to see him. I desired enlightenment.

"What was all that, Jeeves?"

"The disturbance, sir?"

"It sounded as if little Seabury was being murdered. No such luck, I take it?"

"The young gentleman *was* the victim of a personal assault, sir. At the hands of Sir Roderick Glossop. I was not an actual eye-witness of the episode. I derive my information from Mary, the parlourmaid, who was present in person."

"Present?"

"Peeping through the door, sir. Sir Roderick's appearance when she encountered him by chance on the stairs seems to have affected the girl powerfully, and she tells me that she had followed him about in a stealthy manner ever since, waiting to see what he would do next. I gather that his aspect fascinated her. She is inclined to be somewhat frivolous in her mental attitude, like so many of these young girls, sir."

"And what occurred?"

"The affair may be said to have had its inception, sir, when Sir Roderick, passing through the hall, stepped upon the young gentleman's butter-slide."

"Ah! So he put that project through, did he?"

"Yes, sir."

"And Sir Roderick came a stinker?"

"He appears to have fallen with some heaviness, sir. The girl Mary spoke of it with a good deal of animation. She compared his descent to the delivery of a ton of coals. I confess the imagery somewhat surprised me, for she is not a highly imaginative girl."

I smiled appreciatively. The evening, I felt, might have begun rockily, but it was certainly ending well.

"Incensed by this, Sir Roderick appears to have hastened to the drawing-room, where he immediately subjected Master Seabury to a severe castigation. Her ladyship vainly endeavoured to induce him to desist, but he was firm in his refusal. The upshot of the matter was a definite rift between her ladyship and Sir Roderick, the former stating that she never wished to see him again, the latter asseverating that, if he could once get safely out of this pestilential house, he would never darken its doors again."

"A real mix-up."

"Yes, sir."

"And the engagement's off?"

"Yes, sir. The affection which her ladyship felt for Sir Roderick was instantaneously swept away on the tidal wave of injured mother love."

"Rather well put, Jeeves."

"Thank you, sir."

"Then Sir Roderick has pushed off for ever?"

"Apparently, sir."

"A lot of trouble Chuffnell Hall is seeing these days. Almost as if there was a curse on the place."

"If one were superstitious, one might certainly suppose so, sir."

"Well, if there wasn't a curse on it before, you can bet there are about fifty-seven now. I heard old Glossop applying them as he passed."

"He was much moved, I take it, sir?"

"Very much moved, Jeeves."

"So I should imagine, sir. Or he would scarcely have left the house in that condition."

"How do you mean?"

"Well, sir, if you consider. It will scarcely be feasible for him to return to his hotel in the existing circumstances. His appearance would excite remark. Nor, after what has occurred, can he very well return to the Hall."

I saw what he was driving at.

"Good Lord, Jeeves! You open up a new line of thought. Let me just review this. He can't go to his hotel—no, I see that, and he can't crawl back to the Dowager Lady C. and ask for shelter—no, I see that too. It's a dead stymie. I can't imagine what on earth he'll do."

"It is something of a problem, sir."

I was silent for a moment. Pensive. And, oddly enough, for you would have thought my mood would have been one of sober joy, the heart was really rather bleeding a bit.

"Do you know, Jeeves, scurvily as that man has treated me in the past, I can't help feeling sorry for him. I do, absolutely. He's in such an awful jam. It was bad enough for me being a black-faced wanderer, but I hadn't the position to keep up that he has. I mean to say, the world, observing me in this condition, might quite easily just have shrugged its shoulders and murmured 'Young Blood!' or words to that effect, what?"

"Yes, sir."

"But not with a bloke of his standing."

"Very true, sir."

"Well, well, well! Dear, dear, dear! I suppose, if you come right down to it, this is the vengeance of Heaven."

"Quite possibly, sir."

It isn't often that I point the moral, but I couldn't help doing it now.

"It just shows how we ought always to be kind, even to the humblest, Jeeves. For years this Glossop has trampled on my face with spiked shoes, and see where it has landed him. What would have happened if we had been on chummy terms at this juncture? He would have been on velvet. Observing him shooting past just now, I should have stopped him. I should have called out to him 'Hi, Sir Roderick, half a second. Don't go roaming about the place in make-up. Stick around here for a while and pretty soon Jeeves will be arriving with the necessary butter, and all will be well.' Shouldn't I have said that, Jeeves?"

"Something of that general trend, no doubt, sir."

"And he would have been saved from this fearful situation, this sore strait, in which he now finds himself. I dare say that man won't be able to get butter till well on in the morning.

Not even then, if he hasn't money on the person. And all because he wouldn't treat me decently in the past. Makes you think a bit, that, Jeeves, what?"

"Yes, sir."

"But it's no use talking about it, of course. What's done is done."

"Very true, sir. The moving finger writes and, having writ, moves on, nor all your piety and wit can lure it back to cancel half a line, nor all your tears wash out a word of it."

"Quite. And now, Jeeves, the butter. I must be getting about my business."

He sighed in a respectful sort of way.

"I am extremely sorry to be obliged to inform you, sir, that, owing to Master Seabury having used it all for his slide, there is no butter in the house."

★ 16 ★

Trouble At The Dower House

I STOOD there with my hand out, frozen to the spot. The faculties seemed numbed. I remember once, when I was in New York, one of those sad-eyed Italian kids who whizz about Washington Square on roller skates suddenly projected himself with extraordinary violence at my waistcoat as I strolled to and fro, taking the air. He reached journey's end right on the third button from the top, and I had much the same sensation now as I had had then. A sort of stricken feeling. Stunned. Breathless. As if somebody had walloped the old soul unexpectedly with a sandbag.

"What!"

"Yes, sir."

"No butter?"

"No butter, sir."

"But, Jeeves, this is frightful."

"Most disturbing, sir."

If Jeeves has a fault, it is that his demeanour on these occasions too frequently tends to be rather more calm and unemotional than one could wish.   One lodges no protest, as a rule, because he generally has the situation well in hand and loses no time in coming before the Board with one of his ripe solutions.   But I have often felt that I could do with a little more leaping about with rolling eyeballs on his part, and I felt it now.   At a moment like the present, the adjective "disturbing" seemed to me to miss the facts by about ten parasangs.

"But what shall I do?"

"I fear that it will be necessary to postpone the cleansing of your face till a later date, sir.   I shall be in a position to supply you with butter tomorrow."

"But tonight?"

"Tonight, I am afraid, sir, you must be content to remain *in statu quo*."

"Eh?"

"A Latin expression, sir."

"You mean nothing can be done till tomorrow?"

"I fear not, sir.   It is vexing."

"You would go so far as to describe it as that?"

"Yes, sir.   Most vexing."

I breathed a bit tensely.

"Oh, well, just as you say, Jeeves."

I pondered.

"And what do I do in the meantime?"

"As you have had a somewhat trying evening, I think it would be best, sir, if you were to get a good sleep."

"On the lawn?"

"If I might make the suggestion, sir, I think you would be more comfortable in the Dower House.   It is only a short distance across the park, and it is unoccupied."

"It can't be.   They wouldn't leave it empty."

"One of the gardeners is acting as caretaker while her ladyship and Master Seabury are visiting the Hall, but at this hour he is always down at the 'Chuffnell Arms' in the village.   It would be quite simple for you to effect an entrance and establish yourself in one of the upper rooms without his cognizance.   And tomorrow morning I could join you there with the necessary materials."

I confess it wasn't my idea of a frightfully large evening.

"You've nothing brighter to suggest?"

"No, sir."

"You wouldn't consider letting me have your bed for the night?"

"No, sir."

"Then I might as well be moving."

"Yes, sir."

"Good night, Jeeves," I said moodily.

"Good night, sir."

It didn't take me long to get to the Dower House, and the trip seemed shorter than it actually was, because my mind was occupied in transit with a sort of series of silent Hymns of Hate directed at the various blokes who had combined to land me in what Jeeves would have called this vexing situation—featuring little Seabury.

The more I thought of this stripling, the more the iron entered into my soul. And one result of my meditations regarding him was to engender—I think it's engender—an emotion towards Sir Roderick Glossop which came pretty near to being a spirit of kindliness.

You know how it is. You go along for years looking on a fellow as a blister and a menace to the public weal, and then one day you suddenly hear of some decent thing he's done and it makes you feel there must be good in the chap, after all. It was so in the matter of this Glossop. I had suffered much at his hands since first our paths had crossed. In the human Zoo which Fate has caused to centre about Bertram Wooster, he had always ranked high up among the more vicious specimens—many good judges, indeed, considering that he even competed for the blue ribbon with that great scourge of modern times, my Aunt Agatha. But now, reviewing his recent conduct, I must admit that I found myself definitely softening towards him.

Nobody, I reasoned, who could slosh young Seabury like that could be altogether bad. There must be fine metal somewhere among the dross. And I actually went so far as to say to myself with something of a rush of emotion that, if ever things so shaped themselves that I could go freely about my affairs again, I would look the man up and endeavour to fraternize with him. I had even reached the stage of toying with the idea of a nice little lunch, with him on one side of the table and me on the other, sucking down some good, dry vintage wine and chatting like old friends, when I found that I had arrived at the outskirts of the Dower House.

This bin or depository for the widows of deceased Lords Chuffnell was a medium-sized sort of shack standing in what the advertisements described as spacious and commodious grounds. You entered by a five-barred gate set in a box hedge and approached by a short gravel drive—unless you were planning to break in through a lower window, in which case you sneaked along a grass border, skipping silently from tree to tree.

This is what I did, though at a casual glance it didn't seem really necessary. The place looked deserted. Still, so far, of course, I had only seen the front of it: and if the gardener in charge had changed his policy of going down to the local pub for a refresher at this hour and was still on the premises, he would be round at the back. It was thither, therefore, that I now directed the footsteps, making them as snaky as possible.

I can't say I liked the prospect before me. Jeeves had spoken airily—or glibly—of busting in and making myself at home for the night; but my experience has been that whenever I try to do a bit of burgling something always goes wrong. I had not yet forgotten that time Bingo Little persuaded me to break into his house and pinch the dictaphone record of the mushy article his wife, née Rosie M. Banks, the well-known female novelist, had written about him for my Aunt Dahlia's paper, *Milady's Boudoir*. Pekingese, parlourmaids, and policemen had entered into the affair, you may remember, causing me despondency and alarm: and I didn't want anything of that nature happening again.

So it was with a pretty goodish amount of caution that I now sidled round to the back: and when the first thing the eye fell on was the kitchen door standing ajar, I did not rush in with the vim I would have displayed a year or so earlier, before Life had made me the grim, suspicious man I am today: but stood there cocking a wary eye at it. It might be all right. On the other hand, it might not be all right. Time alone could tell.

The next moment, I was dashed glad I had held off, because I suddenly heard someone whistling in the house, and I saw what that meant. It meant that the gardener bloke, instead of going down to the "Chuffnell Arms" for a snifter, had decided to stay home and have a quiet evening among his books. So much for Jeeves's authoritative inside information.

I drew back into the shadows like a leopard, feeling pretty peeved. I felt that Jeeves had no right to say that fellows went

down to the village for a spot at such and such a time when they
didn't.

And then suddenly something happened that threw an entirely new light on the position of affairs, and I saw that I had
misjudged the honest fellow. The whistling stopped, there
was a single, brief hiccough, and then from inside came the sound
of somebody singing "Lead, Kindly Light".

The occupant of the Dower House was no mere gardener. It
was Moscow's Pride, the unspeakable Brinkley, who lurked
therein.

The situation seemed to me to call for careful, unhurried
thought.

The whole trouble with fellows like Brinkley is that in dealing
with them you cannot go by the form book. They are such in-
and-out performers. Tonight, for instance, within the space of
little more than an hour, I had seen this man ravening to and fro
with a carving knife and also tolerantly submitting to having
himself kicked by Chuffy practically the whole length of the
Chuffnell Hall drive. It all seemed to be a question of what
mood he happened to be in at the time. If, therefore, I was
compelled to ask myself, I were to walk boldly into the Dower
House now, which manifestation of this many-sided man would
greet me? Should I find a deferential lover of peace whom it
would be both simple and agreeable to take by the slack of the
trousers and bung out? Or should I have to spend the remainder
of the night racing up and down the stairs with him a short head
behind me?

And, arising out of this, what had become of that carving knife
of his? As far as I could ascertain, he did not appear to have it
on his person during the interview with Chuffy. But then, on
the other hand, he might simply have left it somewhere and
collected it again by now.

Reviewing the matter from every angle, I decided to remain
where I was; and the next moment the trend of events showed
that the decision had been a wise one. He had just got as far as
that bit about "The night is dark" and seemed to be going
strong, though a little uncertain in the lower register, when he
suddenly broke off. And the next thing I heard was a most
frightful outbreak of shoutings and clumpings and bangings.
What had set him off, I could not, of course, say; but the sounds

left little room for doubt that for some reason or other the fellow had abruptly returned to what I might call the carving-knife phase.

One of the advantages of being in the country, if you belong, like Brinkley, to the more aggressive type of loony, is that you have great freedom of movement. The sort of row he was making now, if made in, let us say, Grosvenor Square or Cadogan Terrace, would infallibly have produced posses of policemen within the first two minutes. Windows would have been raised, whistles blown. But in the peaceful seclusion of the Dower House, Chuffnell Regis, he was granted the widest scope for self-expression. Except for the Hall, there wasn't another house within a mile: and even the Hall was too far away for the ghastly uproar he was making to be more than a faint murmur.

As to what he thought he was chasing, there again one could make no certain pronouncement. It might be that the gardener-caretaker had not gone to the village, after all, and was now wishing that he had. Or it might be, of course, that a fellow in Brinkley's sozzled condition did not require a definite object of the chase, but simply chased rainbows, so to speak, for the sake of the exercise.

I was inclining to this latter view, and wondering a little wistfully if there mightn't be a chance of him falling downstairs and breaking his neck, when I found that I had been wrong. For some minutes the noise had grown somewhat fainter, activities seeming to have shifted to some distant part of the house; but now it suddenly hotted up again. I heard feet clattering downstairs. Then there was a terrific crash. And immediately after that the back door was burst open, and out shot a human form. It whizzed rapidly in my direction, tripped over something, and came a purler almost at my feet. And I was about to commend my soul to God and jump on its gizzard, hoping for the best, when something in the tone of the comments it was making—a sort of educated profanity which seemed to give evidence of a better bringing-up than Brinkley could possibly have had—made me pause.

I bent down. My diagnosis had been correct. It was Sir Roderick Glossop.

I was just going to introduce myself and institute inquiries, when the back door swung open again and another figure appeared.

"And stay out!" it observed, with a good deal of bitterness.

The voice was Brinkley's. It was some small pleasure to me at a none too festive time to note that he was rubbing his left shin.

The door slammed, and I heard the bolts shot. The next moment, a tenor voice rendering "Rock of Ages" showed that, as far as Brinkley was concerned, the episode was concluded.

Sir Roderick had scrambled to his feet, and was standing puffing a good bit, as if touched in the wind. I was not surprised, for the going had been fast.

It struck me as a good moment to start the dialogue.

"What ho, what ho!" I said.

It seemed to be rather my fate on this particular night to stir up my fellow man, not to mention my fellow scullerymaid. But, judging by results, the magnetic force of my personality appeared to be a bit on the wane. I mean to say, while the scullerymaid had had hysterics and Chuffy had jumped a foot, this Glossop merely quivered like something in aspic when joggled on the dish. But this, of course, may have been because that was all he was physically able to do. These breathers with Brinkley take it out of a man.

"It's all right," I continued, anxious to set him at his ease and remove the impression that what was murmuring in his ear was some fearful creature of the night. "Only B. Wooster——"

"Mr. Wooster!"

"Absolutely."

"Good God!" he said, becoming a little more tranquil, though still far from the life and soul of the party. "Woof!"

And there the matter rested, while he took in a supply of life-giving air. I remained silent. We Woosters do no intrude at such a time.

Presently the puffing died away to a soft whiffle. He took about another minute and a half off. And, when he spoke, there was something so subdued, so what you might call quavering, about his voice that I came within a toucher of placing a kindly arm round his shoulder and telling him to cheer up.

"No doubt you are wondering, Mr. Wooster, what is the explanation of all this?"

I still wasn't quite equal to the kindly arm, but I did bestow a sort of encouraging pat.

"Not a bit," I said. "Not a bit. I know all. I am abreast

of the whole situation.   I heard what had happened at the Hall,
and directly I saw you shoot out of that door I knew what must
have occurred here.   You were planning to spend the night in
the Dower House, weren't you?"

"I was.   If you have really been apprised of what took place
at Chuffnell Hall, Mr. Wooster, you are aware that I am in the
unfortunate position of . . ."

". . . being blacked out.   I know.   So am I."

"You!"

"Yes.   It's a long story, and I couldn't tell you, anyway,
because it's by way of being secret history, but you can take it
from me that we are both in the same fix."

"But this is astonishing!"

"You can't go back to your hotel, and I can't get up to London
till we have taken the make-up off."

"Good God!"

"It seems to bring us very close together, what?"

He breathed deeply.

"Mr. Wooster, we have had our differences in the past.
The fault may have been mine.   I cannot say.   But in this
crisis we must forget them and—er——"

"Stick together?"

"Precisely."

"We will," I said cordially.   "Speaking for myself, I decided
to let the dead past bury its dead when I heard that you had been
giving little Seabury one or two on the spot indicated."

I heard him snort.

"You are aware what that abominable boy did to me, Mr.
Wooster?"

"Rather.   And what you did to him.   I am thoroughly
posted up to the time you left the Hall.   What happened after
that?"

"Almost immediately after I had done so, the realization of my
terrible position came upon me."

"Nasty jar, I imagine?"

"The shock was of the severest.   I was at a complete loss.
The only course it seemed possible to pursue was to seek refuge
somewhere for the night.   And, knowing the Dower House to
be unoccupied, I repaired thither."   He shuddered.   "Mr.
Wooster, that house is—I speak in all seriousness—an Inferno."

He puffed awhile.

"I am not alluding to the presence on the premises of what appeared to me to be a dangerous lunatic. I mean that the whole place is congested with living organisms. Mice, Mr. Wooster! And small dogs. And I think I saw a monkey."

"Eh?"

"I remember now that Lady Chuffnell informed me that her son had started to maintain an establishment of these creatures, but at the moment it had slipped my mind, and the experience came upon me without warning or preparation."

"Of course, yes. Seabury breeds things. I remember him telling me. And you were snootered by the menagerie?"

He stirred in the darkness. I fancy he was mopping the b.

"Shall I tell you of my experiences beneath that roof, Mr. Wooster?"

"Do," I said cordially. "We have the night before us."

He handkerchiefed the brow once more.

"It was a nightmare. I had scarcely entered the place when a voice addressed me from a dark corner of the kitchen, which was the room in which I first found myself. 'I see you, you old muddler,' was the phrase it employed."

"Dashed familiar."

"I need scarcely tell you what consternation it occasioned me. I bit my tongue severely. Then, divining that the speaker was merely a parrot, I hastened from the room. I had scarcely reached the stairs when I observed a hideous form. A little, short, broad, bow-legged individual with long arms and a dark wizened face. He was wearing clothes of some description and he walked rapidly, lurching from side to side and gibbering. In my present cool frame of mind I realize that it must have been a monkey, but at the time . . ."

"What a home!" I said sympathetically. "Add little Seabury, and what a home! How about the mice?"

"They came later. Allow me, if you will, to adhere to the chronological sequence of my misadventures, or I shall be unable to relate the story coherently. The room in which I next found myself appeared to be completely filled with small dogs. They pounced upon me, snuffling and biting at me. I escaped and entered another room. Here at last, I was saying to myself, even in this sinister and ill-omened house there must be peace. Mr. Wooster, I had hardly framed the thought when something ran up my right trouser leg. I sprang to one side, and in so doing upset what appeared to be a box or cage of some kind. I found myself in a sea of mice. I detest the creatures. I endeavoured to brush them off. They clung the more. I fled from the room, and I had scarcely reached the stairs when this lunatic appeared and pursued me. He pursued me up and down stairs, Mr. Wooster!"

I nodded understandingly.

"We all go through it," I said. "I had the same experience."

"You?"

"Rather. He nearly got me with a carving knife."

"As far as I could discern, the weapon he carried was more of the order of a chopper."

"He varies," I explained. "Now the carving knife, anon the chopper. Versatile chap. It's the artistic temperament, I suppose."

"You speak as if you knew this man."

"I do more than know him. I employ him. He's my valet."

"Your valet?"

"Fellow named Brinkley. He won't be my valet long, mind you. If he ever simmers down enough for me to get near him and give him the sack. Ironical, that, when you come to think of it," I said, for I was in philosophic mood. "I mean, do you realize that I'm giving this chap a salary all this time? In other words, he's actually being paid to chivvy me about with carving knives. If that's not Life," I said thoughtfully "what is?"

It seemed to take the old boy a moment or two to drink this in.

"Your valet? Then what is he doing in the Dower House?"

"Oh, he's a mobile sort of fellow, you know. Now here, now there. He flits. He was at the Hall not long ago."

"I never heard of such a thing."

"New to me, too, I must confess. Well, you're certainly having a lively night. This'll last you, what? I mean, you won't need any more excitement for months and months and months."

"Mr. Wooster, my earnest hope is that the entire remainder of my existence will be one round of unruffled monotony. Tonight I have seemed to sense the underlying horror of life. You do not suppose that there could possibly be mice on my person still?"

"You must have shaken them off, I should say. You were pretty active, you know. I could only hear you, of course, but you seemed to be leaping from crag to crag, as it were."

"Certainly I spared no effort to elude this man Brinkley. It was merely that I fancied I felt something nibbling at my left shoulder-blade."

"You've had quite a night, haven't you?"

"A truly terrible night. I shall not readily recover a normal tranquillity of mind. My pulse is still high, and I do not like the way my heart is beating. However, by a merciful good fortune, all has ended well. You will be able to give me the shelter I so sorely need in your cottage. And there with the assistance of a little soap and water I shall be able to wash off this distasteful blacking."

I saw that this was where I had to start breaking things gently to him.

"You can't get that stuff off with soap and water. I've tried. You have to have butter."

"The point strikes me as immaterial. You can provide butter, no doubt?"

"Sorry. No butter."

"There must be butter in your cottage."

"There isn't. And why? Because there isn't a cottage."

"I cannot understand you."

"It's burned down."

"What?"

"Yes. Brinkley did it."

"Good God!"

"A nuisance in many ways, I must confess."

He was silent for a space. Turning the thing over in his mind. Looking at it from this angle and that.

"Your cottage is really burned down?"

"Heap of ashes."

"Then what is to be done?"

It seemed time to point out the silver lining.

"Be of good cheer," I said. "We may not be so well off for cottages, but the butter situation, I am happy to say, is reasonably bright. We can't get any tonight, but it cometh in the morning, so to speak. Jeeves is going to bring me some as soon as the dairyman delivers."

"But I cannot remain in this condition till morning."

"Only course to pursue, I'm afraid."

He brooded. Hard to see in the darkness, but discontentedly, I thought, as if his haughty spirit fretted somewhat. He must

have been doing some good, solid thinking, too, because suddenly
he came to life with an idea.

"This cottage of yours—had it a garage?"

"Oh, yes."

"Was that burned down also?"

"No, I fancy it escaped the holocaust. It was well away from
the scene of conflagration."

"Is there petrol in it?"

"Oh, yes. Lots of petrol."

"Why, then all is well, Mr. Wooster. I am convinced that
petrol will prove a cleansing agent equally as efficacious as
butter."

"But, dash it, you can't go to my garage."

"Why not, pray?"

"Well, yes, you could, if you liked, I suppose. Not me,
though. For reasons which I am not prepared to divulge, I
propose to spend the rest of the night in the summer-house on the
main lawn of the Hall."

"You will not accompany me?"

"Sorry. No."

"Then good night, Mr. Wooster. I will not keep you any
longer from your rest. I am greatly obliged to you for the assistance you have accorded me in a trying situation. We must see
more of one another. Let us lunch together one of these days.
How do I obtain access to this garage of yours?"

"You'll have to bust a window."

"I will do so."

He pushed off, full of buck and determination, and I, with a
dubious shake of the old onion, trickled along towards the
summer-house.

* 17 *

Breakfast-time at the Hall

I DON'T know if you have ever spent the night in a summer-house.
If not, avoid making the experiment. It's not a thing I would
advise any friend of mine to do. On the subject of sleeping in
summer-houses I will speak out fearlessly. As far as I have been

able to ascertain, such a binge doesn't present a single attractive feature. Apart from the inevitable discomfort in the fleshy parts, there's the cold, and apart from the cold there's the mental anguish. All the ghost stories you've ever read go flitting through the mind, particularly any you know where fellows are found next morning absolutely dead, without a mark on them but with such a look of horror and fear in their eyes that the search party draw in their breath a bit and gaze at each other as much as to say "What ho!" Things creak. You fancy you hear stealthy footsteps. You receive the impression that a goodish quota of skinny hands are reaching out for you in the darkness. And, as I say, the cold extremely severe and much discomfort in the fleshy parts. The whole constituting a pretty sticky experience and one to be avoided by the knowledgeable.

And what made the thing so dashed poignant in my case was the thought that if I had only had the nerve to accompany in- trepid old Glossop to the garage there would have been no need for me to stay marooned in this smelly structure, listening to the wind howling through the chinks in the woodwork. Once at the garage, I mean to say, I could not only have scoured the face but could have hopped into the old two-seater, which was champing at its bit there, and tooled off to London by road, singing a gipsy song, as it were.

And I simply couldn't muster up the nerve to take a pop at it. The garage, I reflected, was right in the danger zone, well inside the Voules and Dobson belt, and I absolutely could not face the possibility of running into Police-Sergeant Voules and being detained and questioned. Those meetings with him the night before had shattered my *moral*, causing me to look upon this hell- hound of the Law as a sleepless prowler who rambled incessantly and was bound to appear out of a trap just at the moment when you could best have done without him.

So I stayed where I was. I hitched myself into position forty- six in the hope that it would be easier on the f.p's than the last forty-five, and had another shot at the dreamless.

The thing that always beats me is how on these occasions one ever gets to sleep at all. Personally, I abandoned all idea of it at an early stage, and no one, accordingly, could have been more surprised than myself when, just as I was endeavouring to give the miss to a leopard which was biting me rather shrewdly in the seat of the trousers, I suddenly awoke to discover that it had been but a dream, that in reality no leopards were to be noticed among those present, that the sun was up and another day had begun, and that on the greensward without the early bird was already breakfasting and making the dickens of a noise about it, too.

I went to the door and looked out. I could hardly believe that it was really morning. But it was, and a dashed good morning, at that. The air was cool and fresh, there were long shadows across the lawn, and everything combined to give the soul such a kick that many fellows in my position would have taken off their socks and done rhythmic dances in the dew. I did not actually do that, but I certainly felt uplifted to no little extent, and you might say that I was simply so much pure spirit, without any material side to me whatsoever, when suddenly it was as if the old tum had come out of a trance with a jerk, and the next moment I was feeling that nothing mattered in this world or the next except about a quart of coffee and all the eggs and b. you could cram on to a dish.

It's a rummy thing about breakfast. When you've only to press a bell to have the domestic staff racing in with everything on the menu from oatmeal to jams, marmalades, and potted meats, you find that all you can look at is a glass of soda water and a rusk. When you can't get it, you feel like a python when the Zoo officials have just started to bang the luncheon gong. Speaking for myself, I have, as a rule, to be more or less lured to the feast. I mean to say, I don't as a general thing become what you might call breakfast-conscious till I've had my morning tea and rather thought things over a bit. And I can give no better indication of the extraordinary change which had come over my viewpoint now than by mentioning that there was a young fowl of sorts not far away engaged in getting outside a large, pink worm, and I could willingly have joined it at the board. In fact, I would have taken pot luck at this juncture with a buzzard.

My watch had stopped, so I couldn't tell what time it was: and another thing I didn't know was when Jeeves was planning to go to the Dower House to keep our tryst. The thought that he might even now be on his way there and that, if he didn't find me, he would give the thing up as a bad job and retire to some impregnable fastness in the back parts of the Hall gave me a very nasty turn. I left the summer-house and, taking to the bushes, began to work my way through them, treading like a Red Indian on the trail and keeping well under cover throughout.

And I was just navigating round the side of the house and making ready for the dash into the open, when through the french window of the morning-room I saw a spectacle which affected me profoundly. In fact, you'd be about right if you said that it seemed to speak to my very depths.

Inside the room, a parlourmaid was placing a large tray on a table.

The sunlight, streaming in, lit up this parlourmaid's hair: and, noting its auburn hue, I deduced that she must be Mary, the betrothed of Constable Dobson: and at any other time the fact would have been of interest. But I was in no mood now to subject the girl to a critical scrutiny with a view to ascertaining whether the constable had picked a winner or not. My whole attention was earmarked for that tray.

It was a well-laden tray. There was a coffee-pot on it, also toast in considerable quantity, and furthermore a covered dish. It was this last that touched the spot. Under that cover there might be eggs, there might be bacon, there might be sausages, there might be kidneys, or there might be kippers. I could not tell. But whatever there was it was all right with Bertram.

For I had laid my plans and formed my schemes. The girl was on her way out by this time, and I estimated that I had possibly fifty seconds for the stern task before me. Allow twenty for nipping in, three for snaffling the works, and another twenty-five for getting back into the bushes again, and one had all the makings of a successful enterprise.

The moment the door closed I was speeding on my way. I recked little whether anybody saw me, and I should imagine that, had there been eyewitnesses, all they would have seen would have been a sort of blur. I did the first leg of the journey well inside the estimated time, and I had just laid hand on the tray and was about to lift and remove, when there came from outside the door the sound of footsteps.

It was a moment for swift thought, and such moments find Bertram Wooster at his best.

This morning-room, I should mention, was not the small morning-room where Dwight and little Seabury had had their epoch-making turn-up. In fact, I am rather misleading my public in alluding to it as a morning-room at all. It was really a study or office, being the place where Chuffy did his estate business, totted up his bills, brooded over the growing cost of agricultural apparatus, and gave the tenants the bird when they called to ask him to knock a bit off their rent. And as you can't get very far with that sort of thing unless you have a pretty good-sized desk, Chuffy had most fortunately had one put in. It stood across one whole corner of the room, and it seemed to beckon to me.

Two and a half seconds later, I was behind it, crouching on the carpet and trying to breathe solely through the pores.

The next moment, the door opened, and somebody came in. Feet crossed the floor, right up to the desk, and I heard the click as the hidden hand removed the telephone receiver.

"Chuffnell Regis, two-niyun-four," said a voice, and conceive the sudden rush of relief when I recognized it as one that I had many a time shaken hands with in the past—the voice, in short, of a friend in need.

"Oh, Jeeves," I said, popping up like a jack-in-the-box.

You can't rattle Jeeves. Where scullery maids had had hysterics and members of the Peerage had leaped and quivered, he simply regarded me with respectful serenity and, after a civil good morning, went on with the job in hand. He is a fellow who likes to do things in their proper order.

"Chuffnell Regis two-niyun-four? The Seaview Hotel? Could you inform me if Sir Roderick Glossop is in his room? . . . Not yet returned? . . . Thank you."

He hung up the receiver, and was now at liberty to give the late young master a spot of attention.

"Good morning, sir," he said again. "I was not expecting to see you here."

"I know, but . . ."

"I had supposed that the arrangement was that we should meet at the Dower House."

I shuddered a bit.

"Jeeves," I said, "one brief word about the Dower House, and then I should like the subject shelved indefinitely. I know you meant well. I know that when you sent me there your motives were pure to the last drop. But the fact remains that you were dispatching me to a nasty salient. Do you know who was lurking in that House of Fear? Brinkley. Complete with chopper."

"I am very sorry to hear that, sir. Then I assume that you did not sleep there last night?"

"No, Jeeves, I did not. I slept—if you can call it sleeping— in a summer-house. And I was just creeping round through the bushes to try to find you, when I saw that parlourmaid setting out food on the table in here."

"His lordship's breakfast, sir."

"Where is he?"

"He should be down shortly, sir. It is a most fortunate chance that her ladyship should have instructed me to ring up the Seaview Hotel. Otherwise we might have experienced some difficulty in establishing connection."

"Yes. What was all that, by the way? That Seaview Hotel stuff."

"Her ladyship is somewhat exercised in her mind about Sir Roderick, sir. I fancy that on reflection she has reached the conclusion that she did not treat him well last night."

"Mother Love not so hot this morning?"

"No, sir."

"And it's a case of 'Return and all will be forgiven'?"

"Precisely, sir. But unfortunately, Sir Roderick appears to be missing, and we can secure no information as to what has become of him."

I was in a position, of course, to explain and clarify, and I did so without delay.

"He's all right. After an invigorating session with Brinkley, he went to my garage to get petrol. Was he correct in supposing that that would clean him as well as butter?"

"Yes, sir."

"Then I should think he was on his way to London by now, if not actually in the Metropolis."

"I will notify her ladyship at once, sir. I imagine that the information will serve sensibly to lessen her anxiety."

"You really thinks she loves him still and wishes to extend the *amende honorable*?"

"Or olive branch? Yes, sir. So, at least, I divined from her demeanour. I was left with the impression that all the old love and esteem were in operation once more."

"And I'm very glad to hear it," I said cordially. "For I must tell you, Jeeves, that since we last got together I have completely changed my mind about the above Glossop. I see now that there is much good in him. In the silent watches of the night we formed what you wouldn't be far out in describing as a beautiful friendship. We discovered each other's hidden merits, and he left showering invitations to lunch."

"Indeed, sir?"

"Absolutely. From now on, there will always be a knife and fork for Bertram at the Glossop lair, and the same for Roddy *chez* Bertram."

"Very gratifying, sir."

"Most. So if you're chatting with Lady Chuffnell in the near future, you can tell her that the match now has my full approval and sanction. But all this, Jeeves," I proceeded, striking the practical note, "is beside the point. The main issue is that I am sorely in need of nourishment, and I want that tray. So hand it across and look slippy."

"You are proposing to eat his lordship's breakfast, sir?"

"Jeeves," I said emotionally, and was about to go on to add that, if he had any doubts as to what I was proposing to do to that breakfast, he could remove them by standing to one side and watching me get into action, when once more I heard footsteps in the passage outside.

Instead of speaking along these lines, accordingly, I blenched, as near as a fellow can blench when his face is all covered with boot polish, and broke off with a brief heart-cry. Once more I perceived that it had become imperative that I vanish from the scene.

These footsteps, I must mention, were of the solid, sturdy, shoe-number-eleven type. It was natural, therefore, that I should assume that it was Chuffy who now stood without. And to encounter Chuffy, I need scarcely say, would have been foreign to my policy. I have already indicated with, I think, sufficient clearness, that he was not in sympathy with my aims and objects. That interview we had had on the previous night had shown me that he was to be reckoned as essentially one of the opposition— a hostile element and a menace. Let him discover me here, and the first thing I knew he would be locking me up somewhere in a spirit of chivalrous zeal and sending messengers to old Stoker to drop round and collect.

Long, therefore, before the handle had turned I was down in the depths like a diving duck.

The door opened. A female voice spoke. No doubt that of the future Mrs. Constable Dobson.

"Mr. Stoker," it announced.

Large, flat feet clumped into the room.

18

Black Work In A Study

I WEDGED myself a little tighter in behind the old zareba. Not so good, not so good, a voice seemed to be whispering in my ear. Of all the unpleasant contingencies which could have arisen, this seemed to me about the scaliest. Whatever might have been said against Chuffnell Hall—and recent events had tended considerably to lessen its charm in my eyes—I had supposed that you could put forward at least one thing in its favour, viz. that there was no possible chance of encountering J. Washburn Stoker on the premises. And, in spite of having my time fairly fully occupied with feeling like a jelly, I was still able to experience quite a spot of honest indignation at what I considered a dashed unjustifiable intrusion on his part.

I mean to say, if a man has thrown his weight about in a stately home of England, ticking off the residents and asserting positively that he jolly well isn't going to darken its doors again, he has no right to come strolling in barely two days later as if the place were an hotel with "Welcome" on the mat. I felt pretty strongly about the whole thing.

I was also wondering how Jeeves would handle this situation. By this time a shrewd bloke like this Stoker was bound to have guessed that his were the brains behind my escape, and it seemed not unlikely that he would make some tentative move towards scattering these brains on the hearthrug. His voice, when he spoke, undoubtedly indicated that some such idea was floating in his mind. It was harsh and roopy, and though all that he actually said by way of a start was "Ah!" a determined man can get a lot of meaning into an "Ah!"

"Good morning, sir," said Jeeves.

This business of lying curled up behind desks cuts both ways. It has its advantages and its drawbacks. Purely from the standpoint of the slinking fugitive, of course, fine. Indeed, could scarcely be bettered. But against this must be set the fact that it undoubtedly hampers a chap in his capacity of audience. The effect now was much the same as if I had been listening-in to a dramatic sketch on the wireless.   I got the voices, but I missed the play of expression.   And I'd have given a lot to be able to see it.   Not Jeeves's, of course, because Jeeves never has any. But Stoker's, it seemed to me, would have been well worth more than a casual glance.

"So you're here, are you?"

"Yes, sir."

The next item was an extremely nasty laugh from the visitor. One of those hard, short, sharp ones.

"I came here because I wanted information about where Mr. Wooster has got to.   I thought that Lord Chuffnell might possibly have seen him.   I never reckoned I should run into you. Say, listen," said the Stoker disease, suddenly hotting up, "do you know what I've a mind to do to you?"

"No, sir."

"Break your damned neck."

"Indeed, sir?"

"Yes."

I heard Jeeves cough.

"A little extreme, sir, surely?   I can appreciate that the fact that I decided—somewhat abruptly, I admit—to leave your employment and return to that of his lordship should occasion displeasure on your part, but . . ."

"You know what I'm talking about.   Or are you going to deny that it was you who smuggled that guy Wooster off my yacht?"

"No, sir.   I admit that I was instrumental in restoring his liberty to Mr. Wooster.   In the course of a conversation which I had with him, Mr. Wooster informed me that he was being detained on the vessel *ultra vires*, and, acting in your best interests, I released him.   At that time, you will recall, sir, I was in your employment, and I felt it my duty to save you from what might have been an extremely serious contretemps."

I couldn't see, of course, but I received the impression from a certain amount of gurgling and snorting which he put in during these remarks that old Stoker would have been glad to have the floor a bit earlier.   I could have told him it wasn't any good. You can't switch Jeeves off when he has something to say which he feels will be of interest.   The only thing is to stand by and wait till he runs down.

But though he had now done so, it wasn't right away that the party of the second part started anything in the nature of a counter-speech. I imagine that the substance of Jeeves's little talk had given him food for thought.

In this conjecture, it appeared that I was correct. Old Stoker breathed a bit tensely for a while, then he spoke in almost an awed voice. It's often that way when you get up against Jeeves. He has a way of suggesting new viewpoints.

"Are you crazy or am I?"

"Sir?"

"Save *me*, did you say, from——?"

"A contretemps? Yes, sir. I cannot make the assertion authoritatively, for I am not certain to what extent the fact that Mr. Wooster came on board the yacht of his own volition would weigh with a jury . . ."

"Jury?"

". . . but his detention on the vessel despite his expressed desire to leave would, I am inclined to imagine, constitute an act of kidnapping, the penalties for which, as you are no doubt aware, sir, are very severe."

"But, say, listen . . .!"

"England is an extremely law-abiding country, sir, and offences which might pass unnoticed in your own land are prosecuted here with the greatest rigour. My knowledge of legal *minutiæ* is, I regret to say, slight, so I cannot asseverate with perfect confidence that this detention of Mr. Wooster would have ranked as an act in contravention of the criminal code, and, as such, liable to punishment with penal servitude, but undoubtedly, had I not intervened, the young gentleman would have been in a position to bring a civil action and mulct you in very substantial damages. So, acting, as I say, in your best interests, sir, I released Mr. Wooster."

There was a silence.

"Thanks," said old Stoker mildly.

"Not at all, sir."

"Thank you very much."

"I did what I considered the only thing that could avert a most disagreeable contingency, sir."

"Darned good of you."

I must say I can't see why Jeeves shouldn't go down in legend and song. Daniel did, on the strength of putting in half an hour or so in the lions' den and leaving the dumb chums in a condition of suavity and *camaraderie*; and if what Jeeves had just done

wasn't entitled to rank well above a feat like that, I'm no judge of
form.   In less then five minutes he had reduced this ravening
Stoker from a sort of human wildcat to a positive domestic pet.
If I hadn't been there and heard it, I wouldn't have believed it
was possible.

"I've got to think about this," said old Stoker, milder than ever.

"Yes, sir."

"I hadn't looked at it that way before.   Yes, sir, I've got to
think about this.   I believe I'll go for a walk and mull it over in
my mind.   Lord Chuffnell hasn't seen Mr. Wooster, has he?"

"Not since last night, sir."

"Oh, he saw him last night, did he?   Which way was he
headed?"

"I rather fancy it was Mr. Wooster's intention to pass the night
in the Dower House and return to London today."

"The Dower House?   That's that place across the park?"

"Yes, sir."

"I might look in there.   It seems to me the first thing I've got
to do is have a talk with Mr. Wooster."

"Yes, sir."

I heard him go out through the french window, but it wasn't
till another moment or two had passed that I felt justified in
coming to the surface.   It being reasonable to suppose by then
that the coast was clear, I poked the head up over the desk.

"Jeeves," I said, and if there were tears in the eyes, what of it?
We Woosters are not afraid to confess honest emotion, "there is
none like you, none."

"It is extremely kind of you to say so, sir."

"It was all I could do to keep from leaping out and shaking your
hand."

"It would scarcely have been judicious, in the circumstances,
sir."

"That's what I thought.   Your father wasn't a snake-charmer,
was he, Jeeves?"

"No, sir."

"It just crossed my mind.   What do you think will happen
when old Stoker gets to the Dower House?"

"We can only conjecture, sir."

"My fear is that Brinkley may have slept it off by now."

"There is that possibility, sir."

"Still, it was a kindly thought, sending the fellow there, and we

must hope for the best.   After all, Brinkley still has that chopper.
I say, do you think Chuffy is really coming down?"

"At any moment, I fancy, sir."

"Then you wouldn't advise my eating his breakfast?"

"No, sir."

"But I'm starving, Jeeves."

"I am extremely sorry, sir.   The position at the moment is a
little difficult.   Later on, no doubt, I may be able to alleviate
your distress."

"Have you had breakfast, Jeeves?"

"Yes, sir."

"What did you have?"

"The juice of an orange, sir, followed by Cute Crispies—an
American cereal—scrambled eggs with a slice of bacon, and toast
and marmalade."

"Oh, gosh!   The whole washed down, no doubt, with a cup
of strengthening coffee?"

"Yes, sir."

"Oh, my God!   You really don't think I could just sneak a
single sausage?"

"I would scarcely advocate it, sir.   And it is a small point, but
his lordship is having kippers."

"Kippers!"

"And this, I fancy, will be his lordship coming now, sir."

So down once more into the lower levels for Bertram.   And
I had hardly fitted myself into the groove when the door opened.

A voice spoke.

"Why, hallo, Jeeves."

"Good morning, miss."

It was Pauline Stoker.

I must say I was a bit peeved.   Chuffnell Hall, whatever its
other defects, should, as I have pointed out, have been entirely
free from Stokers.   And here they were, absolutely over-running
the place like mice.   I was quite prepared to find something
breathing in my ear and look round and see little Dwight.   I
mean to say, I was feeling—bitterly, I admit—that if this was
going to be an Old Home Week of Stokers, one might as well
make the thing complete.

Pauline had begun to sniff vigorously.

"What's that I smell, Jeeves?"

"Kippered herrings, miss."

"Whose?"

"His lordship's, miss."

"Oh. I haven't had breakfast yet, Jeeves."

"No, miss?"

"No. Father yanked me out of bed and had me half-way here before I was properly awake. He's all worked up, Jeeves."

"Yes, miss. I have just been having a conversation with Mr. Stoker. He did appear somewhat overwrought."

"All the way here he was talking about what he was going to do if he ever found you again. And now you tell me he did find find you. What happened? Didn't he eat you?"

"No, miss."

"Probably on a diet. Well, where has he got to? They told me he was in here."

"Mr. Stoker left a moment ago with the intention of visiting the Dower House, miss. I think he hopes to find Mr. Wooster there."

"Somebody ought to warn that poor sap."

"You need experience no anxiety for Mr. Wooster, miss. He is not at the Dower House."

"Where is he?"

"Elsewhere, miss."

"Not that I care where he is. Do you remember my telling you last night, Jeeves, that I was thinking of becoming Mrs. Bertram W.?"

"Yes, miss."

"Well, I'm not. So you needn't save up for that fish slice, after all. I've changed my mind."

"I am glad to hear that, miss."

So was I. Her words were music to my ears.

"Glad, are you?"

"Yes, miss. I doubt whether the union would have been a successful one. Mr. Wooster is an agreeable young gentleman, but I would describe him as essentially one of Nature's bachelors."

"Besides being mentally negligible?"

"Mr. Wooster is capable of acting very shrewdly on occasion, miss."

"So am I. And that is why I say that, no matter if father does tear the roof off, I am not going to marry that poor, persecuted lamb. Why should I? I've nothing against him."

There was a pause.

"I've just been talking to Lady Chuffnell, Jeeves."

"Yes, miss."

"Apparently she has had a little domestic trouble, too."

"Yes, miss.   There was an unfortunate rift between her lady-ship and Sir Roderick Glossop last night.   Now, I am glad to say, her ladyship appears to have thought matters over and decided that she made a mistake in severing relations with the gentleman."

"One does think things over, doesn't one?"

"Almost invariably, miss."

"And a fat lot of use that is, if the severed relation doesn't think them over too.   Have you seen Lord Chuffnell this morning, Jeeves?"

"Yes, miss."

"How was he looking?"

"Somewhat worried, it seemed to me, miss."

"He was?"

"Yes, miss."

"H'm.   Well, I won't keep you from your professional duties, Jeeves: smack into them right away, as far as I'm concerned."

"Thank you, miss.   Good morning."

For some moments after the door closed I remained motionless. I was passing the position of affairs under thoughtful review. To a certain extent you might say that relief was tingling through the veins like some rare wine, causing satisfaction and mental uplift.   In the plainest possible language, weighing her words and speaking without dubiety or equivocation, this girl Pauline had stated that not even the strongest measures on the part of her father would induce her to shove on the old bridal veil and step up the aisle at my side.   So far, so good.

But had she thoroughly estimated that father's powers of per-suasion?   That was what I asked myself.   Had she ever seen him when he was really going good?   Was she aware of what a Force he could be when in mid-season form?   In a word, did she realize what she was up against, and know that to attempt to thwart J. Washburn Stoker, when in spate, was like entering a jungle and taking on the first couple of wildcats you encountered?

It was this thought which prevented my rapture from being complete.   It seemed to me that, in opposing her will to that of a bally retired pirate like this male parent of hers, the frail girl was going out of her class and that her resistance to his matrimonial plans would be useless.

And I was musing thus when I suddenly heard the sloosh of coffee in a cup, and a moment later there came what Drexdale Yeats would have called a metallic clang, and with profound emotion I divined that Pauline, unable to resist the sight of that tray any longer, had poured herself out a steaming beaker and was getting at the kippers. For there was no longer any possible room for doubt as to the correctness of Jeeves's information. It was the scent of kippered herrings that was now wafted to me like a benediction, and I clenched my fists till the knuckles stood out white beneath the strain. I could mark every mouthful and each in turn went through me like a knife.

It's odd, the effect hunger has on one. You can't tell what you will do under the stress of it. Let the most level-headed bird get really peckish, and he will throw prudence to the winds. I did so at this point. Obviously the sound scheme was for me to remain under cover and wait till all these Stokers and what not blew over, and that was the policy which, in a calmer frame of mind, I would have pursued. But the smell of those kippers and the knowledge that with every moment that passed they were melting away like snow upon the mountain tops and that pretty soon all the toast would be gone as well, was too powerful for me. I came up from behind that desk like a minnow on a hook.

"Hi!" I said, speaking with a strong note of pleading in my voice.

It's rummy how experience never teaches us. I had seen the reaction of the scullerymaid to my sudden appearance. I had noted its effect on old Chuffy. And I had watched Sir Roderick Glossop at the moment of impact. Yet here I was, bobbing up in just the same sudden fashion as before.

And exactly the same thing happened again. If anything, rather more so. At the moment, Pauline Stoker was busy with a mouthful of kipper, and this for the nonce cramped her freedom of expression, so that all that occurred for about a second and a quarter was that a pair of horrified eyes stared into mine. Then the barrier of kipper gave way, and one of the most devastating yowls of terror I've ever heard in my puff ripped through the air.

It coincided with the opening of the door and the appearance on the threshold of the fifth Baron Chuffnell. And the next moment he had dashed at her and gathered her in his arms, and she had dashed at him and been gathered.

They couldn't have done it more neatly if they had been rehearsing for weeks.

∗ 19 ∗

Preparations For Handling Father

I ALWAYS maintain that it is by a chap's behaviour on this sort of occasion that you can really weigh him in the balance and judge if he's got the right chivalrous delicacy in him or not. It is the acid test. Come to me and say to me "Wooster, you know me pretty well. Tell me something. To settle a bet, would you consider that I was a *preux chevalier*, as the expression is?" and I reply "My dear Bates, or Cuthbertson, or whatever the name may be, I shall be able to answer that question better if you will indicate what you would do if you happened to be in a room where two loving hearts, after a painful misunderstanding, were in the process of getting together again on a basis of chumminess and mutual esteem. Would you duck down behind the desk? Or would you stand there and drink the performance in with bulging eyes?"

My own views are rigid. When a lovers' reconciliation is in progress, I do not remain goggling. As far as the conditions will permit, I withdraw and leave them to it.

But though, with the desk between us, I could not see these two, I could hear them, and most unpleasant it was. I have known Chuffy, as I say, practically from childhood, and in the course of the years I have seen him in a variety of differing circumstances and in many moods. And I never would have believed him capable of the revolting slush which now proceeded from his lips at the rate of about two hundred and fifty words to the minute. When I tell you that the observation "There, there, little girl!" was the only one I can bring myself to quote, you will be able to gather something of the ordeal to which I was subjected. And, to make matters worse, on an empty stomach, mind you.

Pauline, meanwhile, was contributing little or nothing to the dialogue.   Until this moment I had considered that, in the matter of emotional reaction to my appearance, the scullerymaid had set a mark at which others who met me suddenly might shoot in vain.   But Pauline eclipsed her completely.   She remained in Chuffy's arms gurgling like a leaky radiator, and it was only quite some little time later that she began to regain anything of a grip on her faculties.   The girl seemed goofy.

I suppose the fact of the matter was that at the moment when I manifested myself she was undergoing a considerable mental strain, and that my appearance served, as it were, to put the tin hat on it.   At any rate, she continued to give this radiator impersonation of hers so long that in the end it seemed to strike Chuffy that it was about time he switched off the murmured endearments and got down to first causes.

"But, darling," I heard him say.   "What was it, angel? What scared you, sweetheart?   Tell me, precious.   Did you see something, pet?"

It seemed to me that the moment had come to join the meeting. I rose above the top of the desk, and Pauline shied like a frightened horse.   It annoyed me, I confess.   Bertram Wooster is not accustomed to causing convulsions in the gentler sex. As a matter of fact, usually when girls see me, they incline rather to the amused smile, or, on occasion, to the weary sigh and the despairing "Oh, are *you* here again, Bertie?"   But better even that than this stark horror.

"Hallo, Chuffy," I said.   "Nice day."

You might have thought that relief would have been the emotion uppermost in Pauline Stoker's bosom on discovering that the cause of her panic was merely an old friend.   But no. She absolutely glared at me.

"You poor goof," she cried, "what's the big idea, playing hide-and-go-seek like that and scaring people stiff?   And I don't know if you know it, but you've got a smut on your face."

Nor was Chuffy behindhand in the recriminations.

"Bertie!" he said, in a sort of moaning way.   "My God! I might have guessed it would be you.   You really are without exception the most completely drivelling lunatic that was ever at large."

I felt it was time to check this sort of thing pretty sharply.

"I regret," I said, with a cold hauteur, "that I startled this young fathead, but my motives in concealing myself behind that desk were based on prudence and sound reasoning. And, talking of lunatics, Chuffnell, don't forget that I was compelled to overhear what you have been saying for the last five minutes."

I was pleased to see the blush of shame mantle his cheek. He shuffled uncomfortably.

"You oughtn't to have listened."

"You don't imagine that I wanted to listen, do you?"

Something of defiance or bravado came into his manner.

"And why the devil shouldn't I talk like that? I love her, blast you, and I don't care who knows it."

"Oh, quite," I said, with a scarcely veiled contempt.

"She's the most marvellous thing on earth."

"No, you are, darling," said Pauline.

"No, you are, angel," said Chuffy.

"No, you are, sweetness."

"No, you are, precious."

"Please," I said. "Please!"

Chuffy gave me a nasty look.

"You were saying, Wooster?"

"Oh nothing."

"I thought you made a remark."

"Oh, no."

"Good. You'd better not."

The first nausea had worn off somewhat by this time, and it was a kindlier Bertram Wooster who now displayed himself. I am a broad-minded man, and I reflected charitably that it was wrong to be hard on a fellow in Chuffy's situation. After all, in the special circumstances he could scarcely be expected to preserve the decencies. I struck a conciliatory note.

"Chuffy, old man," I said, "we must not allow ourselves to brawl. This is a moment for the genial eye and the affable smile. No one could be more delighted than myself that you and this old friend of mine have buried the dead past and started all square again together. I may look on myself as an old friend, may I not?"

She beamed in a cordial manner.

"Well, I should hope so, you poor ditherer. Why, I knew you before I ever met Marmaduke."

I turned to Chuffy.

"This Marmaduke business. I want to take that up with you some time. Fancy you keeping that dark all these years."

"There's nothing wrong in being christened Marmaduke, is there?" said Chuffy, a little heatedly.

"Nothing wrong, no. But we shall all have a good laugh about it at the Drones."

"Bertie," said Chuffy tensely, "if you breathe a word of it to those blighters at the Drones, I'll track you to the ends of the earth and strangle you with my bare hands."

"Well, well, we must see, we must see. But, as I was saying, I am delighted that this reconciliation has taken place. Being, as I am, one of Pauline's closest friends. We had some pretty good times together in the old days, didn't we?"

"You bet."

"That day at Piping Rock."

"Ah."

"And do you remember the night the car broke down and we were stranded for hours somewhere in the wilds of Westchester County in the rain?"

"I should say so."

"Your feet got wet, and I very wisely took your stockings off."

"Here!" said Chuffy.

"Oh, it's all right, old man. I conducted myself throughout with the nicest propriety. All I am trying to establish is that I am an old friend of Pauline's and am consequently entitled to rejoice at the present situation. There are few more charming girls than this P. Stoker, and you are lucky to have won her, old man, in spite of the fact that she is handicapped by possessing a father who bears a striking resemblance to something out of the Book of Revelations."

"Father's a good enough egg if you rub him the right way."

"You hear that, Chuffy? In rubbing this bally old thug, be sure to do it the right way."

"He is not a bally old thug."

"Pardon me. I appeal to Chuffy."

Chuffy scratched his chin. Somewhat embarrassed.

"I must say, angel, he does strike me at times as a bit above the odds."

"Exactly," I said. "And never forget that he is resolved that Pauline shall marry me."

"What!"

"Didn't you know that? Oh, yes."

Pauline was wearing a sort of Joan of Arc look.

"I'm darned if I'll marry you, Bertie."

"The right spirit," I said approvingly. "But can you preserve that intrepid attitude when you see Pop breathing flame through his nostrils and chewing broken bottles in the foreground? Will you not, if I may coin a phrase, be afraid of the big bad wolf?"

She wavered a bit.

"We're going to have a tough time with him, of course. I can see that. He's pretty sore with you, angel, you know'"

Chuffy puffed out his chest.

"I'll attend to him!"

"No," I said firmly, "*I* will attend to him. Leave the whole conduct of the affair to me."

Pauline laughed. I didn't like it. It seemed to me to have a derogatory ring.

"You! Why, you poor lamb, you would run a mile if Father so much as said 'Boo!' to you."

I raised the eyebrows.

"I anticipate no such contingency. Why should he say 'Boo!' to me? I mean, a damn silly thing for anybody to say to anyone. And even if he did make that idiotic observation, the effects would not be such as you have outlined. That I was once a little on the nervous side in your parent's presence, I admit. But no longer. Not any more. The scales have fallen from my eyes. Recently I have seen him in the space of something under three minutes reduced by Jeeves from a howling blizzard to a gentle breeze, and his spell is broken. When he comes, you may leave him to me with every confidence. I shall not be rough with him, but I shall be very firm."

Chuffy looked a bit thoughtful.

"Is he coming?"

Outside in the garden, footsteps had become audible. Also heavy breathing. I jerked a thumb at the window.

"This, if I mistake not, Watson," I said, "is our client now."

⋆ 20 ⋆

Jeeves Has News

AND so it was. A substantial form appeared against the summer sky. It entered. It took a seat. And, having taken a seat, it hauled out a handkerchief and started to mop the brow. A bit preoccupied, I divined, and my trained sense enabled me to recognize the symptoms. They were those of a man who had just been hobnobbing with Brinkley.

That this diagnosis was correct was proved a moment later when lowering the handkerchief for a space, he disclosed what had all the makings of a very sweetish black eye.

Pauline, sighting this, uttered a daughterly yip.

"What on earth has been happening, father?"

Old Stoker breathed heavily.

"I couldn't get at the fellow," he said, with a sort of wild regret in this voice.

"What fellow?"

"I don't know whe he was. Some lunatic in that Dower House. He stood there at the window, throwing potatoes at me. I had hardly knocked at the door, when he was there at the window, throwing potatoes. Wouldn't come out like a man and let me get at him. Just stood at the window, throwing potatoes."

I confess that, as I heard these words, a sort of reluctant admiration for this bloke Brinkley stole over me. We could never be friends, of course, but one had to admit that he was a man who could do the right and public-spirited thing when the occasion called. I took it that old Stoker's banging on the knocker had roused him from a morning-after reverie to the discovery that he had a pretty nasty headache, and that he had instantly started to take steps through the proper channels. All most satisfactory.

"You can consider yourself dashed lucky," I said, pointing out the bright side, "that the fellow elected to deal with you at long range. For close-quarters work he usually employs a carving knife or a chopper, and a good deal of clever footwork is called for."

He had been so wrapped up in his own concerns till now that I don't think he had got on to the fact that Bertram was with him once more. At any rate, he stared quite a bit.

"Ah, Stoker," I said airily, to help him out.

He continued to goggle.

"Are you Wooster?" he asked, in what seemed to me a rather awed way.

"Still Wooster, Stoker, old man," I said cheerily. "First, last, and all the time Bertram Wooster."

He was looking from Chuffy to Pauline and back again almost pleadingly, as if seeking comfort and support.

"What the devil has he done to his face?"

"Sunburn," I said. "Well, Stoker," I proceeded, anxious to get the main business of the day settled, "it's most convenient that you should have dropped in like this. I've been looking for you . . . well, that's putting it a bit loosely, perhaps, but, anyway, I'm glad to see you now, because I've been wanting to tell you that that idea of yours about your daughter and me getting married is off. Forget it, Stoker. Abandon it. Wash it right out. Nothing to it, at all."

It would be difficult to overpraise the magnificent courage and firmness with which I spoke. In fact, for a moment I rather wondered if I mightn't have overdone it a little, because I caught Pauline's eye and there was such a look of worshipping reverence in it that it seemed quite on the cards that, overcome by my glamour at this jucture, she might decide that I was her hero, after all, and switch back again from Chuffy to me. This thought caused me to go on a bit quickly to the next item on the agenda.

"She's going to marry Chuffy—Lord Chuffnell—him," I said, indicating C. with a wave of the hand.

"What!"

"Yes. All set."

Old Stoker gave a powerful snort. He was deeply moved.

"Is this true?"

"Yes, father."

"Oh! You intend to marry a man who calls your father a pop-eyed old swindler, do you?"

I was intrigued.

"Did you call him a pop-eyed old swindler, Chuffy?"

Chuffy hitched up a lower jaw which had sagged a bit.

"Certainly not," he said weakly.

"You did," said Stoker. "When I told you I was not going to buy this house of yours."

"Oh, well," said Chuffy. "You know how it is."

Pauline intervened. She seemed to be feeling that the point was being wandered from. Women like to stick to the practical issue.

"Anyway, I'm going to marry him, father."

"You are not."

"I am too. I love him."

"And only yesterday you were in love with this damned sooty-faced imbecile here."

I drew myself up. We Woosters can make allowances for a father's chagrin, but there is a sharply defined limit.

"Stoker," I said, "you forget yourself strangely. I must ask you to preserve the decencies of debate. And it isn't soot—it's boot polish."

"I wasn't," cried Pauline.

"You said you were."

"Well, I wasn't."

Old Stoker got off another of his snorts.

"The fact of the matter is, you don't know your own mind, and I'm going to make it up for you."

"I'm not going to marry Bertie, whatever you say."

"Well, you're certainly not going to marry a fortune-hunting English lord."

Chuffy took this fairly big.

"What do you mean, a fortune-hunting English lord?"

"I mean what I say. You haven't a cent, and you're trying to marry a girl in Pauline's position. Why, darn it, you're just like that fellow in that musical comedy I saw once . . . what was the name . . . Lord Wotwotleigh."

An animal cry escaped Chuffy's ashen lips.

"Wotwotleigh!"

"The living spit of him. Same sort of face, same expression, same way of talking. I've been wondering all along who it was you reminded me of, and now I know. Lord Wotwotleigh."

Pauline charged in again.

"You're talking perfect nonsense, father. The whole trouble all along was that Marmaduke was so scrupulous and chivalrous that he wouldn't ask me to marry him till he felt he had enough money. I couldn't think what was the matter with him. And then you promised to buy Chuffnell Hall, and five minutes later he came bounding up to me and started proposing. If you didn't mean to buy the Hall you ought not to have said you would. And I don't see why you won't, either."

"I was planning to buy it because Glossop asked me to," said old Stoker. "The way I feel towards that guy now, I wouldn't buy a peanut stand to please him."

I felt impelled to put in a word.

"Not a bad sort, old Glossop. I like him."

"You can have him."

"What first endeared him to me was the way he set about little Seabury last night. It seemed to me to argue the right outlook."

Stoker was staring with his left eye. The other had now closed like some tired flower at nightfall. I couldn't help feeling that Brinkley must have been a jolly good shot to have plugged him so squarely. It's not the easiest thing in the world to hit a fellow in the eye with a potato at a longish range. I know, because I've tried it. The very nature of the potato, it being a rummy shape and covered with knobs, renders accurate aiming a tricky business.

"What's that you're saying? Glossop soaked that boy?"

"With a will, they tell me."

"Well, I'm darned!"

I don't know if you've ever seen one of those films where the tough guy hears the old song his mother used to teach him at her knee and you get a close-up of his face working and before you know where you are he's a melted man and off doing lots of good to all and sundry. A bit sudden I've always looked on it as, but you can take it from me that these lightning softenings do occur. Because now before our very eyes old Stoker was undergoing one of them.

One moment he had been absolutely the man of chilled steel. The next, he was practically human. He stared at me, speechless. Then he licked his lips.

"You really tell me old Glossop did that?"

"I was not present in person, but I have it straight from Jeeves, who got it from Mary, the parlourmaid, who was an eye-witness throughout. He put it across little Seabury properly—at a venture, I should say with the back of a hairbrush."

"Well, I'm darned!"

Pauline was doing a bit of eye-sparkling. You could see that hope had dawned once more. I'm not sure she didn't clap her hands in girlish glee.

"You see, father. You got him all wrong. He's really a splendid man. You'll have to go to him and tell him you're sorry you were so snooty and that you're going to buy the house for him, after all."

Well, I could have told the poor cloth-head that she was doing the wrong thing, butting in like this. Girls have no idea of handling any situation that calls for nice tact. I mean to say, Jeeves will tell you that on these occasions the whole thing is to study the psychology of the individual, and an owl could have seen what old Stoker's psychology was like. A male owl, that is. He was one of those fellows who get their backs up the minute they think their nearest and dearest are trying to shove them into anything; a chap who, as the Bible puts it, if you say Go, he cometh, and if you say Come, he goeth; a fellow, in a word, who, if he came to a door with "Push" on it, would always pull.

And I was right. Left to himself, this Stoker in about another half-minute would have been dancing round the room, strewing roses out of his hat. He was within a short jump of becoming a thing compact entirely of sweetness and light. Now he suddenly stiffened, and a mulish look came into his eye. You could see his haughty spirit resented being rushed.

"I won't do anything of the sort!"

"Oh, father!"

"Telling me what I'm to do and what I'm not to do."

"I didn't mean it like that."

"Never mind how you meant it."

Affairs had taken an unpleasant turn. Old Stoker was gruffling to himself like a not too sunny bulldog. Pauline was looking as if she had recently taken a short-arm punch in the solar plexus. Chuffy had the air of a man who has not yet recovered from being compared to Lord Wotwotleigh. And, as for me, while I could see that it was a moment that called for the intervention of a silver-tongued orator, I felt it wasn't much use having a pop at being a silver-tongued orator if one hadn't anything to say, and I hadn't.

So all that occurred was a good deal of silence, and this silence was still in progress and getting momentarily stickier, when there was a knock at the door and in floated Jeeves.

"Excuse me, sir," he said, shimmering towards old Stoker and presenting an envelope on a salver. "A seaman from your yacht has just brought this cablegram, which arrived shortly after your departure this morning. The captain of the vessel, fancying that it might be of an urgent nature, instructed him to convey it to this house. I took it from him at the back door and hastened hither with it in order to deliver it to you personally."

The way he put it made the whole thing seem like one of those great epics you read about. You followed the precedure step by step, and the interest and drama worked up to the big moment. Old Stoker, however, instead of being thrilled, seemed somewhat on the impatient side.

"What you mean is, there's a cable for me."

"Yes, sir."

"Then why not say so, damn it, instead of making a song about it. Do you think you're singing in opera, or something? Gimme."

Jeeves handed over the missive with a dignified reserve, and drifted out with salver. Stoker started to rip open the envelope.

"I shall certainly not say anything of the kind to Glossop," he said, resuming the discussion. "If he cares to come to me and apologize, I may possibly . . ."

His voice died away with a sort of sound not unlike the last utterance of one of those toy ducks you inflate and then let the air out of. His jaw had dropped, and he was staring at the cable as if he had suddenly discovered he was fondling a tarantula. The next moment there proceeded from his lips an observation which even in these lax modern days I should certainly not have considered suitable for mixed company.

Pauline hopped towards him. Solicitous. When pain and amguish racks the brow stuff.

"What's the matter, father?"

Old Stoker was making gulping noises.

"It's happened!"

"What has happened?"

"What? What?" I saw Chuffy start. "What? What? I'll tell you what. They're contesting old George's will!"

"You don't mean that!"

"I do mean that. Read it for yourself."

Pauline studied the document. She looked up, rattled.

"But if this goes through, bang goes our fifty million."

"Of course it does."

"We shan't have a cent, hardly."

Chuffy came to life with a jerk.

"Say that again! Do you mean you've lost all your money?"

"It looks like it."

"Fine!" said Chuffy. "Great. Ripping. Wonderful. Topping. Splendid!"

Pauline gave a sort of jump.

"Why, so it is, isn't it?"

"Of course it is. I'm broke. You're broke. Let's rush off and get married."

"Of course."

"This makes everything all right. Nobody can say I'm like Wotwotleigh now."

"They certainly can't."

"Wotwotleigh, on hearing the news, would have edged out."

"I should say so. You wouldn't have been able to see him for dust."

"It' marvellous!"

"It's magnificent!"

"In all my life, I've never heard of such a bit of luck as this."

"Nor have I."

"Coming just at the right time."

"Exactly at the right time."

"It's topping!"

"It's simply great!"

Their fresh young enthusiasm seemed to affect old Stoker like a boil on the cheek-bone.

"Stop talking that infernal rot and listen to me. Haven't you any sense at all? What do you mean, you've lost your money? Do you think I'm going to lie down and let this go through without making any come-back? They haven't a dog's chance. Old George was as sane as I am, and I've got Sir Roderick Glossop, the greatest alienist in England, to prove it."

"But you haven't."

"I've only to put Glossop on the witness stand, and their case collapses like a bubble."

"But Sir Roderick won't testify for you now you've quarrelled with him."

Old Stoker sizzled a bit. Or fumed, if you care to put it that way.

"Who says I've quarrelled with him? Show me the half-wit who dares to assert that I'm not on the most cordial terms with Sir Roderick Glossop. Just because we had a triffling, temporary difference such as happens to the closest of friends, does that mean that we're not like brothers?"

"But suppose he won't apologize to you?"

"There has never been any question of his apologizing to me. I shall naturally apologize to him. I suppose I'm man enough to admit it frankly when I realize that I have been in the wrong and have wounded my best friend's feelings, aren't I? Of course I shall apologize to him, and he will accept my apology in the spirit in which it is given. There is nothing small about Sir Roderick Glossop. I'll have him over in New York, testifying his head off, inside of two weeks. What's the name of that place he's staying at? Seaview Hotel, isn't it? I'll get him on the wire at once and arrange a meeting."

I had to put in a word here.

"He's not at the hotel. I know, because Jeeves was trying to get him just now and drew a blank."

"Then where is he?"

"I couldn't say."

"He must be somewhere."

"Ah!" I said, following the reasoning and finding it sound. "So he is, no doubt. But where? Quite possibly he's in London by now."

"Why London?"

"Why not?"

"Was he planning to go to London?"

"He may have been."

"What's his address in London?"

"I don't know."

"Don't any of you know?"

"I don't," said Pauline.

"I don't," said Chuffy.

"A lot of use you are to a man," said old Stoker severely. "Get out! We're busy."

The remark was addressed to Jeeves, who had come floating in again. It's one of this man's most remarkable properties, that now you see him and now you don't. Or, rather, now you don't see him and now you do. You're talking of this and that and you suddenly sense a presence, so to speak, and there he is.

"I beg your pardon, sir," said Jeeves. "I was desirous of speaking to his lordship for a moment."

Chuffy waved a hand. Distrait.

"Later on, Jeeves."

"Very good, m'lord."

"We're a little busy just now." ..

"Just so, m'lord."

"Well, it's not going to be so hard to locate a man of Sir Roderick's eminence," said old Stoker, resuming. "His address would be in *Who's Who*. Have you got a *Who's Who*?"

"No," said Chuffy.

Old Stoker flung the hands skyward.

"Good God!"

Jeeves coughed.

"If you will pardon me for intruding the observation, sir, I think I can tell you where Sir Roderick is. If I am right in supposing that it is Sir Roderick Glossop that you are anxious to find?"

"Of course it is. How many Sir Rodericks do you think I know? Where is he, then?"

"In the garden, sir."

"This garden, do you mean?"

"Yes, sir."

"Then go and ask him to come here at once. Say that Mr. Stoker wishes to see him immediately on a matter of the utmost importance. No, stop. Don't you go. I'll go myself. Whereabouts in the garden did you see him?"

"I did not see him, sir. I was merely informed that he was there."

Old Stoker clicked the tongue a bit.

"Well, damn it, whereabouts in the garden did whoever merely informed you that he was in the garden merely inform you that he was?"

"In the potting-shed, sir."

"The potting-shed?"

"Yes, sir."

"What's he doing in the potting-shed?"

"Sitting, sir, I imagine. As I say, I do not speak from first-hand observation. My informant is Constable Dobson."

"Eh? What? Constable Dobson? Who's he?"

"The police officer who arrested Sir Roderick last night, sir."

He bowed slightly from the hips and left the room.

⋆ 21 ⋆

Jeeves Finds The Way

"JEEVES!" bellowed Chuffy.

"Jeeves!" screamed Pauline.

"Jeeves!" I shouted.

"Hey!" yelled old Stoker.

The door had closed, and I'll swear it hadn't opened again. Nevertheless, there was the man in our midst once more, an expression of courteous inquiry on his face.

"Jeeves!" cried Chuffy.

"M'lord?"

"Jeeves!" shrieked Pauline.

"Miss?"

"Jeeves!" I vociferated.

"Sir?"

"Hey, you!" boomed old Stoker.

Whether Jeeves liked being called "Hey, you!" I could not say. His well-moulded face betrayed no resentment.

"Sir?" he said.

"What do you mean by going off like that?"

"I was under the impression that his lordship, occupied with more vital matters, was not at leisure to attend to the communication I desired to make, sir. I planned to return later, sir."

"Well, stay put for a second, won't you?"

"Certainly, sir. Had I been aware that you were desirous of speaking to me, sir, I would not have withdrawn from the room. It was merely the apprehension lest I might be intruding at a moment when my presence was not desired . . ."

"All right, all right, all right!" I noted, not for the first time, that there was something about Jeeves's conversational methods that seemed to jar upon old Stoker. "Never mind all that."

"Your presence is of the essence, Jeeves," I said.

"Thank you, sir."

Chuffy took the floor, Stoker being occupied for the nonce with making a noise like a wounded buffalo.

"Jeeves."

"M'lord?"

"Did you say that Sir Roderick Glossop had been arrested?"

"Yes, m'lord. It was on that point that I wished to speak to your lordship. I came to inform you that Sir Roderick had been apprehended by Constable Dobson last night and placed in the potting-shed in the Hall grounds, the constable remaining on guard at the door. The larger potting-shed, m'lord, not the smaller one. The potting-shed to which I allude is the potting-shed on the right as you enter the kitchen garden. It has a red-tiled roof, in contradistinction to the smaller potting-shed, the roof of which is constructed of . . ."

I had never been, as you might say, frightfully fond of J. Washburn Stoker, but it seemed only neighbourly at this moment to try to save him from apoplexy.

"Jeeves," I said.

"Sir?"

"Never mind which potting-shed."

"No, sir."

"Not of the essence."

"I quite understand, sir."

"Then carry on, Jeeves."

He cast a glance of respectful commiseration at old Stoker, who seemed to be having a good deal of trouble with his bronchial tubes.

"It appears, m'lord, that Constable Dobson arrested Sir Roderick at an advanced hour last night. He was then in something of a quandary as to what means to take for his disposal. You must understand, m'lord, that in the conflagration which destroyed Mr. Wooster's cottage that of Sergeant Voules, which is contiguous, was also burned down. And as this cottage of Sergeant Voules's is also the local police station, Constable Dobson was not unnaturally somewhat at a loss to know where to place his prisoner—the more so as Sergeant Voules was not there to advise him, he, in fighting the flames, having sustained an unfortunate injury to his head and having been removed to the house of his aunt. I refer to his Aunt Maud, who resides in Chuffnell Regis, not . . ."

I did the square thing again.

"Never mind which aunt, Jeeves."

"No, sir."

"Scarcely germane."

"Quite so, sir."

"Then carry on, Jeeves."

"Very good, sir.   So in the end, acting upon his own initiative, the constable arrived at the conclusion that as secure a place as any would be the potting-shed, the larger potting-shed . . ."

"We understand, Jeeves.   The one with the tiled roof."

"Precisely, sir.   He, therefore, placed Sir Roderick in the larger potting-shed, and remained on guard there throughout the remainder of the night.   Some little time ago, the gardener came on duty and the constable, summoning one of them—a young fellow named . . ."

"All right, Jeeves."

"Very good, sir.   Summoning this young fellow, he dispatched him to the temporary residence of Sergeant Voules in the hope that the latter would now be sufficiently restored to be able to interest himself in the matter.   Such, it appears, was the case. A night's sleep, acting in conjunction with a naturally robust constitution, had enabled Sergeant Voules to rise at his usual hour and partake of a hearty breakfast."

"Breakfast!"   I couldn't help murmuring in spite of my iron self-control.   The word had touched an exposed nerve in Bertram.

"On receiving the communication, Sergeant Voules hastened to the Hall to interview his lordship."

"Why his lordship?"

"His lordship is a Justice of the Peace, sir."

"Of course, yes."

"And, as such, has the power to commit the prisoner to in-carceration in a more recognized prison.   He is waiting in the library now, m'lord, till your lordship is at leisure to see him."

If the word "breakfast" was, as it were, the key word that had the power to set Bertram Wooster a-quiver, it appeared that "prison" was the one that tickled old Stoker up properly.   He uttered a hideous cry.

"But how can he be in prison?   What's he got to do with prisons?   Why does this fool of a cop think he ought to be in prison?"

"The charge, I understand, sir, is one of burglary."

"Burglary!"

"Yes, sir."

Old Stoker looked so piteously at me—why me, I don't know, but he did—that I nearly patted him on the head. In fact, I might quite easily have done so, had not my hand been stayed by a sudden noise in my rear like that made by a frightened hen or a rising pheasant. The Dowager Lady Chuffnell had come charging into the room.

"Marmaduke!" she cried, and I can give no better indication of her emotion than by saying that as she spoke her eyes rested on my face and it made no impression on her whatsoever. For all the notice she took of it, I might have been the Great White Chief. "Marmaduke, I have the most terrible news. Roderick . . ."

"All right," said Chuffy, a little petulantly, I thought. "We've had it too. Jeeves is just telling us."

"But what are we to do?"

"I don't know."

"And it is all my fault, all my fault."

"Oh, don't say that, Aunt Mrytle," said Chuffy, rattled but still *preux*. "You couldn't have helped it."

"I could. I could. I shall never forgive myself. If it had not been for me, he would never have gone out of the house with that black stuff on his face."

I was really sorry for poor old Stoker. One thing after another, I mean to say. His eyes came out of his head like a snail's.

"Black stuff?" he gurgled faintly.

"He had covered his face with burnt cork to amuse Seabury."

Old Stoker tottered to a chair and sank into it. He seemed to be thinking that this was one of those stories you could listen to better sitting down.

"You can only remove the horrible stuff with butter . . ."

"And petrol, so the cognoscenti tell me," I couldn't help putting in. I like to keep these things straight. "You support me, Jeeves? Petrol does the trick?"

"Yes, sir."

"Well, petrol, then. Petrol or butter. At any rate, it was to get something that would take the stuff off that he must have broken into this house. And now . . .!"

She cheesed it in mid-sentence, deeply moved. Not, however,

any more deeply than old Stoker, who seemed to be more or less passing through the furnace.

"This is the finish," he said, in a sort of pale voice. "This is where I drop fifty million dollars and try to like it. A lot of use any testimony in a lunacy case is going to be from a fellow who gets himself pinched while wandering around the country in a black face. Why, there isn't a judge in America who wouldn't rule out anything he said on the ground that he was crazy himself."

Lady Chuffnell quivered.

"But he did it to please my son."

"Anybody who would do anything to please a young hound like that," said old Stoker, "must have been crazy."

He emitted a mirthless l.

"Well, the joke's on me, all right. Yes, the joke's certainly on me. I stake everything on the evidence of this man Glossop. I rely on him to save my fifty million by testifying that old George wasn't loco. And two minutes after I've put him on the stand, the other side'll come right back at me by showing that my expert is a loony himself, loonier than ever old George could have been if he'd tried for a thousand years. It's funny when you come to think of it. Ironical. Reminds one of that thing about Lo somebody's name led all the rest."

Jeeves coughed. He had that informative gleam of his in his eyes.

"Abou ben Adhem, sir."

"Have I *what*?" said old Stoker, puzzled.

"The poem to which you allude relates to a certain Abou ben Adhem, who, according to the story, awoke one night from a deep dream of peace to find an angel . . ."

"Get out!" said old Stoker, very quietly.

"Sir?"

"Get out of this room before I murder you."

"Yes, sir."

"And take your angels with you."

"Very good, sir."

The door closed. Old Stoker puffed out his breath in a stricken sort of way.

"Angels!" he said. "At a time like this!"

I felt it only fair to stick up for Jeeves.

"He was perfectly right," I said. "I used to know the thing

by heart at school. This cove found an angel sitting by his bed, writing in a book, don't you know, and the upshot of the whole affair was . . . Oh, all right, if you don't want to hear'"

I withdrew to a corner of the room and picked up a photograph album. A Wooster does not thrust his conversation upon the unwilling.

Fom some time after this there was a good deal of what you might call mixed chatter, in which—through dudgeon—I took no part. Everybody talked at once, and nobody said anything that you could have described as being in the least constructive. Except old Stoker, who proved that I had been right in thinking that he must at one time have been a pirate of the Spanish or some other Main by coming boldly out with a suggestion for a rescue party.

"What's the matter," he wanted to know, "with going and breaking the door down and getting him out and smuggling him away and hiding him somewhere and letting these darned cops run circles round themselves, trying to find him?"

Chuffy demurred.

"We couldn't."

"Why not?"

"You heard Jeeves say Dobson was on guard."

"Bat him over the head with a shovel."

Chuffy didn't seem to like this idea much. I suppose, if you're a J.P., you have to be careful what you do. Bat policemen over the head with shovels, and the County looks askance.

"Well, darn it, then, bribe him."

"You can't bribe an English policeman."

"You mean that?"

"Not a chance."

"My God, what a country!" said old Stoker, with a sort of whistling groan, and you could see that he would never be able to feel quite the same towards England again.

My dudgeon melted. We Woosters are human, and the spectacle of so much anguish in a moderately-sized room was too much for me. I crossed to the fire-place and pressed the bell. With the result that just as old Stoker was beginning to say what he thought about the English policeman, the door opened and there was Jeeves.

Old Stoker eyed him balefully.

"You back?"

"Yes, sir."

"Well?"

"Sir?"

"What do you want?"

"The bell rang, sir."

Chuffy did another spot of hand-waving.

"No, no, Jeeves.   Nobody rang."

I stepped forward.

"I rang, Chuffy."

"What for?"

"For Jeeves."

"We don't want Jeeves."

"Chuffy, old man," I said, and those present were, no doubt, thrilled by the quiet gravity of my tone, "if there could ever be a time when you wanted Jeeves more than you do now, I . . ."   I lost the thread of my remarks, and had to start again.   "Chuffy," I said, "what I'm driving at is that there is only one man who can get you out of this mess.   He stands before you.   I mean Jeeves," I said, to make the thing clearer.   "You know as well as I do that on these occasions Jeeves always finds the way."

Chuffy was plainly impressed.   I could see that memory had begun to stir, and that he was recalling some of the man's triumphs.

"By Jove, yes.   That's right.   He does, doesn't he?"

"He does, indeed."

I shot a quelling glance at old Stoker, who had started to say something about angels, and turned to the man.

"Jeeves," I said, "we require your co-operation and advice."

"Very good, sir."

"To begin with, let me give you a brief synopsis . . . do I mean synopsis?"

"Yes, sir.   Synopsis is perfectly correct."

". . . a brief synopsis, then, of the position of affairs.   I have no doubt that you recall the late Mr. George Stoker.   That cable you brought just now was to say that his will, under the terms of which Mr. Stoker here has benefited so considerably, is being contested on the ground that the testator was as goofy as a coot."

"Yes, sir."

"In rebuttal of this, Mr. Stoker had intended to bung Sir Roderick Glossop into the witness box to testify as an expert that old George was Grade A. in the sanity line. Not a gibber in him, if you see what I mean. And in ordinary circs this move could not have failed. It would have brought home the bacon infallibly."

"Yes, sir."

"But, and this is the nub of the thing, Jeeves—Sir Roderick is now in the potting-shed—the larger potting-shed—with his face covered with burnt cork and a sharp sentence for burglary staring him in the eyeball. You see how this weakens him as a force?"

"Yes, sir."

"In this world, Jeeves, you can do one of two things. You can set yourself up as a final authority on whether your fellow-man is sane or not, or you can go blacking your face and getting put in potting-sheds. You cannot do both. So what is to be done, Jeeves?"

"I would suggest removing Sir Roderick from the shed, sir."

I turned to the meeting.

"There! Didn't I tell you Jeeves would find the way?"

One dissentient voice. Old Stoker's. He seemed bent on heckling.

"Remove him from the shed, yes?" he said, and in an exceedingly nasty voice. "How? With a team of angels?"

He started his buffalo imitations again, and I had to shush him pretty firmly.

"*Can* you remove Sir R. from the s., Jeeves?"

"Yes, sir."

"You are convinced of this?"

"Yes, sir."

"You have already formulated a plan or scheme?"

"Yes, sir."

"I take it all back," said old Stoker reverently. "Forget I said it. Get me out of this jam and you can come and wake me up in the night and talk about angels, if you want."

"Thank you, sir. By removing Sir Roderick before he is actually brought into the presence of his lordship, sir," proceeded Jeeves, "we shall, I think, obviate all unpleasantness. His identity is not yet known to either Constable Dobson or Sergeant Voules. The constable had never seen him before their meeting last night, and assumes that he is a member of the troupe of negroid minstrels who performed on Mr. Stoker's yacht. Sergeant Voules is under the same impression. We have, therefore, only to release Sir Roderick before the matter is gone further into, and all will be well."

I followed him.

"I follow you, Jeeves," I said.

"If you will allow me, sir, I will now sketch out the method which I would advocate for accomplishing this end."

"Yes," said old Stoker. "What is this method? Spill it."

I held up a hand. A thought had struck me.

"Wait, Jeeves," I said. "Just one moment."

I fixed old Stoker with a compelling eye.

"Before we go any further, there are two things to be settled. Do you give your solemn word to purchase Chuffnell Hall from old Chuffy here at a price to be agreed upon between the two contracting parties?"

"Yes, yes, yes. Let's get on."

"And you consent to the union of your daughter Pauline with old Chuffy, and none of that rot about her marrying me?"

"Sure, sure!"

"Jeeves," I said, "you may speak."

I stepped back, and gave him the floor—noting, as I did so, that his eye was a-gleam with the light of pure intelligence. His head, as usual, bulged out at the back.

"Having given this matter a good deal of consideration, sir, I have come to the conclusion that the chief difficulty that confronts us in our attempt upon our objective lies in the presence before the entrance of the potting-shed of Constable Dobson."

"Very true, Jeeves."

"He represents the *crux*, if I may say so."

"Certainly you may say so, Jeeves. Another way of putting it would be 'the snag'."

"Precisely, sir. Our first move, accordingly, must be to eliminate Constable Dobson."

"That's what I said," put in old Stoker rather querulously. "And you wouldn't listen to me."

I squelched him.

"You wanted to hit him over the head with a spade or something. All wrong. What is needed here is . . . what's the word, Jeeves?"

"*Finesse*, sir."

"Exactly. Carry on, Jeeves."

"This, in my opinion, may be readily accomplished by sending word to him that the parlourmaid, Mary, wishes to see him in the raspberry bushes."

I was stunned by the man's sagacity, but not so stunned as to be unable to turn to the others and add an explanatory footnote.

"This Mary, this parlourmaid," I said, "is betrothed to the blighter Dobson, and while I have only seen her in the distance, I can testify that she is exactly the sort of girl any red-blooded constable would come leaping into the raspberry bushes to meet. Full of sex-appeal, eh, Jeeves?"

"An exceedingly attractive young woman, sir. And I think that we might make matters even more certain by including in the message a word to the effect that she had a cup of coffee and a ham sandwich for him. The constable, I find, has not yet breakfasted."

I winced.

"Skim lightly over this bit, Jeeves. I am not made of marble."

"I beg your pardon, sir. I was forgetting."

"Quite all right, Jeeves. You will have to square Mary, of course?"

"No, sir. I have been canvassing her views, and I find that she is extremely eager to convey refreshment to the officer. I would suggest giving her a message—ostensibly from the latter—to the effect that he is waiting at the spot indicated."

I had to interrupt.

"A snag, Jeeves. A *crux*, in fact. If he wanted food, why wouldn't he come straight to the house?"

"He would be apprehensive of being observed by Sergeant Voules, sir. He is under strict orders from his superior to remain at his post."

"Then would he leave it?" asked Chuffy.

"My dear old man," I said. "He has not yet breakfasted. And this girl will be dripping with coffee and ham sandwiches. Don't hold up the run of the dialogue with foolish questions. Yes, Jeeves?"

"In his absence, sir, it would be a simple task to remove Sir Roderick and lead him to some place of concealment. His lordship's bedroom suggests itself."

"And Dobson wouldn't have the nerve to confess that he had abandoned the post of duty. That's what you're driving at?"

"Precisely, sir, his lips would be sealed."

Old Stoker shoved himself forward again.

"No good," he said. "Wouldn't work. I'm not saying we couldn't get Glossop away, but the cops would see that there had been funny business. Their man would have gone, and they'd figure it out that somebody had got him away. They would put two and two together and get wise to us having done it. Last night, for example, on my yacht . . ."

He stopped, not wishing, I suppose, to disinter the dead past, but I saw what he meant. When I had got away from the yacht, it hadn't taken him long to see that Jeeves must have been at the bottom of it.

"It's a point, Jeeves," I was bound to say. "The constabulary might not be able to do anything definite, but they would talk about it, and before we knew where we were, the story would be out that Sir Roderick had been roaming around with his face blacked up. The local paper would get hold of it. One of those gossip-writers you find at the Drones, always waiting with their ears flapping for good stuff about the eminent, would hear of it, and then we should be just as badly off as if the old boy went and picked oakum at Dartmoor or somewhere for years."

"No, sir. The officers would find a prisoner in the shed. I would advocate substituting you for Sir Roderick."

I stared at the man.

"Me?"

"It is vital, if I may be allowed to point it out, sir, that a black-faced prisoner be found in the shed when the moment arrives for the accused to be conducted before his lordship."

"But I don't look like old Glossop. We're built on different lines. Me—slender and willowy; him . . . well, I don't wish to say anything derogatory concerning one who is bound to the aunt of an old friend by ties warmer than those of . . . well, what I'm driving at is that you couldn't by any stretch of the imag. call him slender and willowy."

"You are forgetting, sir, that only Constable Dobson has actually seen the prisoner; and his lips, as I say, will be sealed."

It was true. I had forgotten that.

"Yes, but, Jeeves, dash it, anxious as I am to bring aid and comfort to this stricken home, I'm not so bally keen on doing five years in the jug for burglary."

"There is no danger of that, sir. The building into which Sir

Roderick was breaking at the moment of his arrest was your own garage."

"But, Jeeves. Reflect. Consider. Review the position. Am I supposed to have allowed myself to be pinched for breaking into my own garage and shut up in a shed all night without saying a word? It isn't . . . what is it . . . it isn't plausible."

"It is only necessary to induce Sergeant Voules to believe it, sir. What the constable may think is immaterial, owing to the fact that his lips are sealed."

"But Voules wouldn't believe it for a minute."

"Oh, yes, sir. I fancy that he is under the impression that it is a frequent practice of yours to sleep in sheds."

Chuffy uttered a glad cry.

"Of course. He'll just take it for granted that you've been mopping it up again."

I was frigid.

"Oh?" I said, and you couldn't have described my voice as anything but caustic. "So I am to go down in the history of Chuffnell Regis as one of our leading dipsomaniacs?"

"He may just think him potty," suggested Pauline.

"That's right," said Chuffy. He turned to me pleadingly. "Bertie," he said, "you aren't going to tell me at this time of day that you have any objection to being considered . . ."

". . . Mentally negligible," said Pauline.

"Exactly," said Chuffy. "Of course you'll do it. What, Bertie Wooster? Sacrifice himself to a little temporary inconvenience to save his friends? Why, he jumps at that sort of job."

"Springs at it," said Pauline.

"Leaps at it," said Chuffy.

"I've always thought he was a fine young fellow," said old Stoker. "I remember thinking so the first time I met him."

"So did I," said Lady Chuffnell. "So different from so many of these modern young men."

"I liked his face."

"I have always liked his face"'

My head was swimming a bit. It isn't often I get as good a Press as this, and the old salve was beginning to unman me. I tried feebly to stem the tide.

"Yes, but listen . . ."

"I was at school with Bertie Wooster," said Chuffy. "I like

to think of it. At private school and also at Eton and after that at Oxford. He was loved by everybody."

"Because of his wonderful, unselfish nature?" asked Pauline.

"You've absolutely hit it. Because of his wonderful, unselfish nature. Because when it was a question of helping a pal he would go through fire and water to do so. I wish I had a quid for every time I've seen him take the blame for somebody else's dirty work on his own broad shoulders."

"How splendid!" said Pauline.

"Just what I'd have expected of him," said old Stoker.

"Just," said Lady Chuffnell. "The child is the father of the man."

"You would see him face a furious headmaster with a sort of dauntless look in those big blue eyes of his . . ."

I held up a hand.

"Enough, Chuffy," I said. "Sufficient. I will go through this ghastly ordeal. But one word. When I come out, do I get breakfast?"

"You get the best breakfast Chuffnell Hall can provide."

I eyed him searchingly.

"Kippers?"

"Schools of kippers."

"Toast?"

"Mounds of toast."

"And coffee?"

"Pots."

I inclined the head.

"Well, mind I do," I said. "Come, Jeeves, I am ready to accompany you."

"Very good, sir. If I might be permitted to make an observation——?"

"Yes, Jeeves?"

"It is a far, far better thing that you do than you have ever done, sir."

"Thank you, Jeeves."

As I said before, there is nobody who puts these things more neatly than he does.

Jeeves Applies For A Situation

THE sunlight poured into the small morning-room of Chuffnell Hall. It played upon me, sitting at a convenient table; on Jeeves, hovering in the background; on the skeletons of four kippered herrings; on a coffee-pot; and on an empty toast rack. I poured myself out the final drops of coffee and sipped thoughtfully. Recent events had set their seal upon me, and it was a graver, more mature Bertram Wooster who now eyed the toast-rack and, finding nothing there, transferred his gaze to the man in attendance.

"Who's the cook at the Hall now, Jeeves?"

"A woman of the name of Perkins, sir."

"She dishes up a nifty breakfast. Convey my compliments to her."

"Very good, sir."

I touched the cup to my lips.

"All this is rather like the gentle sunshine after the storm, Jeeves."

"Extremely like, sir."

"And it was quite a storm, what?"

"Very trying at times, sir."

"Trying is the *mot juste*, Jeeves. I was thinking of my own trial at that very moment. I flatter myself that I am a strong man, Jeeves. I am not easily moved by life's untoward happenings. But I'm bound to confess that it was an unpleasant experience coming up before Chuffy. I was nervous and embarrassed. A good deal of the awful majesty of the Law about old Chuffy. I didn't know he wore horn-rimmed spectacles."

"When acting as Justice of the Peace, invariably, I understand, sir. I gather that his lordship finds that they lend him confidence in his magisterial duties."

"Well, I think someone ought to have warned me. I got a nasty shock. They change his whole expression. Make him look just like my Aunt Agatha. It was only by reminding myself that he and I once stood in the same dock together at Bow

Street, charged with raising Cain on Boat Race night, that I was enabled to maintain my *sang-froid*. However, the unpleasantness was short-lived. I must admit he rushed things through nice and quickly. He soon settled Dobson's hash, what?"

"Yes, sir."

"A rather severe reprimand, I thought?"

"Well phrased, sir."

"And Bertram dismissed without a stain on his character."

"Yes, sir."

"But with Police Sergeant Voules firmly convinced that he is either an inveterate souse or a congenital loony. Possibly both. However," I proceeded, turning from the dark side, "it is no use worrying about that."

"Very true, sir."

"The main point is that once again you have shown that there is no crisis which you are unable to handle. A very smooth effort, Jeeves. Exceedingly smooth."

"I could have effected nothing without your co-operation, sir."

"Tush, Jeeves! I was a mere pawn in the game."

"Oh, no, sir."

"Yes, Jeeves. I know my place. But there's just one thing. Don't think for a moment that I want to detract from the merit of your performance, but you did have a bit of luck, what?"

"Sir?"

"Well, that cable happening to come along in what you might call the very nick of time. A fortunate coincidence."

"No, sir. I had anticipated its arrival."

"What!"

"In the cable which I dispatched to my friend Benstead in New York the day before yesterday, I urged him to lose no time in retransmitting the message which formed the body of my communication."

"You don't mean to say——?"

"Immediately after the rift had occurred between Mr. Stoker and Sir Roderick Glossop, involving, as it did, the former's decision not to purchase Chuffnell Hall and the consequent unpleasantness to his lordship and Miss Stoker, the dispatching of the cable to Benstead suggested itself to me as a possible solution. I surmised that the news that the late Mr. Stoker's will was being contested would lead to a reconciliation between Mr. Stoker and Sir Roderick."

"And there's nobody contesting the will really?"

"No, sir."

"But what about when old Stoker finds out?"

"I feel convinced that his natural relief will overcome any possible resentment at the artifice. And he has already signed the necessary documents relating to the sale of Chuffnell Hall."

"So that even if he's as sick as mud he can't do a thing?"

"Exactly, sir."

I fell into a moody silence. Apart from astounding me, this revelation had had the effect of engendering a poignant anguish. I mean to say, the thought that I had let this man get away from me, that he was now in Chuffy's employment, and that there was a fat chance of Chuffy ever being chump enough to put him into circulation again . . . well, dash it, you can't say it wasn't enough to shove the iron into the soul.

It was with something of the spirit of the old aristocrat mounting the tumbril that I forced myself to wear the mask.

"Cigarette, Jeeves?"

He produced the box, and I puffed in silence.

"Might I ask, sir, what you intend to do now?"

I came out of the reverie.

"Eh?"

"Now that your cottage is burned down, sir. Is it your purpose to take another in this neighbourhood?"

I shook the head.

"No, Jeeves, I shall return to the metrop."

"To your former apartment, sir?"

"Yes."

"But . . ."

I anticipated the question.

"I know what you are going to say, Jeeves. You are thinking of Mr. Manglehoffer, of the Honourable Mrs. Tinkler-Moulke and Lieutenant-Colonel J. J. Bustard. But circumstances have altered since I was compelled to take the firm stand I did in regard to their attitude towards the old banjolele. From now on, there will be no friction. My banjolele perished in the flames last night, Jeeves. I shall not buy another."

"No, sir?"

"No, Jeeves. The zest has gone. I should not be able to twang a string without thinking of Brinkley. And the one thing I do not wish to do till further notice is think of that man of wrath."

"You are not intending to retain him in your employment, then, sir?"

"Retain him in my employment? After what has occurred? After finishing first by the shortest of heads in the race with him and his carving knife? I do not so intend, Jeeves. Stalin, yes. Al Capone, certainly. But not Brinkley."

He coughed.

"Then, as there is a vacancy in your establishment, sir, I wonder if you would consider it a liberty if I were to offer my services?"

I upset the coffee-pot.

"You said—what, Jeeves?"

"I ventured to express the hope, sir, that you might be agreeable to considering my application for the post. I should endeavour to give satisfaction, as I trust I have done in the past."

"But . . ."

"I would not wish, in any case, to continue in the employment of his lordship, sir, now that he is about to be married. I yield to no one in my admiration for the many qualities of Miss Stoker, but it has never been my policy to serve in the household of a married gentleman."

"Why not?"

"It is merely a personal feeling, sir."

"I see what you mean. The psychology of the individual?"

"Precisely, sir."

"And you really want to come back with me?"

"I should esteem it a great privilege, sir, if you would allow me to do so, sir, unless you are thinking of making other plans."

It is not easy to find words in these supreme moments, if you know what I mean. What I mean is, you get a moment like this —supreme, as you might say—with the clouds all cleared away and the good old sun buzzing along on all six cylinders—and you feel . . . well, I mean, dash it!

"Thank you, Jeeves," I said."

"Not at all, sir."